BITTER COMRADES—IN A DUEL TO THE DEATH

"DAMN you, Harry—I'll fight you right here. One shot apiece at twenty paces." Thornton McClintock and his longtime comrade, Harry Drayberry, stood in the middle of the dusty Granada street, all friendship forgotten.

"Very well, I accept your challenge," Harry said angrily. "Let's get on with it."

They counted aloud as they stepped the ten paces in opposite directions, Thornton seething with rage as he remembered how Harry had insulted Solange. He'd be damned if he'd let any man insult his woman—not even Harry, whose friendship he had shared since childhood, long before they'd met up with William Walker and come to Nicaragua with Walker's band of mercenaries.

Thornton thought back to the carefree life they'd led in Tennessee, and how they had set out together to find gold and adventure in California. It was strange how quickly the two young "soldiers of fortune" had become bitter enemies, sworn to destroy one another.

As he counted his tenth step, Thornton turned and raised his pistol, placing the head of Harry Drayberry in the sights. He lowered the barrel a fraction of an inch so the recoil would not cause the bullet to overfly the handsome face. Then, his right finger squeezed off a perfect shot . . .

THE
SOLDIERS
OF
FORTUNE

Lee Davis Willoughby

A DELL/JAMES A. BRYANS BOOK

Published by
Dell Publishing Co., Inc.
1 Dag Hammarskjold Plaza
New York, New York 10017

Dell ® TM 681510, Dell Publishing Co., Inc.

ISBN: 0-440-08199-8

Printed in the United States of America

First printing—November 1982

1

THE TIME of year was late in the month of March. It would be springtime in Tennessee, with jonquils and azaleas and yellow bells and tulip trees, wisteria and redbuds, peach trees, apple trees, all of them in flower, and the big willow oaks along the roads unfurling their first green leaves. Here where he was the sun beat down on contorted cactuses, thorny scrub and bare stony soil caked by the heat. Late March 1854, the Republic of Lower California and Sonora was foundering, and its president, William Walker of Nashville, Tennessee, led forty men northeast across the mountains and wastelands below the U.S. border.

William Walker, twenty-nine years old, wore a blue uniform, riding boots and a white broad-brimmed hat with a gold cord and three gold stars. A saber and two heavy pistols hung from his belt. He was a small man, barely five feet tall, with long fair hair, and he did not say much. His men found him not only soft-spoken but courteous—and it would have surprised a stranger to hear that this man was notorious on the duelling field, and had a reputation among his own fighting men for dauntless courage. The one thing in the appearance of William Walker which struck all men—and

5

women—was his eyes, which were gray, calm, and
compelling.

Walker and a few of the others rode horses, and the
rest drove their food supply ahead of them—a hundred cattle and sheep—from waterhole to waterhole.
The men wore an assortment of uniforms according to
their own military fancy. Only a couple of days on the
hot sandy wastes reduced the grandest uniform to
sweat-soaked filthy rags. But these men did not complain. Mostly they were failed goldminers and rough-
neck adventurers who knew no other life than one of
brutal effort in a harsh environment.

The lure now was gold. If they could get their hands
on the precious metal from the mines of Sonora, all
was not lost. The United States had blockaded supplies to the new republic. The Mexican government
had finally shown interest in the area only after it had
been taken from them, and they too blocked the flow
of essential supplies to Walker's new independent state.
But gold from the mines in Sonora could purchase
rifles, lead, powder and food in abundance despite the
edicts of Washington and Mexico City.

William Walker pressed on to the northeast, heading for the narrow strip between the U.S. border and
the Gulf of California, which connects the promontory
of Lower California to the mainland area of Sonora.
They killed cattle and sheep sparingly as they went,
and lived as much as possible off the country through
which they passed, for every one of them knew that
without food, animals and bullets, they had no chance
of survival.

Bands of hostile Indians shadowed them as they
descended the eastern slopes of the Sierra de Juarez.
The days passed and they tramped onward, never
knowing whether the same Indians followed them day
after day or whether one band kept them under sur-
veillance in its territory to be succeeded by another
band in the next territory. Nor did they know whether

the vultures that soared and spiraled above them as they trekked across the deserted windblown landscape were the same carrion-eaters that had glided above them hopefully the previous day and the days before that.

Finally they descended into the green valley of the Colorado River, which they had to cross to get to Sonora, leaving the desolate wilderness behind them. Instead of the wide, shallow, placid river they had seen before, they were confronted with a raging torrent fully half a mile wide.

"The snows are melting in the mountains to the north," William Walker said quietly, dismissing the swirling power of the turbulent waters with this explanation.

He ordered the reluctant men to cut down trees by the river bank and build rafts.

As the men put together the log rafts, working for a spell, then resting and bathing in the river water, looking after the animals, fishing, washing their uniforms, cleaning their weapons, a band of peaceful Indians approached along the river bank. Their leader, a muscular, stocky warrior, spoke some English and Spanish and told Walker that he and his band were going downriver to their summer fishing grounds on the Gulf of California. He said that usually his people traveled on the east bank of the Colorado, but that the Apaches on that side of the river, driven south from Texas by the white man, were so numerous and fierce he feared to travel anymore on the east bank. He watched as Walker's men tied tree trunks together into rafts large enough to carry the cattle and sheep.

"The Apaches will follow you," the Indian said, "until you are in what the white man calls the Desierto de Altar, and they will kill you one by one in the desert for your weapons and your animals."

The men building the nearest raft had stopped work to listen.

The Indian gave them advice. "Do not let the Apaches take you alive. Better to die tied in a bag with a hundred scorpions than slowly at the hands of the Apaches."

The Indian's experience had taught him that the white man would not listen to what he and his people, who had lived in this place since the creation of the world, could tell them. He allowed his people to satisfy their curiosity by gazing at these crazy strangers on their way to their deaths, but made sure that the women were covered well in shawls and out of reach of the white men, and that the braves with their cocked rifles kept apart and ready for action.

"Lieutenant Petrie," Walker called.

The lieutenant, a tall, gaunt man with a heavy mustache who spoke in the same Tennessee accent as his leader, ambled over to him.

"I want six men with me on the small raft," Walker told Petrie. "I want to cross now."

The men were puzzled, and lingered to see what the outcome of this would be. Most had long ago given up hope they would come across a cache of gold to solve their problems. But they believed unquestioningly in William Walker as their leader. He had shown himself to be braver than they were, cleverer, more resourceful. They knew he was not a god, expected there would be setbacks on his campaign, knew their loyalty would be tested, guessed Walker as a matter of principle would not be deflected by a swollen river. The desert and the Apaches on the other bank were what concerned them. Walker had not argued with the Indian or tried to discredit what he had said with laughter. As usual, William Walker had said nothing.

The men had a single unspoken hope, but all felt it would be disloyal to say aloud what each secretly wished for—that Walker would give up and cross the border to the north of them into California. Not that any of them had much to return to, but three months of fighting in the deserts and mountains were enough to give the men nostalgia for what they had before, no matter how humble or unsatisfactory things had seemed back in California. The lawyer-doctor-journalist who had led them on this expedition was a Southern gentleman and a great soldier, they respected him still, but after all these months their once solid expectations had faded to increasingly faint hopes. Now all they could think about was the shambles of their republic in the hands of bandidos, Apaches in the desert beyond the roaring river at their faces, and Fort Yuma inside the U.S. border only about seventy miles upstream from where they stood.

The men pushed the small raft into quiet water below a spit of land which they had been using for swimming. Two men poled the raft out from the river bank, but abandoned the poles as useless when the raft moved into the deep, swiftly moving water. All six men labored with broad paddles, which had about as little effect as the legs of an insect on the surface of the rushing, churning waters. William Walker stood attentively, clutching a rail at the center of the raft. His gray eyes were fixed on the opposite shore, and he ignored alike the struggles and shouts of his men and the currents and roar of the river.

The main current swept them close to the opposite shore at a bend, and the men paddled furiously to get their unwieldy craft out of the flow of water. They finally managed this by clinging to the branches of a large tree overhanging the river and pulling the raft to shore.

William Walker stepped up on the bank, looked about him for a minute without going farther, then stepped onto the raft again and pointed back at the shore which they had just left.

The six men were quietly exultant as they paddled out into the main current. Now they would be going to California! Their leader had crossed the Colorado only to show that neither nature nor man could stop him if he chose to advance. It had to be obvious, even to him, that large rafts with cattle and sheep aboard could not be gotten across.

Below the river bend the current swept them toward the western bank. They pulled the raft ashore and walked upstream some miles along the bank to their encampment. Walker still had said nothing to any of them.

"We return to San Vicente," he announced at the camp.

The men stared at him and muttered among themselves. San Vicente, near the Pacific coast and on the other side of the Sierra de Juarez, had been their starting point on this expedition. The town in Baja California was a hundred and seventy miles away to the southwest of them. He was asking them to retrace their steps.

They were to spend that night by the river and would strike camp at dawn to begin their march. In the morning three men were missing. Walker sent Lieutenant Petrie and four others on horseback after them upriver. They returned in four hours with the three men. The sun was already high in the sky, and this delay had cost them some of the coolest hours of the day in which to travel.

Walker did not raise his voice at the three men. He did not have to ask where they had been going or why.

"I hereby formally charge you with desertion," he told them. "What have you to say for yourselves?"

The three men mumbled shamefacedly, but did not try to excuse their action.

Walker told them in his quiet voice, "The penalty for desertion is death by the firing squad. I find you guilty, as charged, of desertion to the armed forces of the Republic of Lower California and Sonora. Lieutenant Petrie, you will carry out the sentence without delay."

The officer lined the three men against a gravel bank and selected six men for the firing squad. Honoring tradition, one rifle of the six was left without a lead ball, so that each of the men on the firing squad might believe he'd fired the harmless shot. All six might want to claim they had not been the one who had shot a comrade for an offense any of them might have committed under the circumstances. But this was not enough for one man.

"They've all been brave fighters, sir," he told Walker. "I won't be the one to shoot them down."

"If you disobey orders," Walker replied politely, "you may walk over there and stand with them."

In a direct challenge to him, the man handed his rifle to Walker and strode over to where his three comrades stood against the gravel bank. All four turned their eyes on Walker.

"Lieutenant Petrie, you may proceed with your orders," Walker said, joining the firing squad in the man's place.

Petrie gave the command. The six men, including William Walker, raised their rifles to their shoulders and, on Petrie's signal, fired. The blue smoke cleared slowly in the hot, still air. One of the four condemned men lay wounded on the ground, groaning horribly, and the lieutenant had to finish him off with a pistol shot to the forehead.

Walker waited patiently while graves were dug for the four men and removed his white broad-brimmed hat with the three gold stars while prayers were said for their souls.

2

THE WHITE columns of the plantation house gleamed among the dark pines clustereed about it. Two horsemen rode up the cypress-lined avenue which led from the country road to the house. As they rode they surveyed the cotton fields on either side of them, for everyone in this agricultural community kept a close eye on the progress of his neighbor's crops, as well as on his wayward behavior.

Both horsemen were young, handsome and well built. They spent less time eyeing the cotton than their fathers had on their arrival earlier that morning. The young men's minds were more on the all-day picnic that lay ahead.

"Are you going to get drunk again this year and make a fool of yourself over that girl cousin of theirs from Huntsville?" Harry Drayberry asked his companion casually.

"I never mean to get drunk," Thornton McClintock replied.

"That doesn't answer my question. Are you going to make a fool of yourself over that girl? I hear she's coming."

Thornton laughed. "Emily sure gave me hell about

that. Wouldn't let me forget it for months. But that Huntsville girl sure was a beauty, wasn't she?"

"She was," Harry conceded. "Except you got there first and wouldn't let go, I'd have thrown off Elizabeth's harness myself if I'd been given the chance."

"No, you wouldn't," Thornton said, "for fear Elizabeth might not put the bit back in your mouth and you'd be left without the reins."

Harry Drayberry said nothing to this.

Thornton McClintock was not taunting him, but merely stating a fact. Both men shared the same predicament and sought the same solution to it. They were younger sons, not heirs. Born to wealthy plantation owners whose eldest sons would inherit everything except for a fairly modest cash settlement for other members of the family, younger sons and all daughters were expected to fend for themselves—and not wait too long before going about it. Girls had their dowries and were justified to get married willy-nilly or become old maids. For a man, as the saying had it, the world was his oyster.

Neither Thornton nor Harry were going to be worldshakers. They had settled for an understanding of marriage, each to the only children of local plantation owners—fathers whose burden in life it was to bear a daughter instead of an only son. Neither had shown much in the way of academic promise, a lack that was heartily approved of by their families. The Drayberrys detested all forms of book learning, dating back, it was said, to rougher, wilder days when their grandfather shot dead on his own doorstep a process server who had the insolence to suggest he was unable to read the papers being served upon him. The McClintocks believed in reading, but only in one source, the Good Book.

Neither of the young men—they had both turned twenty-one—were a cause of worry to their families.

They were excellent horsemen, were good shots, held their liquor well on most occasions and, most important of all, had Southern pride.

They were country gentlemen, not cut out to compete with the riffraff of the outside world, and both Thornton and Harry knew this instinctively. Both would be content to live out the rest of their lives in privilege on the rich cotton lands around Antrimville in Tennessee, just north of the Alabama border.

"You ever think what it's going to be like with you settled down and all with Emily?" Harry asked finally, allowing his horse to further slow its walk along the avenue up to the plantation house.

"Maybe that's what made me cut loose with that pretty Huntsville girl."

"Your Emily's better looking than my Elizabeth," Harry said dourly.

"Yes, but Elizabeth will have more land and they'll build you a bigger house than I've been offered."

"You're not going to go through with marrying Emily, I can tell," Harry accused him.

"Maybe."

"What are you going to do instead?"

Thornton shrugged. "Maybe go to California to find gold."

"What would Emily say to that?"

"Oh hell, she likes me," Thornton said, "but she's only sixteen. It's not as if we were officially engaged to be married."

"Yet."

"I know," Thornton answered gravely.

The families of the girls were waiting for them to turn seventeen before any announcements were made. Thornton had ten months before that date, and Harry eight. These family-arranged marriages had been set up before the girls had turned thirteen and had always seemed, to the male partners at least, comfortably distant in the future and a good excuse for not doing anything but ride and hunt in the meantime. They both now felt for the first time, since the sixteenth birthday of the girls, that their freedom was being threatened.

They could delay their arrival no longer. They dismounted in the gravel area before the house, and black boys led their horses around to the stables.

Emily's father, Matthew Hardwick, host of the picnic, came to meet them. Having shook hands with him, they went to seek out Emily and Elizabeth immediately. Such behavior was the sort of thing that was noticed. If they had not sought out the company of the young ladies with speed after their late arrival, it would have amounted almost to an insult.

"One day, my boy," Harry uttered in a gruff undertone, "all this is going to be yours."

Thornton grinned bitterly. "The price is dear enough."

Thornton McClintock, like many other high-spirited men of twenty-one, tended to exaggerate his sorrows. Emily Hardwick was quite pretty in a demure way. She had lively brown eyes, a pointed chin and a petite figure. Her mouth was a bit small and its expression was tight. In her radiantly colored hooped dress with her hair raised in a chignon, she looked like a spring flower as she hurried excitedly to meet Thornton.

He sighed inwardly when he saw her delight in his arrival. What he had was an obstinate, possessive child instead of a full-grown, passionate woman, he thought to himself. He meant by this that he had already detected the strong will in this young girl—a will he as a husband would have to contend with. His other complaint was that her small frame would never carry a generous body with full breasts and big hips. Damn, he lusted for a fiery woman with a luscious mouth, a ready laugh and a body he could seize and caress, and not a prim, tiny child-woman

he could only respect—although he liked her in a
way. Were two thousand acres of cotton and a plantation house worth this? For the rest of his life? It
wasn't—Thornton had no hesitation in answering that.
It was only when he had to think of what else he
would do with his life that he smiled dutifully, took
Emily's arm, and went to meet the other guests.

The married women had gathered into groups in
the shade, keeping the sun from their treasured milk-
white complexions. When some chose to walk out
in the sun, there was much fussing with dainty be-
ribboned parasols, and they picked their way about
the lawn among the flower beds. The air was filled
with chatter and high-pitched laughter.

Most of the men stood about in solid, dignified
poses as they spoke to each other of cotton prices
and the latest Yankee outrages. They sipped bourbon with a sprig of mint and a spoon of sugar added.
Quite a few of them seemed to be well warmed with
the potent beverage. A large picnic lunch of pork
and chicken would help steady their heads.

The unmarried young above the age of fifteen,
male and female, moved everywhere, met and parted
after a few words, met again in different company,
flirted, promised dances for the ball which would be
held that night, fluttered with excitement, turned icy
with disdain, blushed at a daring word. . . .

Most mixed, joked and whispered to whoever they
met, since everyone there had grown up together with
only a few exceptions. Certain couples, promised
to each other in marriage, walked arm in arm, proud
possessors of each other.

Thornton and Emily, arm in arm, came to a group
which included the pretty girl from Huntsville, Alabama, to whom Thornton had spent so much time
speaking at last year's picnic and dancing with at the
ball. She flirted outrageously now with Thornton in
order to see if she could once again steal her cou-

sin's beau. Thornton seemed oblivious to the charms she lavished upon him, just as he did not seem to notice Emily's eagle eye watching every expression on his face. He knew he was still on trial and was very careful. He knew by the way Emily clutched his arm when they moved on to the next group that he had crossed the first hurdle.

"Look who's here," Emily gushed when she saw Harry and Elizabeth approach.

For some reason Emily liked Harry, whom many women found attractive but snubbed as a cad, and disliked Elizabeth, who seemed to Thornton to be as prim and proper as Emily herself.

Once when Thornton had tried to bring the two women together as friends, Harry had warned him off by saying, "Do you really want those two to compare notes and gang up on us?"

Elizabeth was plain. Other women felt sorry for her. They need not have. There was not a man at that picnic who sooner or later did not give her body an admiring glance as she passed. It never occurred to Harry that had it not been for Thornton's unsettling influence, he would have been genuinely satisfied with his future mate. Nor did it occur to Harry, any more than it did to Thornton himself, that Thornton's dissatisfaction had more to do with the trap he felt himself caught in than any real objection to sharing his marriage bed with Emily.

Neither Thornton nor Harry went in much for self-examination, being content to spend most of their waking hours on horseback and at the dinner table. Right now they felt like two raccoons upon very slender branches treed by dogs.

3

WILLIAM WALKER led his men on their trek to the southwest, to San Vicente and the Pacific coast of Baja California, which they had left in search of gold in the mines of Sonora. The days grew hotter as they marched south and as the second week in April brought the sun creeping high in latitude. The vast white-gold ball now beat mercilessly on them from dawn until dusk, and they had taken to hiding from it beneath blankets or in the shade of rocks from midday until late afternoon.

The animals were bone-thin. The ones they killed for food had tough meat, scarcely chewable, and it tasted odd. Many of the waterholes they had used previously had now dried up, and the cattle and sheep kept up a persistent lowing and baaing for water which so depressed the men that every now and then they beat the animals for complaining so continuously about conditions which the men themselves found almost intolerable. It was just that a man does not want a sheep or a steer to express his feelings for him. Two horses died of exhaustion, and they ate those, too.

They had expected the town of San Vicente to be deserted by its civilian population. So it was, as it

had been ever since the bandidos had begun mount-
ing their savage attacks against Walker's forces when
they'd been stationed there. But they had expected
to be greeted by the twenty men they had left behind
when they had departed on their march and whom
they now realized Walker had refused to abandon by
crossing into California. They had expected to see
the blue and white flag with the red star, the flag of
the republic, flying proudly over the town. It was
not to be seen.

Silence. They approached the dusty little town cau-
tiously. Nothing moved among the houses, not even
a hungry dog. Doors hung open on their hinges, and
no sounds came from the dark cool interiors. No
snipers shot at them. Their comrades did not respond
to their calls. As they neared their quarters, the men
halted as the stench of decomposing bodies wafted
down the street to their nostrils.

Only William Walker did not break stride. He had
dismounted at the other end of town, and had walked
in his characteristically unhurried and controlled manner in his blue uniform and black leather riding boots
up the center of the dirt street, his spurs jingling,
his saber swinging easily at his side. The sun beat
down on the terracotta tiles of the roofs, the light
danced blindingly off the white walls, and Walker's
small stature cast an extremely foreshortened shadow
before him. For a moment the only sound to be
heard was that made by his spurs, and then his men
stirred and moved forward again in his wake.

They found seven of their men. Although the heat
had speeded the natural processes of decay, it was
nevertheless plain that their ears, noses and genitals
had been cut off. Knowing their enemy as they did,
they guessed these body parts had been cut from
their comrades before they died, and that the same
fate awaited them if they should ever surrender or
be captured alive by the followers of Melendrez. But

they had left twenty men at San Vicente. Where were the other thirteen?

Walker had left instructions that the logbook was to be kept up in his absence. He now consulted it. Three attacks were described. The bandidos had swept through the town, causing the twenty men to use much ammunition to keep them at bay. As the ammunition ran short, thirteen of the men had deserted, leaving their reasons and impolite farewells to Walker in the logbook.

Walker made elaborate funeral arrangements for the seven loyal men who had died at their post. Then, to the amazement of his men, he took up residence in the town and began assigning them to guard duty and dispatching details to repair the fortifications, secure the water supply and build pens and procure forage for the animals that still remained.

The men now spoke openly of rebellion and of Walker's insanity. The talk of mutiny was not meant seriously, since there was nowhere for them to go safely if they did rebel. None of them at any time had ever considered William Walker a normal human being—if they had followed him for a single reason, it was because they hoped to profit from his daring madness. So, although the troops complained, they obeyed orders. They got things done for another good reason: any day now they expected the bandidos to return. They would need the defenses they had been ordered to build.

As the men predicted, it did not take long for the soldados of Melendrez to learn the whereabouts of the president of the republic. They knew that all Walker's supplies had been cut off, that the men in San Vicente they had not killed had already deserted, that the crazy gringo was now back in the town acting as if he were going to stay in spite of dwindling food and what they guessed was a small supply of ammunition.

However, the forces of Melendrez had their own problems. Although the bandit leader sent more than two hundred men to seal off the town of San Vicente from the outside—the rest of Walker's so-called republic having already been lost—these were not disciplined soldiers trained to obey orders whether they agreed with them or not. They were plunderers for the most part. If rich booty was dangled before their noses, they would fight to possess it. They knew they had already taken everything of value from San Vicente, and that Walker and his men were hardly worth robbing. These men did not go into combat for abstract causes, such as love of country or defense of the weak against the strong. They did not like long campaigns—win or lose, they wanted their reward or punishment swiftly.

Melendrez had now been fighting for three months against Walker's forces. His men at first believed they would capture gold and many weapons from the soft and foolish invaders. Instead they had been outmaneuvered and slaughtered without mercy, and worse, they had learned that Walker had no gold, that he was like them, a marauder, a freebooter, looking for a well-fed victim upon whom to prey. But this country was dry, hard and spare. There were no fat lambs here to be led to the butcher block, only subsistence farmers, fishermen and nomadic Indians, all of whom were willing to fight back to retain their few miserable possessions.

Now the crazy Anglo had come back to San Vicente and was flying his stupid flag there and calling himself president again. Trouble was, the Anglo was crazy like a fox. They were tired of fighting him. They just wanted him to go back where he had come from so the farmers and fishermen could go back to work and they would have someone to rob and terrorize again.

Walker's sentries had spotted them scouting the

town, and thus the bandidos' surprise attack was met by well-prepared defenders who allowed the horsemen to approach closely before firing. Bullets were scarce and each one had to count.

As the horsemen galloped down the street, pistols and swords drawn to cut down the unsuspecting Anglos, their advance riders were ripped from their saddles by the impact of lead from the barrels of concealed riflemen. As their bodies fell to the dusty street, the horses galloping behind instinctively shied away from trampling the bodies, thereby upsetting the aim of their riders and unseating a few of them.

In the meantme, each of Walker's men, well trained in these tactics, selected a particular horseman in the confusion, followed him in the sights of his rifle until he had a good shot and brought him down among the charging horses' hooves, or saw him dragged forward with a foot caught in a stirrup, his head making a furrow in the dust.

As soon as the thunder of the galloping horses died down, and it became evident that the horsemen were not going to swing around for a return pass through the town, Walker ordered Petrie to call out the names of the men. All were accounted for. They had suffered not a single injury. In teams of six, so that there was never more than one team exposed in the open at a time, they picked the weapons and ammunition from the dead and dying on the street.

They had almost doubled their arsenal this way. They took the weapons only to deprive the enemy of them. The ammunition was what they desperately needed.

Three hours after the charge had passed through the town, and only minutes after the last of the bandits had died slowly and unaided in the hot sun on the unshaded street, two horse-drawn wagons came into the town. The wagons contained four men apiece, and a tall stick with a white flag attached was tied to the base of the right shaft. Under the watchful eyes of Walker's men, who still maintained their positions, the eight men gathered up their dead onto the two wagons and then drove slowly out of town with their grisly burdens piled high.

It was agreed by general estimate that Melendrez had lost fifty men in the attack, about a quarter of the force that attacked the town. Walker's men were still outnumbered by more than three to one, but now they had much more ammunition than before, despite what they had expended in this battle.

Each succeeding day left them with less food. The horses killed in the battle had enabled them to gorge themselves on horsemeat for a couple of days before the heat rendered the flesh inedible. The bandits kept a loose watch on the town from a distance, knowing that a supply column had to arrive from the outside (which they could ambush), or else Walker would be starved out of his stronghold. Walker's men were now flushed with victory, and so long as they had food to eat and water to drink, they were content to sleep in the shade and unquestioningly follow their leader.

Lieutenant Petrie knew that no supply column was on its way, that the surrounding countryside was ravaged by warfare as well as the hostile climate and could provide them only with famine, that the animals in the pens and the stacks of flour in the larder were at a dangerously low level. He had broached the subject several times to William Walker, but this was almost impossible to do without questioning the judgment of his superior. Petrie felt those gray eyes level on him and examine him calmly, as if measuring him for a firing squad.

Finally the lieutenant felt he had the duty to confront Walker openly on what his future plans were, in view of their rapidly declining food supplies.

Walker listened to him politely. He spent some time gazing out through a window over the barren hills of this godforsaken land before replying.

"No matter how bad things become," he told Petrie, "while I remain here, my flag flies above my head and I am still President of the Republic of Lower California and Sonora."

4

THE OLD gentleman held up his silk handkerchief and motioned the four horses into a straight line abreast. The Tennessee countryside round about was filled with the vigor of late April. The dogwood trees were speckled with white flowers, and the crabapple trees with pink. Honeysuckle crept over the field hedges, and wild violets sprung up out of the tender new grass. The old gentleman held his scarlet handkerchief aloft for a moment, and then swept it down in a descending arc.

The horsemen spurred their mounts and all four sped across the field, neck to neck. They were all even at the bramble hedge at the end of the field. A big bay gelding gained half a length on the others as they jumped, and halfway across the next field this horse was a full length in front of two of the others, with the fourth horse trailing badly. They jumped another bramble hedge into a small field and then leaped a stone wall out of that into another large field.

Now they were on the home stretch. The winning post was a stick driven in the ground and painted white, with a piece of board cut in a rough circle and painted red nailed to its top. The ladies in their bonnets and hooped dresses, with gloves and parasols protecting their skins from the sun, squealed with excitement as the horses approached. They clung to the arms of their men as if the tension might overcome them and they would faint on the spot. The men, dressed in black cutaway riding coats, ruffled linen shirts, mustard or fawn trousers and leather riding boots, supported them and looked equally tense.

The cause of the men's tenseness was not the well-being of their women. Some had bet large amounts of money on a particular horse, and even those who were not big gamblers had at least bet something for luck on his own or a neighbor's son riding some horse. Most of the horses were bred locally, and many of the men there could deliver an account of a horse's breeding back over several generations, remembering the names, dates and outstanding performances of various dams and sires. The same man might be vague about the names of his own brother's children who lived ten miles away.

The riders of the horses were their owners or sons of owners for the most part—that is, gentlemen. However, poor whites when they had a good horse often used the occasion to triumph over their land-rich neighbors who asserted superiority over them in every other way.

The big bay gelding was a full two lengths ahead of the second-place horse at the post. Some of the women who did not know one horse from another clapped with delight, until they saw who was mounted on the winning horse. One of the Jacksons of the Hollow—white trash. The gentlemen and their ladies applauded politely according to the ethics of the sport as the rider brought his panting, sweating horse back to the winning post to collect his prize money. However, there was a lack of enthusiasm in the applause for the added reason that none of the gentlemen present had bet on the poor man's horse.

A few tousle-haired ragged boys led the horse in. They were younger brothers of the rider, because the

Jacksons owned no slaves. Not because they disapproved of slavery—they did not—only because they themselves lived hardly better than slaves, at least slaves on the farms with humane masters. The great difference was that the Jacksons were white and were free men, while slaves belonged like cattle to their master, and even the most decent owner had his off-days when he misused those in his total power.

"Blood!" one man called. "There's blood coming from beneath the saddle."

He pointed to the side of the bay gelding which had won the race, and indeed a trickle of blood ran from beneath the saddle down its heaving, steaming flank.

The rider jumped down and pushed the man away from his horse. He was in his early twenties, a big raw youth with a cast in one eye, broken yellow teeth and huge, work-hardened hands.

"Give me my prize money," he demanded belligerently.

The Jacksons were descended from swamp-dwellers and backwoods folk who had come to the place as trappers when it was still wilderness. They lived off what they grew on their few acres of mediocre land, and on what they shot and trapped. The prize money for the race was very little, not even half the average bet a gentleman would have placed on the race, but that money, little enough as it was, might be the only hard cash any of the Jacksons had handled in months. They needed that money. But every Jackson had Southern pride. No one denied them that.

To insinuate to a prideful Southerner that all was not well with the way he handled his horse was looking for trouble. But the Jackson youth who had ridden the horse was anxious to collect his prize money first; he would take care of the insinuations later. He again pushed the man away from his horse, along with some others who had tried to get a closer look.

"Give me my prize money," he demanded again.

Harry Drayberry circled around to the other side of the big horse and reached under him to unbuckle the belly band that held the saddle. The saddle slipped off on the rider's side, revealing a twig of a locust tree, its long hard thorns placed between the saddle and the horse's back so that the weight of the rider on the saddle would drive the thorns into the horse's flesh, cruelly goading him to further effort.

The Jackson youth knew his prize money was now forfeited. In a rage at being insulted and cheated of his prize, he pulled out a huge bowie knife. If he could not have his money, he knew what he could have— vengeance on the man who caused him to lose it by unbuckling the horse's belly band.

Jackson had to run around the horse's head to get at Drayberry, and as Harry saw him coming with the sharp bowie blade extended before him, he took several rapid steps backward while he pulled a pistol and cocked it. He leveled the gun at Jackson's head.

"Not a step farther or I shoot," Harry said in a cool voice.

Jackson was beyond reason. Or perhaps he decided it was more honorable for him to die in this frenzied attack than to accept another humiliation in being disarmed at gunpoint. Whatever the cause, the big man kept coming for Harry with the bowie knife.

Harry lowered the pistol barrel and the weapon discharged with a loud report and a puff of blue smoke.

Ladies fainted. Most of the women, however, were intrigued and would not have missed a moment of it, no matter how much decorum demanded that feminine delicacy could not withstand such displays of violence. Incidents like this were almost daily events, but few of the women ever got to witness them and had to satisfy their curiosity through their menfolk's accounts.

Today they saw for themselves the cool way that Harry Drayberry handled himself, how he had drawn his weapon so quickly when his life had been threatened, how he had called on his attacker to halt before discharging the weapon, how he had lowered the barrel of the pistol before firing so as not to take the life of his maddened attacker. Truly, despite his wild ways and the things that often were said against him, every woman there saw for herself how Harry Drayberry had behaved like a gentleman.

And then the ladies saw with their own eyes the red hole appear on the thigh of the nasty Jackson boy and how he fell down, howling and clutching his leg. His family took him away on a mule-drawn cart. The doctor went with them, and laughingly told some gentlemen before he left that the bone had not been hit by the bullet, that it was a flesh wound, and the Jackson boy's howls were as much a result of shame as serious hurt.

The prize money was awarded to the second-place horse, and bettors pleased with that result treated Harry to tall glasses of bourbon. It was just about everyone's opinion, they told old Winston Drayberry, that his son Harry was a real Southern gentleman and a credit to the county.

Thornton McClintock won the first race he was entered in. He rode a roan mare owned and bred by Emily's father, and Matthew Hardwick had bet a fistful of gold coins on his future son-in-law. Emily was dizzy with pride when she held the reins of the horse for a moment and accepted the prize money for her father.

"You will have no chance at all against Thornton later today," she told Harry, playfully sniffing at the bourbon he was drinking.

Harry had not been in that race. He had ridden once already that day, but on a green horse that was just being shown the course.

Harry laughed. "I was wondering who had organized all those people to treat me to drinks. I should have guessed it was you, Emily, trying to help your precious Thornton to win."

The racecourse was a casual affair—several level fields that had good jumping fences and quality grass without too many rough tussocks or rodent holes, which could so easily break a swiftly moving horse's leg. The number of races depended on the number of horses brought to the meet, and on who wished to race against whom.

All betting was between individuals, and when personal reputations and long rivalries were involved, the stakes could be high. The riders, mostly young and yet to come into their inheritances, rarely wagered more than a few silver dollars on their mounts. Often enough they were unwilling to bet anything at all on their chances.

Thornton McClintock had three mounts that day, and Harry Drayberry two. They would meet each other in the last race of the day, both riding their favorite horses. As Harry succumbed to successive offers of bourbon, Thornton rose in favor with the bettors looking forward to their race. Thornton's second mount touched the stone wall with its right hind hoof as it cleared the obstacle and stumbled on landing. Thornton was thrown from the saddle and winded by the fall.

He revived himself with a few bourbons while watching other races, so that when it came time for the two young men to race, the general consensus of opinion was that there was little to choose between the condition of these two riders, and interest spread to other entrants in the last race.

At the downsweep of the yellow silk handkerchief—a second old gentleman acted as starter for this race—the seven horses thundered forward neck to neck across the broad field. They cleared the bramble hedge into the next field and crossed that and were all still racing neck to neck when they jumped the second bramble hedge into the small field and headed for the stone wall. The wall could be a brutal test for both horse and rider. One horse fell and another lost so much ground its rider eased up. Of the five horses still in the running, those of Thornton and Harry pulled out by a neck ahead of the third horse. They were still racing nose to nose.

This was a two-mile race, so instead of heading for the winning post straight away, they bore to the left along a course marked by occasional boughs stuck in the grass. They rounded a giant elm tree in the middle of the field and then headed for home.

"Get over!" Harry yelled to Thornton, who was riding high on the marked course and keeping Harry's horse pinned out there with him.

Thornton glanced behind to make sure that he had forced the third-place horse on the outside along with Harry's horse, and that the horses following were far enough behind not to be able to catch up by taking the shorter inner side of the course to the winning post.

Harry could understand what Thornton's strategy was. His horse and the other one were trapped on the outside because he could not get ahead of Thornton to cross him, and if he dropped behind he would never gain the ground again.

"Bastard!" Harry shouted and grinned. He knew there was a trick somewhere and he wanted to turn it against Thornton by seeing it in time.

The last obstacle before the home stretch was a seven-foot-wide brook with the higher bank on the near side. As they leaped the water, Harry saw too late what Thornton had done to him. Thornton's chestnut stallion landed squarely on firm ground, but Harry found his horse had been forced to land on soggy ground whose soft soil had been chopped by horses in earlier races. Harry's horse came in a poor second in the race.

"Devil take you," Harry told Thornton as he reined in at the finish. Thornton had already dismounted and was being congratulated warmly by Emily.

"Harry, such language!" she teased him.

"I had forgotten he had ridden a two-miler previously and knew the ground," Harry said. "My other race was only six furlongs."

"Excuses!" Elizabeth said as she came up to them.

"What do you mean?" Harry asked her, with a smile. "He just cheated me out of a race by running me into soft ground. If it weren't for Emily, I would have already shot the rascal."

There was much laughter and new challenges issued for the next race day as the owners and riders and their families made for the manor house of the plantation on which the races had been held. After the ladies and children had left for home, a group of younger men gathered about the billiards table in the smoking room, and some of their livelier elders held a session of their own in the card room.

It was after nine that night when the men finally broke up. Some were considerably the worse for wear, but most prided themselves on how they could hold their liquor, and carried themselves erect—in their own eyes at least. The moon lit up the countryside, and some of the riders gathered at the main gates of the plantation's avenue, still unwilling to go home.

Thornton and Harry took to arguing about the outcome of their race that afternoon. There was no acrimony in their voices, for they had been racing each other since their early teens and both were aware that neither one exceeded the other as a horseman, or a dozen others in the area for that matter. Riding standards were high around Antrimville.

The two ended up racing each other over the moonlit fields before their horses, already tired from that afternoon's race, slowed and made the competition one of endurance rather than speed. Both men had too much affection for their horses to force them to run when exhausted, and by mutual agreement they slowed to a walk and brought their horses to a stream where they could drink.

Across the moonlit fields a lamp burned in an upstairs window of a large house. It was Elizabeth's home.

"I'm going to throw a pebble up at her window and say goodnight to her," Harry announced.

"You'll probably smash the glass and her father will take a shot at you."

Harry laughed and they rode across the fields toward the house. They stopped talking as they neared a row of slave cabins, so as not to rouse them and have them sound an alarm.

"Hold it," Thornton whispered and caught Harry by the arm.

They stopped their horses side by side beneath a row of tall trees as they watched a figure coming unsteadily down the moonlit path past the slave cabins. It was Elizabeth's father. He had stayed on in the card room after his wife and daughter departed for home.

Harry snickered. "Do you think he's lost his way? Can't find his own front door?"

Thornton hushed him.

The plantation owner had not seen them and was too drunk to pay any attention to the noise they made. He passed the last in the row of slave cabins and went on to one apart from the others in the woods. He tried to push the cabin door in, but it was locked.

He beat on the door with his fist. "Goddamn it, let me in or I'll have your hide. Open up. Now!"

A lamp was lit inside the cabin and soon the door was opened. Holding the lamp was a pretty teenaged black girl with an alarmed look.

The plantation owner caught her by the arm and pushed her inside the cabin ahead of him. The cabin door slammed shut after him.

Thornton and Harry exchanged an uncomfortable look.

Harry said, "He bought that girl last week down in Alabama. I hear he paid a real pile of money for her."

They said nothing more to each other and headed their horses for the main road, ready to call it a night.

5

WILLIAM WALKER remained in San Vicente as president of his republic until the last steer and sheep had been slaughtered and consumed for food. Only then was the blue and white flag with the red star folded carefully and put into one of his saddlebags and the town of San Vicente abandoned. Walker was not the kind of man to address his troops with heroic speeches and thundering rhetoric. No man there had to be told they had been starved out, not beaten as soldiers on the battlefield. They all were convinced that if the United States had not actively interfered by blockading their supplies, their forces under Walker's leadership would have decimated the bandidos led by Melendrez and either tamed or banished the bands of fierce Apaches. Once they had gained a foothold as an independent republic, Mexico would not have been able to organize a force so far from its center of power capable of overwhelming them. They had nothing to be ashamed of. They had fought everyone as soldiers, but in the end had been starved out by the tricky politicians in the north.

They marched up the Pacific coast, a journey that was much easier than their recent trek across the interior. Fresh water was plentiful and, while food was far from abundant along the way, they did not go hungry.

The soldados of Melendrez tracked them like a pack of hungry coyotes waiting for a sign of weakness or hoping for some individuals to go astray and become vulnerable to their attack. When they gave chase, Walker and his men stood and prepared to fight, even though outnumbered by more than three to one, but the bandits always broke ranks and scattered before the orderly rows of their waiting rifles.

Walker was quiet on the journey—not grieving or in a sulk, but silent and inscrutable. The men felt a renewed intensity of loyalty toward him, for he gave their lives importance and dignity. Before him they had been wastrels and layabouts, not independent or fierce enough to become full-time outlaws or professional gunfighters, not smart enough to live on easy pickings or as gamblers, not lucky enough to prosper as miners, not hardworking enough to ranch. These were not the men whose faces appeared on wanted posters for stagecoach and bank robberies. They had been treated as rabble all their lives. They were rabble. But this little man with fair hair and merciless gray eyes gave them dignity! This republic had been lost, but they knew the world had not heard the last of William Walker. They would follow him still.

Lieutenant Petrie did not belong to this mob, though he was rough and ready and hard-eyed as any man of them. Like Walker, the gaunt officer was from Tennessee, and a gentleman, and both men always refrained from asking each other what incidents in their pasts had driven them to their present whereabouts. Petrie knew why he had attached himself as right-hand man to Walker.

It had been only six years—on February the second, 1848, at Guadalupe Hidalgo—since Mexico had ceded to the United States the territory between the Nueces and Rio Grande, together with the whole of New

Mexico and California. Petrie still believed there had been nothing outlandish in Walker's ambitions in founding the Republic of Lower California and Sonora. The new American president, Franklin Pierce, who had been inaugurated only the previous year, 1853, had himself fought against the Mexicans in some of the bloodiest battles as a brigadier general. It was inconceivable to Petrie that this man, who had achieved his nation's highest office through his gallantry as a soldier against the Mexicans, could now renounce the Manifest Destiny of the United States by stabbing in the back a pioneer expansionist like William Walker.

If there were weaknesses in his arguments, Petrie was not the sort of man whom people disagreed with readily or corrected carelessly. He had never fought a duel over a woman, but he had killed three men and wounded two others for their lack of respect in challenging his beliefs. Men with temperaments like that often persist in the error of their ways, unchecked by the remarks or observations of those who know them best.

Walker and Petrie created between them the punctilio of a Southern drawing room in the wastes of Sonora and Baja California, treating each other with elaborate courtesy and formality among the cactuses and rocks, and the white trash they commanded followed their movements with the stupefied fascination of a snake gazing at a mongoose.

While the men feared Petrie and knew he would cut the tongue from the head of any living man who spoke against Walker, they could see that Petrie in turn feared Walker as they did. Petrie at heart was made of the same stuff as they were. Walker was not. Walker did not fear death. Bullets did not harm him. Where others quaked, he gained strength. Walker did not doubt. He could not be fooled or outguessed. Walker gave them all dignity.

It was not a dispirited group of failed adventurers

that marched north along the Pacific to the United States border. These men had tried and succeeded as soldiers. Outnumbered as they were, they scattered the enemy about them still and did not take a single casualty on the march north. But they had been cheated out of their just rewards by the schemers in Washington.

As they approached the border, Melendrez made them an offer that if they laid down their weapons, he would grant them a safe conduct into U.S. territory. Otherwise he would prevent them from escaping. Walker laughed good-naturedly at this and informed the messengers that Melendrez had not the courage to attack him and that he had no intention of bargaining with a coward.

Walker declined his men's offers to gouge out the eyes of Melendrez' messengers or even to chop off their fingers or ears. He made sure they returned in safety bearing his insult to the bandido leader.

Word had gone on ahead of the group that William Walker was coming back to the States to surrender. When they marched within sight of the border, the men cheered as the Stars and Stripes was run up on the flagpole to greet them and a uniformed contingent of the U.S. Army formed ranks behind their mounted officers. Walker was immensely pleased by this. It seemed proper to him that his surrender should be accepted with as much military ceremony as possible. His men began to march in step, form lines from the left and shoulder their rifles to demonstrate to their fellow countrymen that they were disciplined troops, not ragamuffins.

Melendrez had suffered much from this three-month-old republic formed by the loco Anglo out of what had always been regarded as Melendrez territory. His reputation had been irreparably damaged. He had lost untold numbers of men in battles. The entire economy of the region had been wrecked, and the years ahead would yield lean pickings to his predatorial troops. And finally he had been personally insulted by the crazy gringo. Called a coward before his own men, Melendrez was going to teach this Yanqui a lesson. He was going to cut him and his men to pieces in full view of Walker's countrymen on the other side of the border, which they would not dare cross to rescue this political adventurer who had been condemned by the Federal government in Washington.

Just as Walker's men began to get their second wind and pick up their weary feet with renewed vigor for a proud crossing of their border, Melendrez' horsemen swung around on both sides of the small force (numbering thirty-seven, including Walker himself) and the approximately one hundred and fifty armed horsemen formed a barrier between them and the border. Only Walker and Petrie still had mounts. Walker drew his saber and held it up, shouting to his men to maintain marching order and not to slacken pace.

The men were marching five abreast in seven lines, with only three men in the rear line and Walker and Petrie mounted in front. Their horses pulled to one side, and the men halted suddenly. The first row of five men dropped to one knee, while the second row remained standing. Simultaneously both rows raised their rifles to their shoulders, Walker slashed downward with his saber and ten rifles went off. In the line of horsemen between them and the border, ten Mexicans fell from their saddles.

The first two rows of men ran to the back of the troop and reformed as the two rear rows and reloaded their rifles. The new front row dropped to their knees and ten rifles were raised in unison with the saber in Walker's hand. The saber did not have to fall again. Melendrez' men were fierce and brave fighters, but sitting still as targets was not part of their code of heroism. They scattered to the sides in disarray, and to cover their embarrassment at this retreat, most made off to a great distance and could not be recalled to attack.

Walker's little army resumed its dignified march north. The U.S. Army officers on the other side of the border had difficulty in reforming ranks of their cheering, exultant soldiers.

Major MacKistry and Captain Burton saluted William Walker before handing him a paper scroll and asking him and his men to sign it.

PAROLE OF HONOR
The undersigned, Officers and Privates of the (so-called) Republic of Sonora, do solemnly pledge their word of honor to report themselves at San Francisco, Cal., to Major General Wood, of the United States Army, charged with having violated the Neutrality Laws of the United States.

San Diego, Cal., May 8, 1854

There were to be no chains, no arrests. They were expected to behave according to their word of honor. Walker had no illusions about his opponents in the States. If they could have led him bound in disgrace and thrown him in a filthy dungeon, they would have done so.

He looked up to see the undisguised admiration on the faces of the American regular soldiers there to accept his surrender. In an instant of silent communication, Walker in a single look let MacKistry and Burton know that if it came to a challenge, their own men would rally round him, not them. Walker then signed the paper and handed it to Petrie for him and the men to sign.

Only then did Walker ride a few paces forward and become aware of the excited crowd of civilians who waited to greet him beyond the soldiers. It seemed to him that the entire population of the town of San

Diego was there. It began to dawn on Walker that he was returning home a legend and a hero.

Something bothered him. Something about that paper he had signed. What had it been? Yes, he had forgotten. The date. May 8. It was his birthday. He had turned thirty.

He spurred his horse forward and continued north at the head of his troop, clearing the cheering throng.

6

THORNTON MCCLINTOCK and Harry Drayberry bid good-bye to their families, promised to behave themselves and set out for Huntsville, Alabama, in a horse and trap driven by the Drayberrys' family coachman. Both young men were dressed in their finest, and each had brought a single large bag. At Huntsville they boarded the new train south to Mobile. The three hundred-mile journey took the train twenty hours to travel, and they arrived in the Gulf port early on the following day. They transferred immediately to a coastal steamer to New Orleans and traveled the one hundred fifty-mile sea journey in a day and a half.

Harry was awestruck. "Counting the fact that we live fifty miles from Huntsville, we've just traveled five hundred miles in less than three days. Can you believe that?"

"One of the wonders of the modern world," Thornton answered unenthusiastically. He was not a good sailor.

"Five hundred miles in less than three days!" Harry repeated in wonder. "You know, some of the old folks back in Antrimville wouldn't believe this was humanly possible if we told them we'd done it."

Thornton grinned maliciously. "There's a lot of

things about you they might find hard to believe if someone told them you'd done them."

"There's no call for that kind of talk, Thornton. And I know you'll never be the one to tell them since you have so much of your own to hide which would make your fond mother shed bitter tears and reach for her Bible."

"I'm thinking of maybe adding a few things to that store on this trip to New Orleans," Thornton said. "That new railroad and all may get us here very fast, but I still think we had more fun when we had to take the stage overland to Memphis and the riverboat down the Mississippi to New Orleans. That had more style than the damn railroad."

"We had good times on those riverboats," Harry said nostalgically.

"You're forgetting Memphis."

Both laughed uproariously, recalling the year they had set out for New Orleans but had got no farther than the wild nightlife of Memphis. After two weeks in that river town, they had limped home exhausted, broke, a week early.

They stayed in an elegant and very proper hotel in New Orleans. Both men had relatives upon whom duty calls had to be paid. They restricted such social obligations to the afternoons. The mornings they spent on the cotton exchange, talking with merchants and exporters, meeting growers visiting from other parts of the South, looking at new agricultural machinery and hearing of new strains of the upland varieties chiefly grown in the Cotton Belt. Their evenings were devoted to the theater and music hall. After that they looked in on one of the gentlemen's clubs they had introductions to for talk, drinks and billiards or cards. They always finished at a brothel.

In none of these somewhat varied activities was there ever any necessity for either of them to descend below the conduct or surroundings of a gentleman. The portly banker they had met the day before at a cousin's afternoon tea was pleased to stand them bourbon when they ran into him that night at a brothel; a merchant at the cotton exchange warned them against the high-stakes games at a particular club; an architect they met at a club agreed to take them backstage the following night to meet an exotic dancer whose artistry and imagination Thornton and Harry very much admired.

The New Orleans of that time was not free of all Victorian propriety. In fact, the city was a model of Victorian respectability in the sense that a gentleman could do anything he pleased so long as he did not do it in the streets and frighten the horses.

The brothels Harry and Thornton visited each catered to a characteristic clientele. Some featured gorgeous chocolate-brown girls where a young white man reared in the rural South could break hearth-shattering taboos without causing the roof timbers to be set afire. Others specialized in octoroon and Creole beauties with almond-shaped eyes and lemon skins, who spoke in West Indian as well as Louisiana English and French accents and who wore the latest in Paris gowns. Some houses were mixed, some were all-white. Fresh-complexioned English and Irish girls who had gone astray in the New World were always popular. So were Southern belles, whom fortune had cast on these bitter distressful rocks and who now fell prey to the avaricious, lustful clutches of males long teased and frustrated by pretty things in hooped dresses with flirtatious smiles and fluttering eyelashes. There were houses for everyone. Even for those with "special needs."

The house which was *the* place to go that year was Madame Laura's. The madame herself always came to the door, and newcomers had to be known to her or be accompanied by someone she knew before they were admitted.

"Laura . . ." Harry turned the name over in his mind. "Is she a tall woman who smokes cheroots?"

"That's her," their informant said, impressed that these out-of-towners should know Laura.

"Remember that roadhouse we went to year before last on the way to Baton Rouge?" Harry asked Thornton. "The time you and that woman jumped in the lake."

Thornton smiled. "My recollection is vague."

"Laura owned that place," Harry said. "I don't know if she'll let us in her new house, but she sure as hell will remember us."

They walked out to her new establishment one night after leaving a club. The location was on a well-to-do commercial street, deserted after business hours. The street had obviously once been residential, and the business now occupied what were once townhouses. Madame Laura's house must have been built by the most ostentatious, if not important, of these former citizens. The building was an almost perfect cube, three stories high, fronted by a two-tiered wrought-iron balcony with delicate metal trellisework and filigrees. Harry banged the shining brass doorknocker.

The door was opened inward immediately, and Thornton and Harry were faced with two huge men who might have once been Scandinavian sailors.

"My, my, look who's here," a woman's voice came from behind the monolithic guards. "Two hellrakes down from Tennessee. Come in, gentlemen. Make yourselves at home."

"Good evening, Laura," Harry said. "You remember my companion here?"

Laura gave Thornton a wary look. "No taking my girls out for midnight swims tonight. The water is miles from here."

"There's still too much of a chill in the air," Thornton reassured her.

Laura smiled at them tolerantly. At forty-three, she was twice their age but had not yet reached the stage where all she felt for a handsome young man was maternal feelings. She puffed on a cheroot and walked with a wiggle in her daring narrow skirt, the latest fashion from Europe, ahead of the two men into the main room of her establishment.

An enormous chandelier dominated the upper part of the large room, and light was further reflected through the haze of tobacco smoke in beveled-edge mirrors placed on all four pine-panelled walls. The amorphous pearl-gray clouds of smoke turned and rolled like a storm gathering in the sky. The din of laughter and talk and the clinking of glasses almost drowned out the sound of music.

"The violinist is Hungarian and the pianist is Polish," Laura told them indignantly. "Very talented, respectable people, and no one listens to them."

"We'll come early the next night so we can hear them," Thornton joked.

"Sure, come early," Laura invited him. "You and I will share a bottle of champagne. My treat."

"It seems Madame has taken a fancy to you," Harry said after she left. "I think she herself comes with the champagne as part of the treat."

"She made that plain."

"Are you interested?"

"Ask me tomorrow," Thornton said. "You see what I see?"

Harry saw. Two extraordinarily beautiful women waiting to be invited by them into conversation. Both were clad in off-the-shoulder, alluring gowns which revealed the upper parts of their breasts. One had long, straight black hair and blue eyes, and she thrust her narrow hips provocatively to one side and sipped languidly from a stemmed glass as she eyed the two men. Her friend said something to her which made her giggle. Then her friend stole a coquettish look at the two men, her melting brown eyes lingered on them and her knowing smile was suggestive.

This was what Thornton had in mind back in Antrimville when he thought about the kind of women he wanted.

Harry picked Blue Eyes, Thornton liked Brown Eyes. They drank a bottle of champagne. The girls were obviously happy to be in the company of handsome, lively men their own age, and Thornton believed that Brown Eyes' touches and warm looks were not entirely only professional and calculated.

Thornton ascended the staircase, discreetly hidden behind a glass-bead curtain, hand in hand with Brown Eyes. She locked the door of a luxurious bedroom behind them. The massive four-poster bed had fresh linen. Little lamps flickered about the room, creating an intimate atmosphere, and they could no longer hear the din of voices from downstairs.

Brown Eyes sat on the edge of the bed and in a demure, ladylike manner waited for Thornton to act. He had to smile. This lady was clever—she knew exactly what he wanted her to be for him. He asked her if he could kiss her—many women who sold their bodies without giving it a thought reserved this right as their own privacy. She nodded. He enjoyed her sensuous lips and ran his hands over her soft shoulders and arms, softly stroking and caressing her. When she turned away from him, he nuzzled her neck and held her breasts from behind, tenderly but firmly.

Her breasts filled his hands and he felt them swell in his palms beneath the silky material. His fingers slipped inside her gown and felt her unprotected breasts. The nipples of the young firm breasts were upturned. His fingertips circled the aureole around each nipple, occasionally teasing and pinching gently the nipple itself so that it stood erect and longed for more attention.

She peeled her long dress off her body like the covering of a ripe fruit waiting to be devoured. He explored every inch of her with his fingertips, lips and tongue. He waited to enter her until she was trembling and anguished for his healing touch, until there was nothing left of her act as a professional seductress and woman of the night, until he was sure she now wanted him as a woman wants and then needs a man to start the fires of desire in her, build the flames till they consume her and finally quench the burning fever in her flesh.

He mounted her tender, palpitating body which welcomed him with moist warmth, and he pressed forward with his manhood into her shuddering, clasping need.

7

WILLIAM WALKER played his cards well. Where another man might have let the adulation he received from the crowds in San Francisco go to his head, might have begun to believe in his own myth, might have flaunted himself in uniform to entertain and gain favor with the rich and powerful—Walker did none of these things.

On the day appointed he appeared in the courthouse dressed not as a flamboyant soldier of fortune, but in a black frock coat with a black velvet collar, a plain well-starched white linen shirt with a high stiff collar and a black bow tie. He looked more like an undertaker or a divinity student than a soldier. When he spoke to say he wished to conduct his own defense, his Southern courtesy and mild manners contrasted with the self-righteous hectoring of the prosecutor, S.W. Inge, an austere New Englander whose frigid manner caused him great unpopularity at every level of society in the roaring pioneer town of San Francisco.

The prosecutor accused him of being a ruthless filibusterer and adventurer whose main interest in founding the Republic of Lower California and Sonora was not, as he claimed, to bring democracy to the admittedly abused population of the area, but to seize the goldmines of Sonora and thereby enrich himself and his followers at the expense of the foreign nationals of that place.

Walker's defense was simple. He had gone to aid an oppressed people. He stood erect and serious in his black coat and stiff high collar, looking every bit as respectable as the judge himself, and told the court that he had founded the republic solely for the sake of Christ and liberty.

In spite of sneers from the prosecutor and admonitions from the judge, the jury took only eight minutes to find William Walker innocent on all charges.

Byron Cole slapped his plump thigh and his jowls shook helplessly with laughter.

"He's priceless," he finally gasped.

"I'm not so sure he is a trickster," the court reporter disagreed. "I think Walker may really believe in himself. That's what the jury reacted to—as well as believing we should grab Sonora."

"I've nothing to complain about," Cole granted. "He's provided us with a lot of hot copy for quite a while now. Ever since he founded that tinpot republic of his."

Byron Cole was publisher of the *San Francisco State Democratic Journal,* but did not see himself restricted to the role of journalist. Cole viewed himself as an entrepreneur, as someone who could direct the efforts and talents of others to achieve the greatest results.

As a newspaper publisher he was grateful to phenomena like William Walker, but he did not distinguish between Walker and earthquakes, the coming of the railroads or Commodore Perry's landing in Japan—so long as they remained newsworthy, they were to be pursued relentlessly. But the public was fickle, and a new volcano or Indian uprising was always coming along to make today's heroes tomorrow's forgotten men.

As an entrepreneur Byron Cole felt a spark of interest. A man whom the public accepted as a hero and who believed in himself as one was definitely a man with possibilities.

"I hear his troops are loyal to him in spite of misfortune, and that every one of them showed up in court today," Cole said.

"That's right," the reporter answered. "They told me they would follow him through hell or high water."

"I'd like to meet him," the publisher told his reporter.

The background of William Walker was by now common knowledge. Instead of puncturing the myth, the details of his past life served to feed the legend which had continued to build around him.

He was born in Nashville, Tennessee, on May 8, 1824. His father was a wealthy merchant, a Scots immigrant who never got on well with his son. William qualified in medicine at the University of Pennsylvania and then spent a year in Europe, in Paris and Heidelberg. On his return to Nashville, he announced he was bored with being a doctor and apprenticed himself to a law firm in Nashville first and later in New Orleans. While practicing law in New Orleans, he began writing for a progressive Abolitionist newspaper there. He then moved to the new territory of California and gradually abandoned law in favor of journalism. He finally abandoned journalism in favor of becoming a soldier of fortune, having already attained a formidable reputation as a duellist.

This doctor-lawyer-journalist, born of a family wealthy enough to send him on a tour of Europe, small in stature, modest in demeanor, soft in voice, cultured —the sort of man the sturdy pioneers of this gold town and busy port might pretend to defer to with a sly grin and a mocking aside—had bloomed into a soldier of fortune under the California sun. As San Franciscans saw it, California had made a man of him. They were proud of him.

The United States, even then, with its relatively scant

population, was feeling the first limitations of size and power. Since Colonial days, the driving force of the expanding nation had been the push westward, into the wilds of Pennsylvania, of Georgia, the crossing of the Mississippi, the prairies, Texas, the Rockies, California. Halted by the Pacific Ocean, America could go no farther west.

Byron Cole understood this as the impulse that drove William Walker south—the urge to expand America farther beyond its borders, call it Manifest Destiny, because men like Walker always rounded up God on their side like a doting general who could be depended upon to approve anything he was handed.

So William Walker believed wholly in himself as a leader of men. . . . Cole positively beamed with pleasure. Cole felt this was indicative he was no mere newspaperman. Ideas like this came only to great entrepreneurial spirits. First of all he had to meet this Walker fellow personally to make sure for himself he was not a braggadocio or a fly-by-night. Then, if all went well, he would have a serious chat over mutton chops and a bottle of wine with Cornelius K. Garrison of the banking firm of Garrison, Morgan, Rolston & Fretz, of New York, Panama and San Francisco. Cole might have a very interesting proposition for him.

8

THORNTON MCCLINTOCK rode his horse through the chilly fall morning at first light to the stables at the rear of the Drayberry plantation house. Harry was saddling his horse outside its stable door. Even the slaves were still asleep. The shoes of McClintock's horse rang on the cobblestones of the yard, and the animal's breath formed spumes in the morning air. Wind blew brown leaves across the yard. The first frosts of winter were not far away.

"Good morning." That was all Thornton said.

Harry nodded to him, unsmiling.

Neither had to pretend to the other they were confident and happy about what they faced today. Although on the previous day they had felt bound to commit themselves, dawn on the day of reckoning weakened their resolve.

They rode out of the stable yard quietly, set off down the avenue and put the horses into a canter on the county road. They were not late, but wanted to free their minds of apprehension and get their vital juices flowing with this morning gallop.

"Jethro and the others will meet us at Harpers Cross," Thornton yelled to Harry.

He was aware that Harry already knew this, and more dimly aware of what he was really saying—that they must not let their friends see them silent and despondent.

Without thinking about it, Harry understood. "We'll show our friends how we can whip those goddam Northerners!"

This was not the first time either of them had ridden to a duel at dawn. Nor was it the first time they had felt trapped by their own hot words and reckless challenges. But all those other quarrels had been with Southerners like themselves, where in the vast majority of cases a couple of shots fired deliberately wide were enough to settle the matter of honor.

If the quarrel was really rancorous and if ill-feeling survived the dawn awakening the next morning, a bullet aimed for an arm or leg would satisfy honor, but even this was not commonly done. Often an arm or leg wound festered, necessitating amputation of the limb after a time, and even causing death in a number of cases. This was not the kind of revenge a Tennessee gentleman sought in a duel, which in any case he fought only with other gentlemen. A horsewhipping was sufficient for the lower orders, or for serious offenses they were run down with dogs and strung up on the nearest tree.

No one knew what to expect from these Northerners. The previous night Jethro Hadden, Thornton's second, had tried to broach a conversation with opponents' seconds, also Northerners, and nothing had come of it. They were prepared to shoot to kill, apparently.

The quarrel had occurred the previous afternoon when six midshipmen, as the students were known, from the newly reorganized U.S. Naval Academy at Annapolis, Maryland, came to a race meeting near Antrimville. The Northerners had come South for the wedding of a fellow midshipman who lived nearby and who was now in Savannah with his new bride. The six midshipmen had lingered on for a few days on Southern hospitality and bourbon before returning to the rigors of naval training at Annapolis.

"This lout fancies he's won the Epsom Derby on that spavined nag," one midshipman remarked, perhaps more loudly then he intended, of Harry Drayberry returning from a win on a friend's horse.

Harry leaped down from the horse's back to confront this insult at its source. He struck the midshipman a glancing blow on the head before the others separated them.

"I'll race you," Harry shouted at the offending midshipman over the shoulders of those between them. "I'll race you any distance you like for a twenty-dollar gold piece."

"I have no horse," the Northerner shouted back.

At this point Thornton intervened. "I'll get you one. You may have my horse to race him, sir. Or any other you see here at the meet. I'll get its owner to lend it to you so we can all see a display of your horsemanship against this fine Southern rider."

"I see no horses worthy of me here, sir," the obnoxious midshipman retorted.

"Nor gentlemen, either," another midshipman joined in.

Harry had to be held back again.

Thornton remained cool. "I hear it's the fashion in the North to shout insults like a fishwife and expect only insults in return. Here in the South we are real men. We expect others to back what they say with deeds."

When they heard this kind of talk, the locals keeping Harry and Thornton away from the midshipmen drew back, willing to let what they now regarded as justified combat take place.

Not so Emily and Elizabeth. They simultaneously

rushed forward and seized their men by an arm, pleading with them to leave and say no more.

The midshipmen laughed at this. It was the second midshipman who spoke this time.

"Their women look no better than their horses," he said loudly.

His fellow students did not laugh at this. They had seen Thornton grow deadly pale and take a step slowly forward.

"You'll pay for this with your life," he growled in a tone of voice Emily had never heard from him before and which made her shiver.

Harry snarled, "I want the other one's blood on my hands."

Jethro Hadden had been the friend standing closest to Thornton.

"Be my second," Thornton requested of him, "and make all the necessary arrangements for us."

Jethro nodded. Thornton and Harry left, escorting their ladies.

Thus it was that both men rose before dawn on this particular day to avenge in blood the words spoken by a drunken midshipman at their ladies. Harry's anger seemed to stem mainly from the slur made at his horsemanship. The irony was not lost on Thornton that this morning he was going to fight a man and perhaps die because that man had expressed an opinion that Emily and Elizabeth were not ravishing beauties. Harry and himself had said a lot worse to each other about their ladies and had been taunted from time to time by friends. However, the stranger's insult had been intended to humiliate the men publicly and wound the feelings of the two women, and for that he would justifiably find himself fighting for his life this morning.

They came upon Jethro and the others at Harpers Cross and rode out together to the edge of the woodlands where duels in the area traditionally were fought.

Tradition too dictated dawn as the time for the contest. In Europe and the Eastern states the hour guaranteed a lack of interference from the authorities, whose attitude at best was always ambiguous toward duelling. But at this time and in this part of Tennessee, there was nothing to prevent men from fighting each other at any hour of the day, as indeed they often did. Yet gentlemen had always fought duels at dawn, so at dawn it would be.

They arrived on the field before the others, Jethro had brought two pairs of fine old duelling pistols. He proceeded to prepare them for loading and priming, which the seconds would do after the weapons had been assigned.

"Maybe the Northern milksops won't show," Harry said, unable to conceal a hopeful note in his voice.

"They'll be here without fail," Jethro said. "I spoke with their seconds late last night. They had ridden out here and know the place."

"I thought maybe they had run home North," Harry said.

"They have to go back to the Naval Academy," Jethro pointed out. "When their friend gets back from Savannah, he would hear of their cowardly behavior and soon everyone at the Academy would know of it. They have no choice. They must come here."

Thornton wondered as they waited whether Harry had had the same family scene to endure as he had. A weeping mother, resigned father, concerned brothers and sisters . . . the whole county had heard of the racecourse incident in a matter of hours. Yet appearances had to be kept up. And each man rode out alone that morning, as if avenging his honor was a casual occurrence.

The midshipmen arrived in a hired carriage, driven by one of them. According to tradition, no further verbal exchanges took place between the combatants.

They kept their distance from one another as their seconds conferred and selected the weapons.

The duelling rules had been settled the previous night. The duel would take place simultaneously. The combatants would stand back to back, with fifteen paces laterally between the pairs. Each man would then take ten paces forward, so that there would be a distance of twenty paces between each pair of antagonists. The midshipmen, as those challenged, would have the first shot as well as the pick of the pistols, which Jethro would supply. Assuming that the first shots missed, Harry and Thornton would then have a shot apiece. If all shots failed to find their mark, the four men would again stand back to back and pace off again, but this time to only seven paces, and the process would be repeated. If all those shots missed, honor would be satisfied and the duel closed. The men at that point had the choice of establishing friendly relations or not. Whatever they chose to do, no further recriminations could take place then or in the future. The incident would be closed.

"Gentlemen, when you are ready!" Jethro called.

The four men, all right-handed and holding their pistol barrels skyward close to their faces, avoided eye contact, turned back to back and marched ten paces. They turned to present their right side to each other, the position of the pistol affording a certain amount of protection for the head of the man being fired upon. Thornton and Harry pulled in their bellies and presented as narrow a side-on target as possible to their antagonists. Obviously a fat man with a large gut would be at a disadvantage in duelling with a thin man. All four of the combatants this day were lean and fit.

Thornton watched, his heart beating wildly, as the midshipman who had started the quarrel with his loud remark about Harry now took his shot at him. He missed. Harry's glance met Thornton's. There was a look of veiled anger on Harry's face which Thornton recognized the significance of. The midshipman had shot to kill, at Harry's head. Now it was Thornton's turn to be the target.

The pistols were smooth-bored and therefore not very accurate. They fired a lead ball roughly the size of the later .45 caliber bullet. The advantage of this size of projectile was that any contact made by it, even at nonvital points, would cause massive tissue damage, at the very least disabling the person struck.

Thornton held himself erect, his right side toward the midshipman holding the pistol. He held his breath, kept his face expressionless and hoped the trembling in his legs was not evident to others. This was the ultimate test of a gentleman's courage—to present himself as an unmoving target to an opponent in a duel.

A hiss of air before his face, then the sound of the shot, the recoil of the pistol in the midshipman's hand and blue smoke rising in the morning air as the shot echoed in the woods. . . .

As with Harry, the midshipman had aimed for his head. These Northerners wanted to return home with Tennessee scalps on their belts. Harry exchanged an exultant look with Thornton. This would be their chance, and their only one unless they were very lucky. Next they would have to present themselves for a head shot at a total of fourteen paces instead of twenty, and those Northerners would not miss at that distance.

Harry leveled his pistol with a flourish and fired. The midshipman's body lifted into the air and sprawled backward onto the grass. A scarlet stain spread on the chest area of the prone man's ruffled white shirt.

Thornton's opponent made a move toward his fallen friend as the pistol was being leveled on him. This was against their rules. Thornton rapidly sighted along the barrel, caught the man's jawbone with the bead in the notch and squeezed the trigger.

The top of the midshipman's head shattered into fragments as he took his first step, and the almost decapitated man took another two steps forward before plunging into the earth of Tennessee.

9

WILLIAM WALKER was erect and calm. He gravely accepted congratulations on his exoneration by the jury and invitations to visit some of the "better people" in San Francisco. Hardly anyone guessed that Walker was penniless. Byron Cole sensed it immediately and offered him a job on the *Democratic State Journal*. Walker accepted, and Cole found him decent lodgings and settled the few small bills Walker had run up.

Cole had been impressed by the little man with eyes of cold gray steel. Walker did not strike him as a feisty bantam, like so many men of high spirit and low stature. Walker was cold, patient and polite. He had the dedicated watchfulness of an untamed predator, Cole decided. When the right prey came along, Walker would spring. And not before.

The editorials written by Walker, although not of literary brilliance, were above average and helped raise the tone of the journal as well as get it new subscribers curious about the opinions of this celebrity. Walker wrote frequently in favor of the abolition of slavery and against the depredations of the robber barons of American industry.

The jovial Cole, himself a Southerner from South Carolina, exerted himself to keep Walker entertained.

He had noticed that when Walker was left to his own
devices, he simply sat in his lodgings alone. He was not
studying or working or anything like that—Cole was
always careful never to intrude on his privacy, if that
was what he needed. Just sitting there alone. Walker
always seemed glad when Cole called on him in the
evening and always accepted whatever invitation was
extended to him. He seemed in good spirits, or at least
never spread an aura of gloom. But when left on his
own, that was all Walker did, sit alone in his lodgings.

There had been just one incident of friction between
the two men, and it had been so fleeting, Cole was still
not sure what to make of it. Cole admitted to himself
that he had perhaps been a little overbountiful on that
particular day in his hospitality, beneficence and jovi-
ality, when Walker had coolly informed him that he
behaved like a man with financial worries who saw the
glitter of gold almost within his reach. The calculating
gray eyes bored into him for a moment, and then
averted their stare like a panther retracting its claws.
Cole was more careful after that.

Walker remained a mystery to him—which satisfied
Byron Cole perfectly for the purposes he had in mind.
A man whose inner depths were too easily perceived
was not what would be needed. Cole announced that
he was leaving on a trip to Nicaragua and left the
newspaper in Walker's hands.

When Cole returned after a month, he was delighted
to find that Walker had continued the publication without a hitch and without making the major changes by
which a lesser man might have asserted his personality.
So far Walker had passed every test. Cole judged it was
time to present him with the final one.

Since Cole's return, Walker had listened with interest to discriptions of the conditions in the Central
American republic of Nicaragua.

"Everyone in that country can be put in one of two
groups," Cole told him, "the Shoe-Wearers and the

Barefooted, as their Spanish nicknames translate. More correctly they are known as the Legitimists and the Liberals. The Legitimists are in power now, and the oligarchic families bleed the country of its wealth and press down ever more heavily on the already burdened poor. There's no middle class of businessmen and professional men as there is here and in most European countries. In Nicaragua you have only the very rich and the very poor. For the most part the poor have been kept ignorant and illiterate, but they have their champions. These men of conscience, many of them outcasts of the oligarchical families responsible for the repression, with other professional soldiers from non-political military families, form the Liberal party in opposition to the Legitimists. They have their own provisional president and hold their own capital city." Cole added warmly, "It was a joy for me to behold gallant men gathered together to fight despotism. It would have warmed your heart to see them, William."

Cole carefully planted the seeds of interest in Walker's mind, painting a picture of heroic deeds, stout hearts, noble military men and, most importantly, power, grandeur, glory, gold and being on the side of the angels. Cole did not think it opportune at this time to mention that in the past six years Nicaragua had had fourteen presidents, with power alternating back and forth between the Legitimists and the Liberals and the capital city switching back and forth between Granada and Leon so often that the common man no longer knew or cared who ruled, since his life of drudgery and near-starvation never changed.

However, Cole did mention that the terrible contrast between rich and poor also existed in the five other countries in the narrow neck of land connecting Mexico to South America.

"Guatamala, Honduras, El Salvador, Costa Rica and Panama, along with Nicaragua, in the opinion of the most highly informed men that I spoke to, are ripe to be brought into a federation of states—perhaps the United States of Central America—but only after Nicaragua has been stabilized. Nicaragua is the key."

There had been a flash of fire in the gray eyes.

"Why is Nicaragua the key?"

The fish was nibbling on the bait.

Byron Cole refilled his port glass from the cut glass decanter and sipped at the ruby liquid. Walker still had not touched the drink poured for him an hour ago.

"Nicaragua has the Transit Road," Cole told him.

Contrary to what became the popular image later, the majority of people going from the East to California, before the railroads stretched from coast to coast, did not do so by covered wagon overland. Some sailed all the way down the Atlantic coast and around the tip of South America and all the way back up the Pacific coast. Most sailed only as far as one of the Central American countries, usually Nicaragua or Panama, crossed the narrow neck of land, and took another ship up the Pacific coast to California.

Walker saw Cole's point immediately. "You think that a military force which occupied the Transit Road across Nicaragua could finance their operations from the tolls imposed on travelers using the road." When Cole nodded, Walker went on, "First the stabilization of Nicaragua and then possibly the United States of Central America. . . . That's a very interesting idea, Byron."

Cole glowed. This was the first time Walker had seriously complimented him on anything. Cole thought to himself that Walker could recognize a genuine entrepreneurial spirit.

While this mutual admiraton lasted, Cole produced a document from his inside pocket and handed it to Walker. He watched uneasily as Walker unfolded it and read. It was a request in the handwriting of General Francisco Castellon, provisional president of the Liberals, to William Walker to organize a force of mercenaries for the purpose of occupying the Transit Road across Nicaragua, for which generous payment in gold and land was detailed. The cat was now out of the bag. Walker would know now why he had gone to Nicaragua. Cole watched apprehensively for Walker to finish reading the document, which Castellon had signed before witnesses.

Cole's heart sank when Walker tore the document in two. He listened silently to the paper being torn into successively smaller pieces, and as if this were not enough, Walker strode to the fireplace and fed the pieces to the flames.

Walker recrossed the room and sat before Cole. He said, "Did you really think that I, a lawyer, having already once been accused of breaking the Neutrality Act of 1818, would sign such an incriminating document as that?"

"I thought the terms of the offer were good," Cole said defensively.

"I am not talking about the terms. Has anyone seen this offer made to me to raise a band of mercenaries?"

Cole shook his head.

"Are there any copies?"

Again Cole shook his head.

Walker was relieved. "Even though I had not signed it, that paper was enough to incriminate me. I want you to return to Nicaragua immediately, Byron"—there was no doubt as to who was in charge now—"and get a written offer from this general to me requesting a group of *colonists* to stabilize the area through which the Transit Road runs."

Walker went into a list of specific things the offer should contain. It was almost as if he had been expecting the request to be made to him and had reviewed the laws carefully to see how the expedition might be undertaken without breaking United States laws. It also occurred to Cole that Walker now seemed to know a great deal more about Central America than he had

earlier pretended. But this was not the time to entertain
doubts, Cole told himself; he had set the ball in motion
and he must keep up now that it was gathering momentum.

Cole was away for a month on his second trip to
Nicaragua. This time he returned with a document
signed by General Francisco Castellon requesting the
arrival of William Walker together with three hundred
American colonists for the agricultural settlement of the
area around the Transit Road. Walker and his men
would be granted immediate Nicaraguan citizenship
upon arriving in the country and would have the
permanent right to bear arms. He and his men would
be paid in gold and would receive a grant of twenty-one
thousand acres of land after their victory over the Legitimists. Walker signed the document immediately.
Cole witnessed his signature and added the date, December 7, 1854.

Byron Cole soon had to admit to Walker that he was
almost bankrupt.

Walker's only comment was, "Then you'll have to
join us, won't you?"

Cole resigned as publisher of the newspaper to devote
his full time to raising funds for the expedition. Walker
resigned from the paper at the same time. One of the
last editorials he wrote was a scathing attack on
Cornelius Vanderbilt, founder of the Accessory Transit
Company, owner of the Transit Road across Nicaragua.

Money for the project did not flood in. Cole observed
that Walker regarded the expedition as a popular one
which should be funded by shares bought by the
patriotic American public. Cole had a more realistic
approach, but found that his main backers, the bankers
Garrison and Morgan, while still enthusiastic about the
project, remained unconvinced about the personality of
William Walker. It was only by personally volunteering
to accompany Walker on the mission himself—at great
personal cost, he claimed—that Cole extracted from the

bankers a minimal starting fund of less than ten thousand dollars. Cole got a promise for a sum twice this amount as soon as something had been achieved. In the meantime Garrison did not want his name associated with Walker's, and he would dole out the sum committed to them over the next few months as they made progress in organizing the expedition, rather than endowing them with a lump sum.

Cole swallowed his pride and accepted these conditions. He said nothing to Walker about them. In fact, he discovered that Walker, like all visionaries, seemed supremely uninterested where the cash came from to finance his dreams. Walker relegated such matters as finance to Cole with a wave of dismissal.

Cole noticed the subtle change taking place in Walker. In his talks and daily work with the dependent needy journalist on his newspaper, Cole had almost forgotten the part of Walker that was ex-president of the Republic of Lower California and Sonora. Now Walker had become a leader of men again. His gray eyes seemed to transmit new power, and his whole body was charged with energy as he patiently checked and rechecked items they would need and searched for the men who had followed him from San Vicente to the border.

Cole privately had his doubts about Walker persuading these men to come. Would any of them be crazy enough to sign on with Walker for a second time? Cole was intrigued when he discovered that all the men, without exception, had committed themselves to the new expedition—without even being told its destination! Secrecy had to be maintained. The men just signed on with Walker, as they had told Cole's court reporter, to follow him through hell or high water.

10

CORNELIUS VANDERBILT'S voyage aboard the *North Star* was one of the most celebrated diversions of the time. The luxury yacht cost him $500,000 to build and $1500 a day to run. The Episcopal clergyman Vanderbilt brought along on the trip wrote a dutiful book: *The Cruise of the Steam Yacht* North Star, *A Narrative of the Excursion of Mr. Vanderbilt's Party to England, Russia, Denmark, France, Spain, Italy, Malta, Turkey, Maderia, Etc.*, by the Rev. John Overton Choules, D.D., published in Boston and New York in 1854.

The interior of the yacht was fitted in precious hardwoods, and chandeliers hung in the staterooms. Advance notice was given to U.S. consuls at ports which the yacht intended to visit, and landing parties cleared areas of undesirables before the ladies in their crinolines set their dainty feet on foreign soil. Mr. Vanderbilt's party was received by European royalty, and lavish banquets were given everywhere they went.

At the time of his voyage, although Vanderbilt had already sold the Staten Island Ferry, his fortune was still chiefly based on being a shipowner. His railroad millions were as yet in the future. He had told a friend before leaving on his voyage aboard the *North Star* that he was worth $11,000,000 and had it invested so that he gained a 25% return on that sum each year. Obviously a man of such vast wealth took some pains to leave his interests in responsible hands before leaving for his sojourn overseas. The first successful laying of a transatlantic telegraph cable would not take place for a few years yet (from Trinity Bay, Newfoundland, to Valentia Bay, Ireland, in 1858) so that while Vanderbilt was away, he in effect had to surrender complete control of his business interests to those he so entrusted.

One of the more lucrative of his investments was the Accessory Transit Co. Vanderbilt's ships from New York to San Francisco had originally sailed around Cape Horn at the southern tip of South America. Crossing the narrow land strip of Central America shortened the journey considerably, but sometimes only in theory. Despite the treacherous seas off Patagonia and frequent shipwreck on Cape Horn itself, for some time it remained easier to ship heavier goods by this route than through the tropical jungles of the Central American crossing. Many of the travelers West brought heavy mining machinery and all their worldly goods with them. There were others who found the risks of the high seas preferable to those of a three-day trek through the jungles of Panama by way of villages whose Indian populations had been corrupted by unscrupulous outsiders and where yellow fever, malaria and dysentery vied with murderous humans for the lives of unwary travelers.

A canal joining the Atlantic and Pacific Oceans through the narrowest part of Central America, in Panama, would have been the ideal solution, but the engineering problems and huge outlays of capital involved in such a scheme were beyond the capabilities of the times.

Cornelius Vanderbilt had come up with an alternative—not an ingenious answer of his own conception but one which he as a man of action had the courage to put into reality. His ships sailed to Greytown on the

Atlantic coast of Nicaragua. From Greytown special steamboats traveled up the San Juan River to Lake Nicaragua and crossed the lake to the town of La Virgen on its western shore. From La Virgen to the port of San Juan del Sur on the Pacific, the distance was only thirteen miles. Vanderbilt's company built a hard-topped road through the jungle to connect the two towns, and at that time the road was better in quality than most if not all roads in North America.

Queen Victoria in England and Emperor Louis Napoleon in France had been eyeing Nicaragua, for the potential of a Nicaraguan canal was well known, but it was Cornelius Vanderbilt who first went into Nicaragua. The Accessory Transit Company signed an agreement with the Nicaraguan government undertaking all costs of construction and supplying ships in exchange for a sole franchise of the crossing, with a licensing fee of $10,000 a year and 10% of the profits going to Nicaragua after the company's initial costs had been recouped.

Cornelius Vanderbilt was the discount merchant of his day—he started a fare war with other companies, offering cut price passages and setting up all sorts of sales promotions. The minimum time for a voyage around Cape Horn was one hundred and twenty days. For $35 a passenger could now travel from New York to San Francisco in twenty-one days. Vanderbilt hoped to replace the Transit Road soon with a canal, further shortening the travel time by reducing loading and unloading.

Before Mr. Vanderbilt set out with his party aboard the *North Star* on his odyssey to picturesque European locations, he resigned as president of the Accessory Transit Co. He turned over the operation of the company to Charles Morgan of New York, who succeeded him as president, and to Cornelius K. Garrison of San Francisco. Morgan and Garrison were the senior partners of a banking firm, and one of Garrison's acquaintances was Byron Cole, publisher of the *San Francisco Democratic State Journal*.

On his return from Europe to New York, Cornelius Vanderbilt stepped off his luxury yacht and went straight to his offices at 5 Bowling Green, a stone's throw from Wall Street on Manhattan's lower tip. He demanded to know what the devil had happened to the Transit Company and why he had lost so much money on it and why its shares had dropped in price so much on the market. His terrified accountants produced the records for him. They did not have to explain that Morgan and Garrison had manipulated company shares on the stock market to their enrichment and Vanderbilt's loss. The two men had even set things up so that Vanderbilt no longer even owned a controlling interest in the company.

It was evident to the great financier that these two scoundrels, Morgan and Garrison, intended to take over the Transit Company themselves. He initiated lawsuits against them, but soon saw that the delay of lengthy legal proceedings would fit in with the men's plans.

Vanderbilt paced his walnut-panelled office in a towering rage. He was being robbed! His family had been robbed before, as he never tired of telling his snooty competitors proud of their English descent. His family had been large landowners outside the old city of New Amsterdam, and when the Dutch lost the city to the British and it was renamed New York, the first act of the rapacious invaders was to burn the city hall and its records of land ownership. In this way his family had been denied nearly all of their possessions.

From a tiny farm on Staten Island, Cornelius had fought his way to the top of the financial world. If a couple of glib-mannered bandits thought they could dip their fingers in the till while he was away, escorting his family and friends on a cultural tour, they would find to their cost that he had not gone soft—they would find that Cornelius Vanderbilt was sound and solid to the very core.

He dispatched agents to buy up Transit Company shares everywhere they could so that he could regain control over the company. Spies were sent to investigate other investments of Morgan and Garrison, to suggest ways in which they could be sabotaged, thus causing financial pressures from other sources on the two men. And he ordered a secretary to pen a short note to Morgan and Garrison, to which he appended his signature.

> *Gentlemen:*
> *You have undertaken to cheat me. I will not sue you because the law takes too long. I will ruin you.*
>
> > *Sincerely yours,*
> > *Cornelius Vanderbilt*

11

THE STEAMER churned upstream against the current of
the San Juan River. From the upper deck, the country
on both sides could be seen stretching away into hot
dismal swamps. Small Indian settlements of a few
thatched huts and slow-moving children were scattered
here and there. The sticky air and stagnant marshes
spelled one word clearly in everybody's mind—fever.

The river formed the border between Nicaragua and
Costa Rica to the south. It drained Lake Nicaragua
into the Atlantic.

Cyrus Figgis was hard put to maintain his dignity
at the sight of this depressing landscape. He was a portly
young man, twenty-three at the most, and his skin had
an unhealthy pallor and some pimples. He displayed
his contempt for the climate by wearing the clothes he
would have worn on a normal work day to the Transit
Company's Manhattan offices—a frock coat, striped
pants, a linen shirt with a well-starched collar and a
simple cravat, and of course a hat.

Cyrus Figgis had known that this assignment was not
going to be a matter of entertainment. Mr. Vanderbilt
—Cyrus never doubted for a moment but that the great
man would soon be back in control of the company—
needed white men he could trust to run the Transit

across Nicaragua. Cyrus had applied for the overseas job because of the supervisory opportunities it would provide for him straightaway. He had thought it over carefully. He was young, single and ambitious. Fifteen more years at his desk in New York would see his gradual climb into a position of relative importance within the company as he stepped into openings vacated by retirees. He had no illusions about the slow, inexorable, bitter wait this would involve, wondering when old So-and-So was going to retire or whether he had decided to die at his desk. And always there would be younger men at his heels, waiting for him to move on or weaken.

Cyrus had seen the light when a man in his early thirties had come back from service overseas with more management experience to his credit than many senior members at the New York offices and had been made head of his department, chosen over one of the sedentary seniors. Cyrus had balanced the threat to his health from the malevolent climes in which he would have to work against the strain of remaining chained to his desk for another fifteen years, perhaps then to be usurped by some more adventurous returnee with much experience abroad. He had chosen. But not these gray miasmal swamps!

To reassure himself, he spoke to the two gentlemen whose acquaintance he had made on the voyage south from New York.

"I've heard," he said, "that very few people live in the eastern half of Nicaragua. This area is supposed to have the highest rainfall in the world."

Having received only polite nods, Cyrus went on, "Most of the population lives between Lake Nicaragua and the Pacific. I'm sure it will be very different there. I'll be living in La Virgen, the Transit Company's terminal on the western shore of Lake Nicaragua."

"Sounds pleasant enough," Thornton McClintock said commiseratingly.

This fat, self-important little man irritated Thornton, but he felt sorry for him, as he would for anyone committed to living for any time in the surroundings they were now passing through.

Harry Drayberry spat over the rail into the water.

Cyrus Figgis recoiled from this ungentlemanly act and was silent.

Harry had been depressed almost constantly since they had left Antrimville. The appearance of this landscape after their ocean voyage from New York lowered his spirits still further.

After the two midshipmen had died in the duel, they had heard nothing further for a few weeks. Then they were told that the dead men's father, for they had been brothers, was a New Hampshire member of the House of Representatives and was now campaigning in Washington for what he called justice to be done in the deaths of his sons. The New Hampshire congressman used the simmering ill feeling between North and South as leverage in his plea and implied that it would no longer be safe for innocent Northerners to venture into the South if these savage murders went unpunished.

The McClintocks and Drayberrys ignored the vengeance-inspired and unsportsmanlike behavior of the New Hampshire congressman as long as they could, which was as long as the Tennessee state authorities could ignore him. Then an apologetic emissary from the state capital arrived to tell the families that a warrant for the arrest of the two young men was about to be served. There was no chance that any Southern jury would find them guilty, he said, yet the families might wish to avoid the unpleasantness of a murder trial, even if there was no doubt about the verdict, by sending the two young men abroad for a year.

Thornton had refused to go to Europe. He wanted gold more than he wanted culture. He was willing to go to California, but not England or France. Harry said he would like California too. So California it was.

They took the railroad to New York City. Both had been there several times before on stopovers during family summer visits to Saratoga. They boarded a Transit Company ship and headed for San Francisco by way of Cornelius Vanderbilt's route through Nicaragua.

As he leaned on the deck rail, Thornton hoped very strongly that California did not look like the swamps of eastern Nicaragua.

"Well, look at that," Harry said. "That's downright impressive."

Two smoking volcanoes, connected by a strip of land, rose high out of the lake.

Harry cheered up for the first time on the trip. "Like to see what folks would say if one of those popped out of the ground back in Tennessee."

Cyrus Figgis was feeling better too. The breezes of Lake Nicaragua had restored his optimism that La Virgen would prove, if not an ideal habitation, at least habitable.

Cyrus, a fund of information once more, told Harry, "The lake is about a hundred miles long and fifty at its widest point, and it's often more than a hundred and fifty feet deep. They say it was once an inlet of the Pacific that got cut off by a lava flow, which is why it has fresh water sharks and swordfish.

Harry peered down into the blue waters as if to look for them.

The steamer, called *La Virgen*, treaded its way among the islands of the lower lake toward the western shore. In the late afternoon the jungle-shrouded land appeared on the horizon. As they neared it, a small town became visible, and in that town a single building stood high above the others. In a while they were able to read the huge letters painted on the side of this building: TRANSIT HOUSE.

When the steamer came close to shore, they saw

them, "and leave your resting place before dawn the next day, you are not so easy to catch while you sleep."

While Thornton and Harry digested this useful piece of information and assumed they would be spending a night under canvas in the jungle, Gonzalez waved to a halt his corps of about thirty men as a reasonably clean house on the outskirts of the town. The door of the house was thrown open and a dozen women in pretty dresses came rushing out, chattering and waving to the men. They were assisted into the horse-drawn wagon with the Tennesseans' baggage. It seemed that the colonel's idea of "a simple soldiers' camp" was a bit different from theirs.

Their "campsite" proved to be a magnificent hacienda requisitioned by the forces for the night. The owner's family had sequestered themselves in one wing of the building, and the colonel forbade his men to go there or cause damage or steal under pain of death. He looked very much like he meant what he said.

The colonel, his lieutenant, Thornton and Harry occupied the family quarters, while the men took over the kitchen and servants' quarters. Gonzalez selected the four prettiest women—a choice neither Thornton nor Harry had any argument with—and gave the rest of the women to his men.

"Everyone is being well paid in gold," Gonzalez told them, "so pay no attention to complaints, especially those of the vampire who owns this hacienda. I have told him that when we take over the country, I will visit him even more often and maybe ask him for the hand of his daughter." He laughed at his joke. "You must call me Enrique. Thornton, Harry, I will give your first choice of our pretty companions."

All four women were part Spanish, part Indian. They had high cheekbones, straight black hair, full bosoms, playful hips and ready laughs. After excellent steak and hearty red wine, in spite of their lack of Spanish,

12

WILLIAM WALKER had signed the "colonist" agreement, witnessed by Byron Cole, on December 7, 1854. His expedition was ready to sail from San Francisco in early May 1855. The initial months had been spent in mostly wasted effort to raise money through colonist bonds. Walker had finally given up on this and allowed Cole to assume the responsibilities of fund-raising. The money started to come in.

Walker could depend on the men who had fought with him in Baja California to form the backbone of his fighting force. Because of lack of funds, he could not expand his force very much beyond them before leaving for Nicaragua. Men were not the problem. Men were cheap and would fight for almost nothing on the promise of a rich reward after victory. But rifles cost money, and so did powder and lead, not to mention horses to ride and cattle, sheep and pigs to eat.

What Walker needed desperately was a corps of officers. Lieutenant Petrie was coming with him. If Walker was to obtain the balance of his troops in Nicaragua, he wanted American officers loyal to him to command them. He ran into difficulties here. Gold had been discovered in the Sacramento Valley in January 1848. San Francisco had become a boom town. Even in these

Spanish returned with four Americans, equally decrepit in appearance.

"You want some women?" one of the Americans asked.

"We can find them for ourselves," Thornton told him.

"That's not a friendly attitude to take to someone who's trying to help you," the man said with a threatening leer.

"We didn't ask for any help."

"Listen." The man approached so that the reek of his unwashed body filled their nostrils. "I know this place. What you see here is all trash. You come with me and I'll really show you something. My friends will carry your bags."

He motioned to the others without waiting for Thornton's reply. The men, nine in all, began grabbing the bags. Thornton whipped out his bowie and slashed one man across the knuckles. With a howl, the man dropped the bag and stared at the blood running down his fingers onto the grimey floor.

Harry pulled his knife and cut one man down the right forearm and another across the left cheek. Neither had attempted mortal thrusts with their blades. They merely wanted to show they could defend themselves. They had not drawn their pistols because they had been warned of the danger to foreigners of killing a Nicaraguan national, even in self-defense.

Neither Thornton nor Harry saw the American who backed away from the others and pulled a pistol from under his coat. The unshaven man drew a bead on Harry and his broken-nailed finger was tightening on the trigger when he felt a touch of ice-cold steel beneath his left ear.

The man lowered the pistol and swiveled his bloodshot eyes to see what had come behind him.

"Drop the pistol," a pleasant voice told him in Spanish-accented English.

that the Transit House was made to look more imposing here than it might have looked elsewhere by the sheer, rundown misery of the rest of the town's buildings. Most of them were grouped along a single street leading down to the water's edge. Their thatched roofs were in bad repair, and their filthy walls had not been painted in years. Establishments bearing the dignified names of Lafayette Hotel, Jackson House and Washington Hotel, on closer inspection, after they had left the ship, proved to be nothing but vermin-infested hovels. The women in the town were all whores, and the men, including some North Americans who had never made it farther than this place, were all touts and thieves.

Thornton and Harry each kept a pair of pistols concealed and ready, plus a bowie knife apiece. They sat on their luggage in an inn, drinking rum and wondering if this was how they would spend their entire night before taking the Transit Road to the Pacific at dawn.

"At least we're moving on," Thornton said. "Poor Cyrus Figgis is staying here."

Harry laughed. "Try to imagine him in his Sunday suit in a year's time here. I bet he will look the same, a bit threadbare and battered, but boring as ever and still saying, 'Mr. Vandberbilt wants this, Mr. Vanderbilt wants that'. I feel sorry for him to some extent, but no man has to do the things he does if he does not want to. If it takes a place like this to change him, so be it. But I doubt if even La Virgen could get through his thick skin."

They waved away some ragged men who were pestering them, and shook their heads wearily at haggard prostitutes. Perspiration ran down their skins, and although hungry they did not eat the rancid-smelling pork. Both settled for a plate of rice and beans, which was not unlike the New Orleans version of the dish. It tasted quite good washed down with dark heavy rum.

The ragged men who had been bothering them in

good times it was easy to find misfits ready to risk their lives for a somewhat obscure cause in a faraway land. They had come this far without finding what they had been looking for, and had no choice now but to search farther afield. Such men made hard and gallant fighters, but they were essentially loners and not given much to thought even when they had brains. In other words, they did not make good military officers.

The sort of man who would be suitable as an officer already had every kind of opportunity open to him in California, then only in its first years of statehood. Walker knew that if a man needed time to think about coming to Nicaragua with him, the final answer would be no.

His only major success was Lindsay Newton, another Southerner, this time from Alabama. Newton had landed with Gen. Lopez as one of six hundred men in an attempt to seize Cuba from the Spanish in 1850. Having failed to arouse support on the island for their cause, the Lopez forces retreated to Key West, closely pursued by a Spanish war-steamer. The following year Lopez organized another company of four hundred and eighty men, including Lindsay Newton, sailed from New Orleans and landed on the north coast of Cuba. This time forty thousand Spanish troops were waiting for them on the island. Lopez was attacked and defeated. His army was dispersed, and he himself, with a number of his followers, was executed in Havana. Newton and others had their lives saved because of U.S. pleas for clemency because of their youth.

Walker appointed Newton a lieutenant. This was the rank he intended to automatically bestow on all officer material. The individuals could work their way up or down from that rank as ability and fortune dictated.

Cole came up with a big find—Gaston de Brissot. While Lindsay Newton was a big-boned man who could hew trees for a log cabin as well as read a map, de Brissot was a French aristocrat who made no apologies for the fact and expected others to acknowledge his superior breeding, refinement and sensibilities. In a word, he was arrogant. Since he readily backed his attitudes with pistol or rapier, and had a score of casualties to his credit west of the Mississippi alone, few people tangled with his pretensions. His two beautiful daughters accompanied him everywhere.

De Brissot was a big find because he was a professional soldier of fortune who had honed his skills over the years. He had achieved a reputation as a fierce soldier in the French colonies, Cole told Walker, and had only just emerged covered with glory from the disastrous French campaign in the Crimean War. A less preoccupied man than Walker might have questioned further the appearance of this military paragon. It was obvious to Petrie and Newton that de Brissot had received a big payment up front, while they lived on promises.

The third new member added to the officer corps was the staff physician, Dr. Jones. In a brief conversation with him Walker was satisfied, from his own medical experience, that the doctor's qualifications were genuine. He did not ask the medical man why he wanted to join the expedition.

Over the months Byron Cole despaired frequently and often loudly. Walker was imperturbable. In spite of himself, Cole found that he looked to Walker when in need of inspiration and example.

At one point, when things really seemed to have fallen to pieces, Walker calmed Cole down and even made him laugh by reading aloud from a book the contents of a letter George Washington had written more than a hundred years previously. Washington complained bitterly in the letter that the merchants under contract to supply his troops during the Revolution protested each time he moved his army because it made their deliveries more difficult and thus lowered their profits. Washington claimed that he had actually been forced to move troops under his command into less than the most advantageous positions against the enemy in order to accommodate these merchants.

Cole could not beat that, and with the aid of a bottle of port, his customary good cheer and optimism soon returned.

It was Cole who chartered the brig *Vesta*. Walker could hardly believe the low price of the charter until he saw the vessel. He was no seaman, but even he could tell there was a question whether this ship was in shape to brave the seas as far as Nicaragua. However, on the bright side, Walker now had a ship, the means to travel, and he decided to keep his doubts about the 34-year-old craft to himself unless something better came along. Battered though she was, the *Vesta* gave concrete reality to his project after all the planning.

Finding a captain to sail her was another matter. Walker and Cole were turned down with either a scowl or a joke by the local ship's masters—by all except one. Robert R. Roberts said he would sail her. He had only one stipulation. He would not assume command aboard the *Vesta* until two full kegs of West Indian rum were delivered to his cabin for his exclusive use. Walker complied.

Next Byron Cole announced that he should go ahead of the expedition proper to Nicaragua to meet with Castellon and smooth the way for Walker and his men.

Walker remarked drily, "I can see now, Byron, why you were not more concerned with the seaworthiness of the *Vesta*."

"How could you think that of me, William?" Cole flustered. "You have cut me to the quick. I am a man of extreme sensitivity, you know."

"I need someone to go ahead of me," Walker told him. "Take de Brissot with you. I don't want his damn daughters driving the men crazy on the voyage down. Remember, when I arrive in Nicaragua, the first thing

I will demand is a personal reassurance from Castellon that everything is still as we agreed. Be sure to arrange that."

After the departure of Cole and de Brissot, Walker began the final preparations for departure. He stored the arms aboard ship in crates marked MACHINERY, and the gunpowder in crates labeled SUGAR, a time-honored tradition among soldiers of fortune. When the munitions were stowed away and secured, he sent out a final call to his men. He purchased the food supplies, leaving the more perishable items and fresh water till last. He then installed Captain Roberts in his cabin with the two full kegs of rum.

William Walker ordered his officers and men aboard the brig *Vesta* on the morning of May 4, 1855. The pilot was already on board, with his charts of San Francisco Bay and his small boat tied alongside. The pilot informed Walker that he would have to wait for the sun to burn the morning fog off the bay before they could set sail. It would be a matter of a couple of hours. Walker noticed there was no sign of the captain on the bridge.

Lieutenant Petrie beckoned urgently to Walker. When they were out of earshot of the pilot, Petrie told him, "There's a deputy sheriff aboard, sir. He has papers entitling him to seize the ship."

"The government again?"

"No. It is over some debts owed by a previous charterer of the *Vesta*. The sheriff says you can't sail till you pay off the debt."

"He waited for an opportune time to seize the ship," Walker observed grimly. "Where is he now?"

"I showed him into Captain Roberts' stateroom. The captain was good enough to pour him some grog."

Walker was alert. "Did the sheriff accept?"

"Indeed he did, sir. He looks like a man who would enjoy his drop, even at this hour of the morning."

"Does he know I am aboard?"

"I have not told him, sir."

"Good man, Petrie. Post an armed guard at the cabin door so that neither man leaves, but tell the man to be discreet. They must not know it. Drop in from time to time to say I am due shortly and make sure the sheriff's glass is refilled, if you have to do it yourself."

"As you say, sir." The lieutenant paused. "Permit me to say that it feels good to be in action again."

"Funny you should say that, Petrie. I was just thinking the same thing myself."

As the fog began to lift, the pilot ordered the sails hoisted. Walker had intimidated the man and he did not make the jokes he would have liked to about the worn, patched, rent sails that were being run up on the masts. The mooring ropes were untied from the capstans, hauled aboard and coiled on deck. The ship began to move away from the stone jetty out into the calm waters of San Francisco Bay and head for the opening to the Pacific Ocean. Walker's expedition was under way.

Having acknowledged the rousing cheer from his men as the ship set sail, Walker headed for the captain's cabin. He dismissed the armed guard outside the door, rapped loudly on it and entered. The cabin was filled with the sweet stink of rum mixed with the aroma of burning Virginia tobacco. The captain and sheriff sat at a table, red-faced, talkative, and oblivious of the fact they were heading out to sea.

The deputy sheriff served his papers on Walker.

Walker waved them away. "I'm sorry, sheriff, I have no time to read them now, but I promise to later on our voyage to Nicaragua."

"You're not going anywhere aboard this ship, Mr. Walker. I'm taking possession of her."

"I suggest you look out the porthole, sheriff." Walker

stopped on his way out the cabin door. "If you hurry, you may still get a lift back to land with the pilot. Otherwise you are welcome to join us."

After the pilot and his unhappy passenger had cast off for shore, the *Vesta* turned south along the California coastline under full sail in bright sunshine.

Walker nodded to Petrie.

The lieutenant ran up the blue and white flag with the red star.

13

THORNTON MCCLINTOCK and Harry Drayberry walked along the cobbled street of the Spanish colonial town of León. A saber swung at the side of each man. They were dressed in a mock military style of their own devising, and each carried a pistol in his belt. They swaggered down the street in their finery, for the present masters of their own fate and answerable to none.

At dawn they had awakened in the hacienda outside the town of La Virgen, and they had taken Colonel Gonzalez' suggestion that they not miss this opportunity to see the real Nicaragua. California would always be there waiting for them, but here was a chance of adventure and novelty they might never have again. Their baggage was stowed at a safe house near the Transit Road, and they set off on horseback with Gonzalez and his men for a quick look at the real Nicaragua.

They parted from Gonzalez along the way so they could see towns held by the governing party, the Legitimists. Gonzalez seemed to be more concerned about their safety than he was about his own. Apparently the civil war in this country, which had lasted for generations, was more complex than a simple war.

The first town they visited was Rivas, not far from the Transit Road between Lake Nicaragua and the

Pacific. In Rivas the Conquistadores, led by Gil Gonzalez de Avila, met the Indian leader Nicarao in 1522. Nine thousand Indians were immediately baptized. They saw the double-armed "cross of Spain" erected by Avila to commemorate the event.

Granada, the present capital of the nation while the Legitimists held power, had been founded two years later, in 1524, on the shore of the lake that came to be named, along with the Spanish colony, after the Indian leader Nicarao. Mombacho Volcano loomed above the town, and cracks caused by earthquakes were visible in the thick walls of the Spanish-style buildings. The hugh fortress-cathedral of San Francisco, whose belfries towered above the roofs of Granada, bore the fighting shield of Hernandez de Cordoba on its facade. The people were courteous and friendly. Rivas and Granada had proved to be very different from the thatched-roof huts in the swampland.

The rival capital of Leon, which they reached after a pleasant week of sightseeing, was just north of Lake Managua and not far from the Pacific. Like Granada, Leon was built at the foot of a volcano, Momotombo, and displayed just as many earthquake-cracked walls and pavements.

When they arrived, Gonzalez invited them to meet a fellow Southerner, Byron Cole. The heavy, jovial Cole soon got them to confess they were at loose ends and that the deaths of the congressman's sons were the cause of their journey.

"Ah, fighting men," Cole said speculatively.

"Not really," Thornton replied modestly. "We just grew up with guns in our hands and, like that, you just naturally get to be a dead-eye shot. Same with riding horses. It gets to be second nature."

Cole was now very interested. "I've come to Nicaragua to help the Liberal side. We have an all-American division on its way and we still need a few officers. Would you boys like to join us?"

"No, sir," Thornton told him. "We're flattered, but we're on our way to California to find gold."

Cole erupted into gales of laughter. He then coughed until his jowls grew bright red. He sipped a glass of port and spoke in a wheezy voice.

"Lads, you know I've just come from San Francisco. Now if I'd met you two on your way there six or seven or even five years ago, I would have told you to hurry and wished you Godspeed. But it's too late now for you to go there. Men have been arriving in thousands. The hills swarm with men like fresh dung under flies. There's nothing left for inexperienced newcomers at this late date. Even three or four years ago I would have urged you on, but would have told you to forget about gold. I'd have said, 'Fellows, sell tools and supplies to hopeful miners on a cash basis with not a cent in credit.' It's too late even for that now. Barring news of fresh strikes in new areas, you'll find nothing in California except high prices and desperate men."

Cole had managed the transition from helpless laughter to sympathetic gloom with the expertise of a professional actor. He was helped by the fact that, for once in his life, Byron Cole was presenting the unadorned truth.

Thornton and Harry had heard rumors of such conditions before, but this account was less easy to laugh off than the others had been.

"You are both fighting men . . . ," Cole went on reflectively. "Fighting men in search of gold. We would pay you in gold to join us."

"We'll think about it," Thornton said.

Meanwhile the days passed pleasantly for them in the Spanish colonial town of Leon. The civil war remained quiescent, and apart from some skirmishes near the border with Honduran troops, who supported the Legitimists, all was quiet.

They were introduced by Cole to Gaston de Brissot, the aristocratic French soldier of fortune who had preceded William Walker to Nicaragua with Cole. They met his two beautiful daughters, Solange and Brigitte, who had attended convent school in New Orleans and spoke excellent English. The two ladies immediately seized upon Thornton and Harry as their beaux.

Solange, eighteen, was brunette, hazel-eyed and very outspoken. Her sister, Brigitte, was younger by a year and left most of the talk to her sister. Yet she was equally beautiful, her hair a mixture of brown and gold, and her eyes green beneath long lashes. They both wore the narrow dresses becoming fashionable with independent-minded women rather than the crinolines which imposed so many restrictions on a woman's movement. Of course a woman in such a costume would have been regarded as half-naked on any of the Antrimville plantations back in Tennessee.

In spite of their daring dress and progressive opinions, when it came to men, Solange and Brigitte were every bit as prim and proper as their dear departed mother could have wished. And according to the customs of those times, it hardly even occurred to Thornton and Harry to treat them otherwise. These were ladies. They were gentlemen. The men went elsewhere for the immediate gratification of their desires. Thus neither Thornton nor Harry found it odd to squire the two ladies around during the early evening and, on leaving them safely in their home, to go straight to a bordello to ease the sensual urges the young French women had aroused.

Cole judged the time was ripe. He offered Harry and Thornton generous expenses in local currency while they waited for action and final payment in gold and land on the victory of their side.

The threat of action seemed so far away in this make-believe war, and Solange and Brigitte were such a happy improvement over Emily and Elizabeth back in Antrimville, that this time Thornton and Harry did not have to think about it before accepting. Even if there were gold left in California, they had now learned that they would have been expected to dig and scoop it out themselves. The thought of undertaking such menial work had more to do with them abandoning their California dreams than Cole's dire predictions. Here in Leon they could escort beautiful women, spend freely and live by the sword. Why should they struggle knee-deep in a muddy stream with a pan?

Harry and Thornton accepted the rank of lieutenant in this bizarre American unit that Cole liked to brag about. The rise and fall of the Republic of Lower California and Sonora and trial of its erstwhile president, William Walker, had not caused much of a stir in their part of Tennessee. In fact, Thornton and Harry had to confess they had never heard of the man.

Thus it was that they played soldier, striding along the cobbled streets in riding boots and spurs, sabers at their sides, pistols in their belts, masters of their fate, answerable to none.

14

THE BRIG *Vesta* sailed into the bay of Realejo on June 1, 1855, and dropped anchor in the sound. William Walker stood on the bridge and surveyed the abundant tropical growth behind the grove of coconut trees along the shore. The captain shuffled up from his cabin to join him and gazed out from bleary eyes into the painfully bright sunshine.

"Congratulations on our safe arrival, Mr. Roberts," Walker said to him ironically.

"You were lucky to find a master mariner to sail this hulk, Mr. Walker," Roberts shot back.

Walker did not smile or reply. His eyes had not left the shore. "Mr. Petrie," he called, "issue weapons to the men."

Long dugouts paddled by Indians were putting out from the jungle-lined shore. Walker ordered his men to fix bayonets to their rifles and board the dugouts for the trip to shore.

"Captain, you and your crew remain aboard the *Vesta*. Perform whatever repairs you have to without delay and be ready to sail at an hour's notice."

With a perfunctory nod to the skeptically grinning, drunk captain, Walker climbed down from the bridge onto the deck and prepared to go ashore.

"Dr. Jones, I trust you are bringing an adequate supply of medicines with you?"

"I was considering staying aboard the ship," the doctor replied uncertainly.

"You will be indispensable to us, doctor," Walker informed him briskly, dismissing thereby the man's unwillingness to go ashore.

Lieutenant Petrie permitted himself a rare moment of humor behind Walker's back. "A great leader sees only his men's strengths; he ignores their weaknesses."

The doctor sighed and went below to fetch his medical kit.

The Indians paddling the canoes spoke no Spanish but otherwise seemed friendly. Their tattooed copper bodies flexed as they strove with the paddles, and the dugouts loaded with men rode the surf onto the shore without mishap.

A heavily built man of mostly Spanish blood stroked his goatee as he gravely watched the landing parties. He strode forward to introduce himself to Walker.

"I am Colonel Enrique Gonzalez. I welcome you on behalf of General Castellon, Provisional Director of the Republic."

Walker shook hands. "Where is General Castellon?"

"In Leon."

"Let's go there."

The colonel supplied horses for the officers and mule-drawn wagons for the supplies. However, when they came to the town of Realejo, about five miles inland, Colonel Gonzalez called for them to halt.

"We all need a rest," he said pleasantly.

"I perhaps am the best judge of that," Walker responded coldly, but he did not issue a counter-order to his men.

It soon became evident that Gonzalez' idea of a rest would involve an overnight stay when they saw his men clear an area outside the town for their camp. Walker nodded to Petrie that his men should follow suit. He still said nothing.

Early the next morning the colonel still seemed in no hurry to move. Walker did not press him. The sun was high in the sky when Gonzalez suggested that he and Walker ride on alone to Leon to meet General Castellon. Walker agreed without hesitation.

"I don't like it, sir," Petrie told Walker. "You shouldn't go alone."

Walker smiled. "I think you miss the point, Mr. Petrie. It is they who are terrified of us. All this delay, and having a senior officer watch for us on the shore, signifies nervousness on their part. They would not have asked me here in the first place were their movement not in a shambles."

Petrie shook his head doubtfully and promised to march on Leon if he had not heard from Walker within forty-eight hours.

Thornton and Harry looked back curiously at the little man whose gray eyes examined them. He was barely five feet high. Gonzalez had introduced him as "Mr. Walker." De Brissot called him that too. They found it a relief that the little man had not selected some ridiculously grandiose military title for himself. Thornton felt this was close enough to being comic opera without that.

"Where's Byron Cole?" Walker asked.

"He left a week ago," de Brissot answered, "without saying where he was going."

"You *know* he went somewhere—or did he just disappear?"

De Brissot shrugged elegantly.

"He went somewhere," Thornton volunteered. "He packed his belongings the previous night, but would tell me nothing."

Walker turned to Colonel Gonzalez. "See if General Castellon is ready to see me now." After the colonel had left the room, he said to Thornton, "You come as my translator."

"I haven't learnt that much Spanish since I've been here."

"You can start now," Walker answered nonchalantly.

They waited in silence. Walker paced slowly up and down the large room, not in an impatient way but as a man might pace in the security of his own home while considering some problem.

Gonzalez returned. "Don Francisco welcomes you and awaits the pleasure of your company."

Thornton trailed after Walker. He had never set eye on Castellon since arriving in Leon. The leader of the Liberals was supposed to be a reclusive aristocrat whose reputation for honor and incorruptibility was far stronger than his reputation for leadership. Colonel Gonzalez, he had learned, had studied at the military academy at West Point, which accounted for his excellent English.

The three men marched across the tiled floors, and their steps echoed down panelled corridors and through high-ceilinged lobbies of the ornate colonial building.

The Provisional Director of the Republic, General Francisco Castellon, sat at his desk in a huge room filled with heavy dark furniture. Large windows looked out on an enclosed dusty courtyard in which a few yuccas struggled in the shade. The general rose to greet them. He was frail and tired-looking, and extended a delicate, well-manicured hand to Walker.

Walker got down to business without delay. He spoke passable Spanish, Thornton noted, much better than he had learned himself. Walker presented General Castellon with a paper for him to sign.

"It reaffirms the grant to me and all my men of immediate Nicaraguan citizenship, and the permanent right to bear arms," Walker informed him.

The general handed it to the colonel to read, and when the latter nodded he signed the paper with a smile and a flourish.

Walker folded the document and put it in the left inside pocket of his coat.

"Colonel Gonzalez has told me that he reports directly to a General Munoz," Walker said quickly. "Since General Munoz is head of your armed forces, General Castellon, perhaps I should meet him."

Castellon raised his hands in a gesture to show he had no objection.

The colonel left the room. The three men waited in silence for a while. Thornton looked from one to the other. Walker seemed preoccupied with his thoughts, and apparently it never occurred to him that it might be useful for him to strike up a friendly accord with the head of the Liberal revolution, the man who had sent for him in the first place. Thornton saw the Nicaraguan glance warily for a moment at Walker and then decide to maintain his own dignified silence. Not the best of all possible starts, Thornton judged.

Gonzalez returned with a short man with stiff, closely cropped hair and an expressionless face with heavy features. The two bantams immediately squared off.

"I want my division to be part of the Liberal army, the *Ejercito Democratico*," Walker told Castellon, "but the division must maintain its individuality and be under my sole command."

"General Carlos Munoz is commander in chief of the *Ejercito Democratico*," Castellon informed him.

"As such, I would report to him of course," Walker volunteered.

Munoz was visibly cheered by this, but still suspicious. "You say it is necessary for your men to be incorporated into the *Ejercito Democratico*. Why?"

"For all the obvious reasons," Walker said. "The most obvious of them is that we must not appear to be a group of foreign mercenaries. The *Falange Americana*—"

"Pardon me," Munoz interrupted, "what is the *Falange Americana*?"

"The division of men I command in your forces, General," Walker answered meekly.

"You will report to me?" Munoz wanted this repeated.

"Yes. But only to you. And to General Castellon."

Munoz looked at Castellon, and Castellon looked at Munoz.

"You have brought only sixty men," Castellon said, "instead of the three hundred I requested."

Walker smiled. "That means that each of my men must try harder, general."

Castellon raised his eyebrows. "What do you—how do you intend to start your campaign?"

"Capture Rivas and seize the area around the Transit Road from Lake Nicaragua to the Pacific."

Munoz whirled about and looked at him. "When?"

"Without delay."

"This is the rainy season," Munoz said. "How will you keep your powder dry?"

"By using it," Walker replied.

Gonzalez spoke. "There's a garrison of two hundred soldiers at Rivas. Lieutenant McClintock here has been to the town—he can tell you it is well defended."

Walker turned to Thornton. "You have been there?"

"There are two hundred soldiers there all right," Thornton said, "but you could hardly say they were disciplined or on a state of alert."

"We will overcome them with a surprise attack," Walker announced. "Sail down the coast on the *Vesta* and cross overland."

Castellon seemed enthusiastic for the first time. "You will need some more men. How many can you spare, Munoz?"

Munoz did not reply.

"I will give you two hundred men," Castellon offered.

"They will be under the command of Colonel Gonzalez," Munoz said stiffly, saluted and left.

15

HARRY COULD hardly believe it when he heard they were to leave aboard a ship to attack the town where the Conquistadores persuaded the Indian chief Nicarao and his followers to be baptized.

"When Walker heard I had been in Rivas, I think he made up his mind I should lead the charge," Thornton said. "You had better shut up about being there too."

"But the town is crawling with soldiers," Harry protested.

"We're going to take them by surprise."

They exchanged a look. They were both thinking of the same thing: was this the time to collect their baggage and leave for California?

Solange burst into tears. She threw her arms about Thornton's neck and clutched him tightly to her. Sobbing, she declared, "I'll pray for you every moment you are gone, Thornton. Please come back to me. I couldn't live if anything happened to you."

She buried her head on his shoulder, and at that moment Thornton decided not to hightail it for the goldfields of California.

They had been told about Walker. Now they were finding out for themselves. He had arrived only that

day in Leon, and already that very evening they were
to leave on horseback for the coast, to sail that night
and to attack Rivas early the next day. Harry and
Thornton, who had never commanded more men than
a slave to bring out their horse's saddle or a railroad
porter to fetch their bags, who had never marched in
step in their lives, whose sole knowledge of military
tactics came from hunting deer and squirrel, who had
not even the vaguest notion how their side differed
from the other, who could not go home because a
stupid Northern congressman could not accept the fate
of his stupid sons, now found themselves officers in
the army of a tiny man from Nashville who confided
in nobody.

As always, Harry had allowed himself to be led by
Thornton. He embraced Brigitte, who promised also
to pray for him. The two girls then both promised to
pray for their father while he was away, which an-
noyed Thornton, who had considered himself promised
all Solange's thoughts and prayers in his absence, although of course he did not complain.

As the three men rode out to meet Walker, the
French aristocrat surprised them by his newly familiar
tone with them. Previously he had welcomed them as
escorts for his daughters, but he had always maintained
a parental distance from them and treated them with
a smooth formality. Now it seemed they were all soldiers together and he shared their own feelings exactly
about Walker's arrival.

"Our days of leisure have drawn to a close, I'm
afraid," de Brissot said with an elegant sweep of his
hand. "Just when he begins to enjoy the ways of peace,
the soldier of fortune is called on by someone who has
a sacred purpose to fulfill—and has the gold to back
it," he added ironically.

"I suppose you've gone to many battles like this,"
Thornton said.

"Many, many . . ." de Brissot replied. "You learn the skills of fighting like any other skills. All you have to do is survive long enough to learn, which makes it a bit different, I suppose. One thing to remember. Although you must never be foolishly reckless, you must not forget the enemy is equally frightened as you, and often a mere gesture of bravado will be enough to convince him you are the stronger. Strong men run before the antics of weaker, cleverer men. Then again, sometimes they do not."

He laughed and changed the subject. DeBrissot knew better than to lecture young men going into their first battle.

Captain Roberts seemed indifferent as his loaded vessel sailed south close to the reefs in utter darkness. He steadied a mug of rum in his right hand and a compass on gimbals with his left and called out directions to the helmsman. Lieutenant Petrie, unable to understand how Walker could have such confidence in this irresponsible sot, listened nervously for the telltale sounds of waves breaking over rocks as the wind bellied out the sails and the ship rushed headlong into the darkness.

But the captain's tattered charts and battered brain proved reliable, and the *Vesta* sailed into the bay of San Juan del Sur as the gray fingers of dawn crept up the sky to landward.

Although Castellon had promised Walker two hundred men, only a hundred and ten appeared in time to sail. At Munoz' request these men were under the command of Colonel Gonzalez, who in turn reported to Walker. Then Walker discovered that Munoz had assigned a second officer to him, one Colonel Sanchez, as a liaison officer.

This time the *Vesta* had three flat-bottomed landing craft, and the men disembarked in these for the shore.

The Americans and Nicaraguans gathered in two separate groups on the land.

"We should send scouts ahead of the main body of troops," Gonzalez suggested.

Walker agreed. Gonzalez selected eight of his men. Walker insisted that an American accompany them. After the scouts had been gone an hour, Walker wanted to move on without further loss of time, but both Gonzalez and Sanchez disagreed and claimed that it would be suicidal to do so. After the nine men in the scouting party had been gone more than two hours, Walker turned to Thornton McClintock.

"Take six Americans with you and find out what's going on," Walker said in an undertone.

When Thornton tried to take Harry Drayberry with him, Walker said, "Leave him. I need my officers. Take six men."

Thornton, who had at first felt himself specially chosen, now wondered if he was being sent as the most dispensable officer. But action leaves a man little time to second-guess his superiors, and in minutes Thornton and six men were making their way on foot inland on a narrow path through the luxurious vegetation.

They had not gone more than a mile when Thornton held up his hand for his men to halt. His sharp sense of hearing had caught the sound of voices. They waited and listened. Since the murmur of voices did not seem to be approaching, they moved forward again. In a clearing on the pathway they saw the eight scouts sent out by Gonzalez, sitting and passing the time in conversation. There was no sign of the American who had gone with them.

With pistols drawn, McClintock and his men walked suddenly among them.

"Where's Maguire?" Thornton demanded.

"He was shot back that way," one man replied.

"Who shot him?"

"Snipers. In the trees. We were on our way back and stopped here to rest."

Thornton looked about. "Where's Maguire's body?"

"A long way back there."

"Take me to it."

"Señor, there are snipers in the trees."

"And I have a pistol in your back," Thornton said menacingly. "Let's go."

Without disarming them, they marched the Nicaraguans ahead of them along the path. Only a short distance forward, the Nicaraguans came to a stop and pointed down a narrow side path.

"Keep them here," Thornton said to his men. He selected the man he had spoken to before. "You and I will go to see. After you."

Maguire's body had been dumped in a gully by the side of the path. It had obviously been dragged there, probably from the main path, Thornton decided. He forced the Nicaraguan to help him lift the body back up out of the gully. The man had been shot in the heart. The wound seemed to Thornton to have been inflicted by a pistol rather than a rifle, at close range rather than from the top of a tree. Added to this, the eight scouts could not have needed a rest, nor would they have taken one such a short distance from a sniper shooting. They had been gone more than two hours when Thornton set out, yet it had taken him but twenty minutes to get here.

"Give me your pistol," Thornton demanded from the man with him.

The man handed it over. Thornton smelled the barrel and handed it back. The weapon had not been fired recently. They returned to the clearing. Thornton smelled each of the pistols. Only one had been discharged recently.

"This is yours?" he asked the man as he handed the pistol back to him.

"Yes."

"You did not lend your gun to anyone?"

"No."

"Time to even the score."

Thornton raised his pistol, cocked it and pulled the trigger. The other man was still pulling back his gun's hammer when Thornton's bullet hit him in the heart.

The other Nicaraguans accepted the death of their comrade in silence.

"Leave him there," Thornton ordered. "We'll bury both bodies when we get here with the main force."

William Walker only nodded when Thornton told him of what had happened and of his own opinion that the scouts had gone ahead to warn lookouts and that the American had been shot because he had witnessed this.

"I think you should consider shooting the remaining seven men as traitors, sir," Thornton told him.

Walker shook his head. "They were only obeying orders. But it's a good thing you took the life of the one who killed our man. They have to understand they can't do that."

Walker did not complain at the delay in burying the two men. It was almost noon, and again he did not complain when Gonzalez and Sanchez claimed that it was now too late to attack Rivas that day. His men set up a separate camp from the Nicaraguans at opposite ends of a clearing. However, Walker did insist that Colonel Sanchez, as his liaison officer, remain in his camp at all times rather than in that of Colonel Gonzalez.

At dawn the next morning, after an uneventful night, Walker again agreed when Colonel Gonzalez suggested that their troops split up and attack Rivas from two approaches. But Walker insisted that Sanchez stay with him.

Thornton seriously thought about questioning some of Walker's decisions, but allowed himself to be restrained by de Brissot.

Walker's forces arrived on the outskirts of Rivas a couple of hours after dawn. The enemy forces were in place, ready to defend the town.

"So much for surprise," Petrie complained.

"And where the hell are Gonzalez' men?" de Brissot asked.

"Gentlemen, I think we have to show both friend and foe what we are made of," Walker said in what was for him a loud voice.

Without another word, he led the advance on the town. The approximately sixty men moved slowly and methodically against the rifle lines of the defending forces, concentrating on a single line of defense until they had broken the discipline of the soldiers through heavy casualties and a slow constant advance against them. When the line broke, the battle-hardened Walker troops, veterans of Baja California, were the ones to charge forward and occupy the position.

Casualties were heavy among the Legitimist soldiers, who seemed unaccustomed to such a cold-blooded, slow, tactical advance which relied on accuracy of marksmanship and the fear that an implacable advance generates in a foe.

Thornton McClintock led his men on an attack against a row of riflemen who ducked down out of sight and stayed there. After a short advance, McClintock and his men took on a second line of defense behind and parallel to the hidden men. With a bit of luck and some crack shooting, they picked off seven in the second line, causing the rest of them to pull back to better cover. The cowardly first line now panicked on finding themselves abandoned to the advancing enemy. The men threw down their weapons and ran, causing the terror to spread to other ranks.

"Hold your fire!" Thornton called to his men.

Seeing that others were successfully fleeing the battle without being fired upon, more defenders joined the flight. Those who stayed to fight were hopelessly weakened and demoralized, and their officers called a general retreat into the streets of the town.

With wild whoops of triumph, Walker's troops chased after them, but were pinned down and took moderate casualties when the defenders held the houses with snipers and fired on them from street corners. Although a few cowards had upset their whole battlefield, these brave Legitimist troops held a very successful rearguard action. For this was what their tactics were proving to be. They held the town as long as they could, to allow their main force to regroup after the retreat. They fired down with rifles and pistols from open upstairs windows and fought back with fixed bayonets on staircases.

At the end of the day—which consisted of the brutal slaughter of a few defenders at a time for a few yards of street, in which the smell of fresh human blood wafted on sickly drafts of torrid air, in which every dark hallway could contain a frightened child left behind or a fear-crazed soldier ready to bring as many Yanquis as he could with him through Death's Gate— at the end of the day Walker and his forces found themselves in possession of an empty shattered town. They knew they would not be able to hold Rivas against the numerically superior army gathering in full view on a hillside a couple of miles away.

Walker took a roll call. He had lost Lindsay Newton and eighteen men, a third of his meager force—for a town he could not hold. There was still no sign of the hundred and ten men commanded by Gonzalez, and no hope now of marching on to the Transit Road. Walker gave the order for his men to rest and told them they would wait till nightfall before evacuating the town. Walker did not say creep away under cover of darkness all the way back through the jungles to their ship, assuming its drunken captain had waited for them—he did not say this and he did not have to.

16

THEY WERE met the next day by messengers from Gonzalez as they trekked to the coast. The men told an elaborate story as to how Gonzalez had come across a minister of the rebel government and had been obliged to delay in order to provide him with protection. Gonzalez had then assumed that because of this delay, Walker would have called off the attack on Rivas and so he and his troops had boarded a Costa Rican ship and sailed back up the coast to Leon. The messengers looked nervously into Walker's impassive face. They had shrewdly kept their good news till the end. On the way to meet Walker, they had heard from locals that the garrison of the coast town of San Juan del Sur had gone to defend Rivas and had left the port defenseless. All Walker had to do was march south and take the town.

Walker brightened. San Juan del Sur was the Pacific terminal of the Transit Road, where ships loaded for the voyage to San Francisco. This would at least give him a toehold on the Transit. Just as importantly, he would not have to return to Leon empty-handed, with nothing to show for his military expedition but the loss of a third of his men.

"We'll go south," Walker announced.

Colonel Sanchez advised against it. They did not know who had given the messengers this information, he said. It could be a trap, an ambush, a diversion. . . .

"That's enough to decide me on the truth of the story," Walker said. "If Colonel Sanchez is against it and Colonel Gonzalez doesn't know about it, it has to be in our favor."

The colonel paled and his eyes blazed with anger.

Walker was not finished. "I hereby accuse you, Colonel Sanchez, of collaboration with the enemy, of conspiring with others to send scouts ahead of our force to warn the enemy of our arrival—no doubt after having initially warned them of our intentions from Leon, of being responsible for the death of one of my men who witnessed the actions of these scouts, of further causing delays in our troop movements to allow enemy reinforcements to arrive and take up positions against us, and now of further trying to divert and harass us in our unstoppable progress in this just struggle which we undertake." The lawyer in Walker had come to the fore. "What have you got to say for yourself?"

"These charges are despicable and beneath my contempt," Sanchez snapped.

"You are guilty," Walker intoned. "I sentence you to die by the firing squad."

Walker nodded to Petrie. The colonel followed Petrie to a giant tree after having been disarmed and stood quietly as directed before the huge trunk. He refused a blindfold. The firing squad lined up and was ready and willing. Each of the men had lost one or more friends in the attack on Rivas and wanted to avenge them on this sidewinder.

Six rifles went off in a deafening volley, and the colonel was thrown back against the tree by the impact of the slugs on his body. He slowly slipped to the ground, writhing and grimacing, the blood running from the multiple bullet punctures.

* * *

San Juan del Sur became Walker's town without a fight. He and his men took over where the Legitimist garrison left off, and life went on as usual. Walker did not interfere with Transit traffic, and no one interfered with him. They heard nothing more from the Legitimists. The Liberals and Castellon seemed glad to be rid of them from Leon. In a matter of days the men began to feel as if they had been stationed in this easy-going port town for months. The sun came up and blazed down on the town every day, except for a few hours around midday when it rained in torrents. Solange and Brigitte came down from Leon, and Thornton and Harry promenaded with them in the cool evening breezes off the ocean.

Since the arrival of Walker, Thornton and Harry had been forced to operate independently of each other. It was as if Walker had left instructions they were not to be assigned duties together. However, they had nothing to complain about. Both were chosen by Walker frequently to perform special missions for him. He had complimented each of them for their bravery in the attack on Rivas.

They themselves had been kept too busy except at the very beginning of the assault on Rivas to observe their leader in action. From what they had seen, the stories of the Baja California veterans seemed true. Walker waded into battle as convinced as a medicine man that bullets could not harm him. His courage struck those who saw him not as suicidal but gallant— and the majority of his fighting men were convinced he was impervious to injury.

Walker these days was rarely seen about the town. He kept to his barracks quarters, and often when someone sought his advice on some matter at an odd hour, they would find him alone, sitting placidly in the chair at his desk with nothing before him, wide awake, attentive and polite as ever. He rarely bawled out the men, never meddled in minor disciplinary matters and usually left the day-to-day running of affairs to the judgment of his officers. Most of the time, it was as if he did not exist.

The town grew festive. The townspeople soon learned that these soldiers were not allowed to shoot them, rape their daughters, steal from them or even beat them. The businessmen found the new soldiers to be good customers. The Transit was kept running. Everywhere there were cheers for the Liberals and the Yanqui liberators. De Brissot mentioned often that the life of a soldier of fortune has some sweet pauses, and he toasted William Walker at their late evening dinners with his daughters beneath the flowering tropical trees.

Then Byron Cole arrived.

"Congratulations! You are a hero!" he told the cold and aloof Walker.

"My attack fails, I lose a third of my men, my allies betray me, I end up isolated in this small town which neither friend nor foe seems to care that I possess, and you congratulate me!" Walker smiled bitterly. "You made sure you were out of harm's way for my arrival. I should have you shot as a deserter."

Cole laughed and poured himself a glass of port from a decanter on the sideboard. "William, you say that you are a failure, that I am a deserter and that no one cares you are here. You are wrong on all three points."

Cole made himself comfortable in a tall-backed chair and proceeded, "You are the hero of Leon. Of the whole Liberal cause in Nicaragua! Leader of a force of sixty Yanquis who killed a hundred Legitimists at Rivas and wounded a hundred and fifty more while outnumbered ten to one. Fantastic!"

"Ten to one?" Walker enquired.

"The garrison at Rivas numbered two hundred men. Three hundred came from Granada as reinforcements. Plus the entire garrison of this town, San Juan del Sur, one hundred men. Six hundred against sixty, and they suffered two hundred and fifty casualties against your twenty or so. Of course you're a hero."

Walker recovered quickly from his surprise. "Which no doubt accounts for your arrival here."

"You wrong me, William. But before I defend myself, I have more important things to discuss with you."

With a flourish, Cole removed a folded paper from his pocket. "No doubt your suspicious turn of mind has not accepted what I have told you. On the way here I stopped in Leon and spoke with General Castellon. I suggested that he put in writing his recognition of your heroism—not empty words of gratitude but firm commitments to you."

He handed the paper to Walker and made a running commentary as Walker read it. "The Transit Road area is confirmed as your colonization territory. The town of San Juan del Sur is ceded to the *Falange Americana* as its garrison town and your headquarters. The number of American colonists you may bring in has been raised from three to five hundred. The permanent right of your men to bear arms has been reconfirmed, with the specific mention that this includes artillery. Every man under your command will receive a hundred dollars monthly in pay and, after the campaign, five hundred acres of land. You now have the right to impose taxes and tolls. And you have the rank of general and answer to no one except Castellon himself."

Byron Cole leaned back in his chair, sipped his port and watched the little man in front of him with shrewd eyes. Walker was reading the document for the second time. Cole did not let the caution of the ex-lawyer fool him for a moment. He had brought Walker news of the recognition he so desperately needed. Walker, for his part, had proved he was a viable military leader who could drive large numbers of Legitimists before him with a small force. From now on, Cole was going to be around. This project was beginning to come along very nicely.

"Is it satisfactory?" Cole asked Walker when he still said nothing.

"You've done very well, Byron."

"It was simply your just reward, William, nothing to do with me. I've spent the last couple of months in Honduras, looking over goldmines in the hill country of Olancho. There are some claims there which could finance all your campaigns here ten times over, but the Honduran army would be a major problem. It would involve a full-scale war. I doubt if the ore could be moved out under such circumstances. When I arrived here ahead of you and heard about that gold, I knew it could solve all our problems and had to be checked out. Even though it did not work out as I had hoped, you may want to consider it as a future resource in a widened campaign. So it's not a total loss. While there, I recruited a Prussian cavalry officer for you—the real thing! Baron Bruno von Satzner, a lieutenant with the Royal Prussian Guard Dragoons."

"He came all the way with you from Honduras to join me here?"

"Of course! Your fame has spread to Honduras and beyond. Here was his big chance to join the famous William Walker. The man is not a fool. Of course he came. He never hesitated!"

Cole saw the little man preen under this treatment.

"The third thing you mentioned," Cole said, "was that no one cares you have occupied San Juan del Sur. I disagree in one way and agree with you in another. Let us say they don't care. Then why they don't care is worth discussing. With Castellon, it's easy to guess. You are all alone down here in the southern part of the country and not stirring things up for him in Leon. Castellon is a bumbler, an incompetent. All he wants is to be left undisturbed, unthreatened."

Walker nodded his agreement to this assessment.

Cole continued, "With the Legitimists, it's harder to analyze their thinking. I suspect they are so hidebound by their traditions and so caught up in the past patterns of their civil war they cannot recognize any new initiatives. They see the war as a fight for control of the colonial towns and the ranchlands of the north and west. That's the territory the Legitimists have always fought the Liberals for. But what does someone outside Nicaragua care about who controls the cathedral towns and haciendas? What would they care about? Why, the only concern in this country that is a big earner of foreign exchange, of American dollars."

"The Transit."

"Absolutely."

Byron Cole's constant promotion of the leadership and greatness of William Walker galvanized the town into new action. A small but steady flow of new recruits came by the Transit steamers. Word of Walker's enterprise was spreading. The men who came were rovers and adventurers for the most part, for whom stable and organized society held few attractions. Some were running from the law, it was reasonable to assume, although no one asked questions like that. And as in every outpost of this kind, there were quiet, educated men whose demeanor indicated they had led quiet respectable lives until very recently and who now, without explanation, had suddenly thrown in their lot with rough men who knew no other kind of life.

Baron von Satzner set about training a volunteer cavalry unit which he called the Lancer Squadron. The ramrod-straight Prussian had tightly clipped hair and a red face. He wore a monocle and barked heavily accented commands to his horsemen in the town plaza. They moved in rigidly controlled formations, which changed into new groupings at a single command. They practiced cavalry charges, attacks on the flank, the cutting down of fleeing soldiers with sabers. . . . The ring of harsh commands and thud of horses' hooves were a reminder to others that this was a military town. But even the Lancer Squadron disappeared from the plaza during siesta, when the sun ruled dominant as supreme lord of all Nicaragua.

Cole found strange Walker's insistence that General Munoz, his former superior, be sent to the firing squad for having alerted the enemy at Rivas and for having sent two colonels to delay and hamper him. Walker's execution of Colonel Sanchez had caused a stir in Leon, and Munoz and Gonzalez had been quick to rouse military resentment, already primed by Walker's fine show against the enemy without their help. To have executed the only Nicaraguan soldier with his force, Walker in their view had insulted the Liberal armed forces. Cole could not dissuade Walker from demanding Munoz' execution, but he did succeed in finding a succession of reasons why for delay in sending the demand to Leon.

A dour, silent Englishman named Doubleday arrived with a squad of men, all crack shots, well fed, well clothed and well paid, with no pretense to be anything but mercenaries on the side of the highest bidder. Walker did not probe Cole's story that "supporters and admirers back in the States" had paid for their services.

Word came that cholera had broken out in Managua, a Legitimist-held city halfway between the rival capitals of Granada and Leon. The epidemic had already decimated the population of the city. Walker sent for Dr. Jones, his staff physician, and the two local doctors in San Juan del Sur. Jones knew better, but the two local practitioners arrived at the barracks ready to deliver their weighty professional opinions on the disease. However, Walker did not ask their medical opinions. He told them to isolate any cases even on the suspicion of cholera. No one with symptoms of the disease was to be permitted to enter the town, that foodstuffs were not to be imported from near the infected area, and that drinking water was to be boiled before being drunk.

Again Dr. Jones knew better, but the two local doctors tried to argue with Walker about what they called his unscientific, groundless notions. It would be more than thirty years before Louis Pasteur open his institute in Paris, and almost thirty before Robert Koch discovered the causative agent of cholera. Little was known of such work at the time, particularly in the New World. Walker stilled the objections of the local doctors by calling Lieutenant Petrie and Lieutenant Drayberry into the room, repeating his instructions and empowering them to shoot on sight anyone caught breaking these rules, including any of the gentlemen present.

17

THE LIBERAL administration in Leon seemed increasingly worried about their American ally esconced in San Juan del Sur, if the increasing number of messengers and written directives were anything to go by. Byron Cole had appointed himself Walker's executive secretary and granted or refused interviews with the general according to his own judgment. He read all incoming documents, and no one knew which ones he spared Walker the trouble of reading.

Cole made one memorable mistake. He tried to extend his authority over the access of the officers to Walker. He chose for his test case Harry Drayberry.

Harry took his word the first time Cole said Walker was not available. When he came back the second time a few hours later, Harry got the same treatment. Again he left and thought nothing of it. The third time Harry got the message.

"Why don't you tell me what you want to see him about?" Cole asked him. "Maybe I can get to him for you."

"No thanks. I'll do it myself. This time I'll wait."

"No you won't," Cole snapped bossily. "In future you will direct your business with General Walker through me."

119

Harry leaped to his feet and drew his saber.

"My God, no!" The flabby ex-publisher rose unsteadily as Harry advanced on him, raising the broadbladed sword above his head.

The saber swung in a silver arc, and Cole uttered a loud scream as the flat of the blade harmlessly smote his fat backside.

Cole ran howling in terror from the room. Harry whirled when he saw a movement in a doorway. It was William Walker. His gray eyes were fathomless.

"Lieutenant Drayberry, come in," Walker said. "It's always a pleasure to see you."

After that, Cole restricted his executive treatment to the enlisted men and strangers.

Messages continued to arrive in General Castellon's handwriting. Mostly they amounted to nothing more than reminders to Walker that Castellon was still boss. Walker refolded them carefully and placed these letters in the left inside pocket of his coat. It was as if he were carefully collecting documentary evidence to defend himself in some future court trial. Once a lawyer, always one, Cole thought to himself. If we fail here it won't be documentary evidence we'll need to stop them from standing us against the nearest wall and filling us with lead.

One message from Castellon was taken by Walker from his pocket on repeated occasions. It announced the death of General Munoz in a border skirmish with Honduran troops—so that the question of his execution for betraying Walker at Rivas was no longer something that Cole had to divert his mind from. The second part of the message bore what superficially seemed to be even greater news. General Castellon had appointed Walker in Munoz' place as commander in chief of all the Liberal forces, the *Ejercito Democratico*.

"It's very clear to me that I have few friends in the *Ejercito Democratico*," Walker told Cole on several occasions. "Castellon knows this as well as I do. What does he expect? For me to come to grief trying to control rebellious army officers?"

"It might not be a bad plan to use up your energies in bureaucratic in-fighting," Cole said, musingly.

"Yes, in one way. But think of the risk he is running by appointing me head of his armed forces. No, I think Castellon has been turned against me by my enemies and wants to lure me to Leon."

"Why doesn't he just send for you?" Cole put to him.

"Because I would not go without the protection of my men and without adequate reassurances. This way he thinks that greed and ambition will blind me and that I will rush there with my head bare to receive laurels and wield power, only to have a bullet put in my brain."

"Castellon has always been afraid of you."

"You're right," Walker agreed. "The day I first set foot in Nicaragua, Gonzalez stopped me from marching my men on Leon and, after a delay of twenty-four hours, took me there by himself. To this day the men who sailed with me here on the *Vesta* have not been permitted into Leon."

"Castellon was anxious to give you the town of San Juan del Sur."

"Yes, he has always been generous with enemy-held territory."

In these conversations Byron Cole thought at first he was seeing a wavering of Walker's will, a vacillation in his decision-making. Later he realized that Walker had never considered for a moment going to Leon to accept his new responsibilities. His frequent discussion of the offer was only his way of venting his frustration at having a carrot dangled before his nose—an irresistible morsel to an ass, but a poison root to William Walker.

Cole had long since grown used to the feeling of

being a puppeteer whose puppet now controls him.

Another group of "colonists" arrived from San Francisco aboard a Transit steamer. They unloaded wooden crates marked MACHINERY and SUGAR and reported to the barracks for duty. Walker gazed thoughtfully at Cole after he had seen the new arrivals and their equipment. The men, he knew, were easy to recruit. But guns were expensive. Someone had paid for them, someone who would want something from Walker in return. Cole treated the shipment in the spirit of a grateful missionary abroad who has received parcels from the home parishes—God is good, He will provide, have faith, question not. William Walker did not ask questions.

Instead, he acted. The new arrivals were given three days of intensive training and allowed to rest on the fourth. Before dawn on the fifth day after their arrival, Walker spread the general call to arms. After a breakfast of strong coffee and spicey goat stew over cassava roots, the men formed in companies outside the town at first light. The officers ran a check of weapons and equipment. Some squads were assigned, much to their disappointment, to remain behind to guard San Juan del Sur. The bulk of the forces set out at a fast walk over the Transit Road.

The mounted men and Von Satzner's Lancer Squadron were in the vanguard, followed by the men on foot. The mule-drawn supply wagons were last, protected by a rearguard of men on foot. The long column made rapid progress eastward over the hard surface of the Transit Road.

Only thirteen miles separated the towns of San Juan del Sur on the Pacific and La Virgen on Lake Nicaragua. They did not see a single human being on the first five miles of road. Then they came to the first guard post. Their own spies and recent travelers had told them this was manned by five soldiers, and that after this post there were three others, each manned by two to five soldiers. Their function was more to prevent trouble among travelers than to protect the road against armed invaders. Certainly the five soldiers in the first guard post saw it this way, and surrendered without a shot being fired when taken by surprise by the Lancer Squadron.

General Walker gave instructions in person to his men that the captives were to be well treated. It was hardly necessary for him to do so, because the good treatment his men received from him and their officers made them humane in turn to others. Except in combat. The men at the next guard post refused to surrender and died in a hail of lead. One enemy soldier at the next guard post shot a mule carrying panniers of ammunition, and some of the men set the little stockade with its thatched roof aflame with lighted brands. The sun-dried lumber and straw were consumed in tall red flames, and the column stood and listened to the dying screams of the men trapped inside.

At the last guard post before La Virgen, the three soldiers surrendered when assured they would not be harmed. Walker was interested to hear that the captured men found it hard to believe they would not be bayoneted. This was the standard treatment of prisoners by both Legitimists and Liberals.

Harry Drayberry and Thornton McClintock each rode at the head of his own company of infantrymen. Each company contained four platoons. A sergeant commanded each platoon of twenty-four men, which was further divided into three squads of eight men apiece. The eight-man squad, including the corporal who commanded it, was the basic fighting unit. In combat the squad was often as not completely on its own.

In theory, of course, it was different. According to

the books, Harry or Thornton would have gone into battle with his hundred-man company and would have issued commands to his platoon sergeants, who in turn would order the squad corporals. It always started out that way. Then the sergeants, under the pressures of battle, had to make their own decisions. Finally it came down to each squad looking out for itself, and the survival of its members often depended on the judgment of its corporal, and how well the squad operated as a team.

Harry and Thornton's only experience of a full-scale military encounter had been the attack on Rivas. During that they had simply yelled, charged at the head of their troops, hoped for the best and shot at anything that moved. They had learned a lot about military strategy since then, but had no opportunity as yet to put this knowledge into practice. And every military man recognizes that action is the only test, and that a brilliant soldier can turn any enemy's military theory into highfalutin' nonsense.

The sergeants and corporals were mostly the men who had served with Walker and Petrie in Baja California. They respected the courage of Thornton and Harry and did not question their authority. Both of the Tennesseans were wise enough to let their sergeants and corporals do the actual running of the fighting units. There was friendly but fierce competition among the squads as to which qualified as the most hell-bound, gut-tearing, bloodthirsty and glory-hungry in the company.

Thornton had learned much about life in the time he spent with these men. Harry had fitted in much more naturally than he had. After all, a gentleman from Tennessee might be expected to live out his entire life without coming into close contact with ruffians like these. Back in Antrimville some of these fellows would have been on the gallows within a week, and many of the rest soon after. He saw the grim humor of his company's banner, a gold rope noose on a green background, with the motto stitched in red: BORN TO HANG.

18

THE SCOUTS rode back to say they had sighted the town of La Virgen ahead. People were moving about on its street, but no alarm of their approach had yet been sounded. Their attack would be a surprise.

"Is there a Transit Company steamer at the dock?" Walker asked.

"No, sir."

"Good. We don't need the added complication of U.S. citizens losing their lives or being injured. Lieutenant McClintock, I want you to take the town with your company of men, while the rest of us attack the military enclosure outside the town. Remember, no harm must come to U.S. citizens no matter what kind of rogues they are. Mr. Cole will ride with you to place the Transit offices under his protection." Seeing the disappointed look on Thornton's face, he added, "When the town is secured, leave a minimum of your men to guard it and join our attack at whatever point you judge best."

Thornton and his men separated from the column of troops on the approach to the town and swept into the main street of La Virgen.

Thornton's orders to his men were simple. "Empty every house of people and gather them all in the

Transit House compound. Tell them you'll shoot any looters—but I don't want anyone shot. The faster you get that job done, the quicker you'll be able to join the real fight. Mr. Cole, you will follow me."

Byron Cole scowled but obeyed the order. He had had trouble before with these whipper-snapper officers he himself had signed on for Walker. He rode after Thornton down the street to the water's edge with a squad of infantry. The two men dismounted at the building whose tall letters painted on its sides proclaimed it the Transit House. They went inside and Thornton asked where the manager's office was.

"I'm not sure he is free to see you, sir," an American clerk informed him with an insulting lack of interest.

Thornton said quietly, "I didn't ask to see the manager, I asked where his office was."

The clerk pointed in a bored way. "Up those stairs, but you can't go up without an appointment."

They strode up the stairs and saw a large office behind glass-panelled doors on the second floor.

Thornton pushed through the doors. "Cyrus Figgis, upon my soul, what a beautiful view of the lake you have from here."

The pasty-faced bookkeeper he and Harry had endured on the voyage down from New York dropped his pen in amazement at this intrusion. He shook hands in a flustered manner and then stooped to clean the ink blot his dropped pen had made on the page of the ledger.

"I—I thought you and Harry had gone to California," he said.

"What? Leave this beautiful country, this land of opportunity, leave all this for that? Not on your life, Cyrus."

Cyrus Figgis' eyes still goggled at the change which had come over this polite, reserved Southerner whom he had found such a pleasant companion during the idle hours of their voyage to Nicaragua. He could visualize Harry Drayberry turning into something like this, but not Thornton McClintock. This man looked and behaved like a freebooter, a pirate, a filibuster! It was then that the shooting started in Walker's attack on the army enclosure. As fusillade after fusillade of shots rang out on the morning air, a look of terrible comprehension crept across the pudgy face of Cyrus Figgis, which now turned from pale to fish-belly white so that the pimples stood out like red, burning points.

"My God!" he gasped, sinking back into the chair behind his desk. "Wait till Mr. Vanderbilt hears about this!"

Thornton introduced Figgis and Byron Cole to each other. Moments later the babble of human voices and raucous female laughter began to sound outside, almost loud enough to drown out the sound of gunfire.

Cyrus Figgis' eyes rolled wildly as he tried to guess what was happening now without getting up from his chair. He could stand it no longer and jumped up and ran to the window.

"What—why are all those . . . uh, people coming into the compound?" he asked.

"For shelter while the fighting is going on," Thornton told him.

"But this compound is private property! You need permission. Written permission! I won't allow it. You do not have my permission!"

Thornton laughed and said nothing.

The bookkeeper was trembling with rage as he stared out the window at the people streaming into the compound.

Thornton joined him at the window. It was quite a sight. Scores of prostitutes in various states of undress at this hour of the morning joked, laughed, and passed rum bottles to each other. Various male touts, thieves and hangers-on looked less pleased about this unexpected outing than the women.

"Interesting group of people your Transit Company

has gathered about it here," Thornton remarked lightly.

But the thrust was a mortal wound to the Puritan hypocrisy and Victorian respectability of Cyrus Figgis. For anyone to even imply that he was in any way connected to these miserable, sinful creatures was practically more than his sensibility could stand. He hadn't known it was going to be like this! And now these animals were on his doorstep and the gentlemen on the ship had turned into filibusters and soldiers of fortune! What on earth would become of him? Would Mr. Vanderbilt hold him responsible for all this? What could he have done to stop it? My God, this was unimaginable!

Cyrus Figgis made his way unsteadily back to his chair. He looked up to see Thornton McClintock wave cheerily as he left the office. The horrible fat man with the oily leer who had been introduced as Byron Something sat in an armchair. Why was he staying?

"You wouldn't have a glass of port, would you?" Cole asked.

Figgis pointed wordlessly at decanters on a shelf.

Cole gave him a lingering smile as he poured two full glasses. "We're going to be seeing a lot of each other. I'm the new Transit Commissioner."

Thornton left a few men to guard the company enclosure filled with the townspeople, and a couple of men on the street to prevent looting. He rode ahead of the rest of his company to see where they could be most useful in the fighting. The walls of the military enclosure had been breached, but the garrison inside had apparently repelled the attackers and now occupied positions outside the gaps in their fortifications.

Men were firing rifles from behind every rock, shrub and piece of cover they could find. Many lay flat on their bellies on the ground and fired at the enemy as fast as they could reload.

Only General William Walker spurned all cover. He

rode up and down, waving his saber and exhorting, praising and encouraging his men. As Thornton rode up, he saw before his eyes a bullet strike Walker in the chest and lift him clean out of the saddle.

Thornton abandoned all caution and galloped to the spot where his fallen leader lay. He leaped from his horse and ran to the prone body. As he did so, Thornton was aware of the increasing silence. Their men had stopped firing, trying to see what had happened to Walker.

As Thornton bent over the still form, suddenly Walker's gray eyes flicked open. Thornton could not help being startled. It was like the dead come to life.

Walker sat up and rose to his feet. "Lieutenant McClintock, would you be so kind as to catch my horse for me?"

Thornton did.

In a minute the little man was riding up and down as before, waving his saber and urging his men on. A huge cheer went up and his troops took up their fighting with a new bloody intensity. Platoons near the hostile positions outside the breached walls made a savage bayonet charge and skewered the defenders too amazed at this suicidal onslaught to retreat behind the walls of the enclosure. But even these attackers could penetrate no farther.

Thornton stayed with Walker, thinking his behavior was a result of shock and he would soon weaken from loss of blood. He himself had seen Walker hit by the bullet. Walker noticed him examining the bullet entry hole in the front of his coat.

The general grinned and pulled out a wad of letters from his left inside pocket. "They are all from that whining old fool in Leon, Francisco Castellon. But he is of some use—look!"

Walker plucked a distorted bullet out of the letters and tossed it over his left shoulder.

"This is between you and me, Lieutenant," he said.

"It does no harm for my men to have a miraculous leader, and I have few enough miracles to offer them."

And the incident was received as a miracle. They had all heard of the fearless little man who ignored enemy bullets, who rode around a battlefield as casually as he would a public park. The men who had fought with him in Baja California all swore that no enemy could hurt him, that he was possessed of magical power. He had been dauntless at Rivas, they all agreed on that. But here was actual proof! Not hearsay. Hundreds of men, both his own and the foe, saw it happen. He was knocked from his horse by a bullet in the chest and, after three minutes, he rose again.

The enemy troops had definitely seen it too. They had heard of the loco Yanqui's white hair and terrible gray eyes, worse than those of any wolf. They had heard how he had sold his soul to El Diablo, how nothing they could do would ever harm him, not even silver bullets! Every man of them wore a cross around his neck, and those of them that had not done so before now pulled out the crosses from beneath their shirts so that the holy emblem hung on each man's chest in full view, preventing the gray evil eye of the Yanqui devil from resting on them.

Thornton was deploying his men in battle formation when Walker rode up to him.

"Bring me the eight captives we took on the Transit Road," Walker said. "Restore their weapons to them."

Thornton had come a long way since joining Walker. He now no longer questioned the orders of his leader, he simply obeyed and waited to see what would happen.

Walker's instructions to the captives were direct and forceful. He had an interpreter repeat them for the men in better Spanish than his own.

"I will call a ceasefire by our side for fifteen minutes. You will walk into the enclosure and tell your fellow soldiers—not just the officers, you must tell the men— that I do not want their lives, just their absence. They may leave La Virgen, unharassed and bearing all their arms and goods if they begin to do so within the fifteen-minute ceasefire. If they do not agree, I will not accept a surrender later, and I will starve, torture and execute every single one of you."

Walker's bugler sounded a ceasefire. The eight frightened men walked forward, waving a white flag. They glanced behind them, expecting to be shot in the back. And they moved forward slowly, not knowing whether their own officers would have them shot as traitors.

Stillness reigned over the battlefield. The men busily cleaned their weapons. Only Walker did nothing. He sat motionless on his charger and stared across the battlefield at the enemy-held fort.

An officer rode out of the enclosure on a chestnut horse. A second officer joined him. Then a third. When they were not fired upon, the men began streaming out. All eyes turned as the Legitimist flag was lowered from the mast.

The enemy force was bigger than they had expected. Reckoning that they had lost about a hundred men, their original force had numbered about six hundred, outnumbering Walker's force by two to one.

At the very end of the departing column of Legitimist infantrymen, an officer rode on a magnificent gray stallion. Instead of turning north along the lake shore after his men, he approached Walker. Weapons were leveled on him in case he attempted some last desperate act. Walker gestured for his men to put their guns aside.

The officer's uniform was that of a colonel. He was a powerfully built, red-faced man with a bushy mustache, perhaps in his middle forties. The sun reflected on the numerous medals, gold braid and highly polished buttons of his uniform. He reined in his horse so that he faced Walker at a distance of twenty paces. Then he briskly saluted.

Walker raised his right hand to return what he

thought was a salute. But the Legitimist colonel's right hand held a small pistol, which he put to the side of his head for an instant and pulled the trigger.

The colonel's body fell sideways from his horse and thumped on the ground.

All eyes turned to Walker.

His face was grave. "Bury him with full military honors. I will attend the funeral."

19

WILLIAM WALKER knew exactly what he had done. With a small group of armed men, he had in effect seized one of the most important commercial rights-of-way in the world, a connection between the Atlantic and Pacific, between the East and the West of a growing America.

He told Byron Cole, "Cornelius Vanderbilt may own the Transit on paper, but I am standing on it."

There were those who waited for a lightning bolt to fall. Indeed it was shortly after Walker's seizure of the Transit Road that the British started shipping arms to the Indians of the Mosquito Coast, the Atlantic shore of Nicaragua. French men-of-war were increasingly seen in the area. But naturally it was the United States, as the great nation most affected by Walker's seizure of the Transit Road, that trouble could be expected from. Yet nothing happened, for two reasons.

First, Walker had not interfered with the Transit business and therefore, so far as the Transit Company was concerned, he might even be good for them if he could introduce some stability into the area. All that the company cared about was the narrow strip of land across which their route lay. Whoever kept that open to them was their friend. Cornelius Vanderbilt was still in the process of gaining back control of the company. However, his enemies Charles Morgan and Cornelius Garrison still sat on the board of directors. Thus divided, the company's protests to Washington were not vigorous enough to get anything done.

Second, even if the protests had been more vigorous, it is far from certain anything would have been done, for the simple reason that Washington had more difficulties of its own than it could handle. The United States was too busy in a bloody dress rehearsal for the Civil War.

The trouble originated in January 1854 when Senator Douglas presented a bill for the organization of two new territories to be known as Kansas and Nebraska, with the proviso that the Missouri Compromise should not apply to them. The Missouri Compromise cut off this region from slavery as part of the Louisiana purchase from France in 1803. According to the senator's bill, the occupants of these territories could decide for themselves whether they wanted slavery when they applied for admission to the Union as soverign states. Although the bill caused great conflict in Congress, it passed both houses and was signed into law by the President in May 1854.

Pro-slavers and anti-slavers rushed into Kansas. The Massachusetts legislature incorporated a company called The Emigrants' Aid Society which during 1855 sent out thirteen hundred anti-slavers. Southern states urged their supporters to resettle in Kansas and claim the territory as a new state of their own. Pro-slavers won the initial elections and set up laws for the convention. However, the anti-slavers claimed the elections were invalid because of the large number of Missouri residents who crossed into the territory only to vote. They held their own elections and set up their own governing body in Topeka to pass laws. Thus there were two sets of authorities, each claiming to be lawfully chosen. Civil war was the result.

The territory soon came to be known as "bloody Kansas." One nineteenth-century account summed it up by saying that "outrages of every kind were committed." The Kansas fighting lasted through the year 1856, and was stopped only by the President's appointment of a new governor with wide military powers.

The activities of a swashbuckling filibuster in faraway Nicaragua were not yet a concern to Northerners among the nation's rulers in Washington. However, certain Southern politicians, whose hopes for separation into a confederacy were now growing from day to day, recalled that William Walker was from Nashville, Tennessee.

Thornton McClintock was bored. He, Harry Drayberry and four others had been playing draw poker for some hours. The stakes were reasonably small, and Thornton's run of hands had been quite good. But his heart was not in the game, and his winnings were not what they might have been had he taken full advantage of some of his best hands.

Lamps illuminated the large room in which they sat around a table. The furnishings were crude but clean and well kept. General Walker had insisted, as he had in San Juan del Sur, that the houses used by his troops in La Virgen were free of dirt, that their food was fresh and properly cooked and that all drinking water was boiled. Those who thought they knew better followed these regulations as tolerable eccentricities of Walker, whom they dared not oppose.

Thornton picked up his hand. He had a pair of nines. Another man opened, and four bought more cards. The man who opened bought one card, and the others three. Thornton picked up a third nine. The opener checked. Two pairs. Harry bet half the pot. Thornton guessed he was bluffing and made it the pot. The fourth man dropped out. So did the dealer. And then Harry. Thornton scooped in the money and got to his feet.

"You can't leave after winning a pot," Harry said.

Thornton laughed. "I'll pay for the drinks."

He paid the woman who ran the house for the bottle of light Panamanian rum on the table.

"You want a nice girl, sir?" she asked.

She thought Thornton was leaving for one of the other houses that Walker's troops frequented in La Virgen. They generally avoided the filthy hovels and medically untreated women elsewhere in the town so ironically, these days, named after the Blessed Virgin.

"I'll be back later," Thornton told her.

"I think Isabellita is expecting you in her room upstairs," the woman tried again.

"I don't believe so."

She caught his arm. "There's the new girl from Rivas. You've never been with her."

Thornton went out the door into the night. The stars looked huge in the sky. Frogs and crickets made a racket in nearby sedges at the lake's edge. A refreshing nocturnal breeze blew in from over the water, not quite cool but at least banishing the heat of the day. He missed the salt tang of the air at San Juan del Sur.

He was aware that it was unusual for someone born and raised a good distance inland like himself to start missing the ocean breeze, but he was less willing to admit it might be something else in San Juan del Sur that he was missing. Such as Solange de Brissot. Since he had been stationed in La Virgen, from the time of its capture, he had always managed to visit her at least twice a week.

He rode his horse over the Transit Road, usually in the company of others looking for a change from La Virgen. Thornton was not alone in tiring of the little town's atmosphere of soldiers, Transit travelers and whores. He had to smile when he recalled how he and

Harry had looked forward to getting out of Antrimville once a year to the wild nights of New Orleans. Now here he was trying to escape the nonstop debauchery available in La Virgen. Not so Harry. He did not come to San Juan del Sur very often. Brigitte was upset but tried not to show it. Solange and Thornton often brought her with them on their walks.

Thornton had spoken to Harry. "At least tell her not to expect you for a couple of weeks so that she will not be waiting for you."

Harry gave him a sardonic smile. "I'm sorry if it inconveniences you, Thornton. I mean, that's what your concern for her is based on. She makes you feel uncomfortable, so you turn on me. That's *why* she goes out of her way to embarrass you, so that you will pester me to come with you rather than have to look at her sad face and hear her soulful sighs."

"Then break it off."

"Break what off?" Harry asked. "I never promised her anything. Unlike you, who promised Emily."

Harry had him there. When they had left Antrimville, he had broken with Emily, telling her not to wait for him, that he would never be back. Harry had promised Elizabeth he would return to marry her. As he later explained to Thornton, if things went well in California he could forget her, and if things went badly she was something he could always return to.

Now Harry drank, gambled, whored and soldiered as if he had never lived otherwise in his life. He did not want to hear about the rest of the world—everything he needed in life was in the tiny town of La Virgen.

But Thornton McClintock was no philosopher who spent time reflecting on what was not. In his opinion a man had to be content with his lot. He had to make his world out of what was at hand, or at least within his reach. A few minutes out with the croaking frogs in the dank night under the merciless eyes of the stars were enough for him. He went back in the house.

"Where's that new girl from Rivas?" he asked the woman.

Pilar, the new girl, had run away from a husband who beat her. Why had he beaten her? Because she could not cook. Just for that? For other reasons too. What? She had slept with other men while her husband was in the fields.

Thornton had always been too filled with animal hunger, with physical need, ever to speak seriously with any of these women before. Perhaps he had wanted to see them only as one-dimensional ladies of the night, caricatures of women draped in silk and sin. Now he was bored with that, or did not believe it any longer. Now he wanted to know the person who would lie with him to slake his lust.

His conversational Spanish had become quite good. The only trouble was, the more the girl told him about herself, the less he understood her. Some time before, he would have decided she was a little insane or could not think straight, but more recently he had noticed that there were whole areas even of Solange's mind he could not understand, either. As a true man of his time, Thornton drew the only conclusion obvious to him from this: that women's brains were like short-winded horses; they could not go the distance that male logic demanded.

In spite of her mild insanity or whatever it was, Thornton felt a fierce physical attraction for Pilar. She too apparently had needed someone to talk to and although she cannot have imagined he comprehended what she was telling him, she knew he sympathized with her. He was not one of the cold, self-gratifying brutes who were her usual customers. She was warm and affectionately grateful to him, surrendering to her urge to be desired by a handsome male whose passions she had stirred by her beauty.

Pilar was beautiful. She had an unusually narrow face, big brown eyes and black hair that hung down about her shoulders. Her breasts were big and firm, and undulated gently when she walked. When she saw that he was aroused, after she had run her hands along his pants leg, she stripped quickly, with a prostitute's greater respect for her clothes than her body.

Thornton saw her shapely legs for the first time.

"I don't think it's fair to make women wear long dresses that cover their legs," she said, looking down admiringly at herself.

Thornton was amazed by this idea. "Then how could men walk on the streets without being overcome by sexual hunger at such a display? They would get erections in public places if women bared their legs."

She laughed merrily at this. Thornton by this time had removed his clothes too. She walked over and caught his erect organ in her hand and stroked it softly. Then she sank to her knees before him and allowed the head of his engorged manhood to slip softly into her moist, warm mouth.

20

"SCRUPULOUSLY DISHONEST" and "ruthless as a crocodile" were two contemporary descriptions of American robber barons. Another was called "a living, breathing, waddling monument to the triumph of vulgarity, viciousness and dishonesty"—and he hired the man who called him that because he liked his way with words.

The great robber barons may have been coarse and ruthless, but in a way their intellects and conduct reflected the most advanced thinking of their time. With Charles Darwin's *Origin of the Species*, first published in 1859, the concept of "survival of the fittest" became widely known. The industrial magnates saw themselves on the pinnacle of human achievement, and might acknowledge that to get there some weaker specimens had to be trodden upon. Others saw the robber barons as tyrannosaurs slouching across the marshes of poverty and ignorance—and in the prints they left in the mud behind them, tiny, broken creatures squirmed.

But in these early days, the 1850s, the robber barons were almost always great pioneers also, forging new routes, putting new ideas into effect. It was not until the financial boom of the Civil War and the years after that their manipulations of the market and bribery in

141

Washington were first seen as being against the national interest.

Cornelius Vanderbilt's pioneering effort was the Transit across Nicaragua. He never got to build the canal he wanted there. But almost a decade later, in 1864, while he was seizing control of the New York Central and Erie railroads connecting New York City to Chicago, he could not see the sense of extending the railroad to California. He dismissed the project by saying, "Building a railroad from nowhere to nowhere at public expense is not a legitimate enterprise."

The Transit was Vanderbilt's baby; he was its father. Paternity was not in doubt.

Morgan and Garrison had thought they could seize control of the Transit Company while he was away on his yacht. By buying shares in odd lots on the market under a variety of names, he had now gained a controlling interest in the firm. He would make his presence felt at the board meeting in the new year.

Vanderbilt was not particularly concerned about the seizure of land adjoining the Transit Road by this soldier of fortune called William Walker. Walker had not dared to interfere with traffic on the Transit, that was the important thing. Vanderbilt knew the sort. He could handle him. In fact, there might be something in this for Cornelius. His arrangement with the Nicaraguan government was satisfactory, but it mattered little to him who he dealt with—and a Southerner would be preferable to those Latin Americans. Walker might be able to bring political stability to the area. If Vanderbilt could depend on that, he would be willing to invest heavily there in cattle ranches and mining ventures.

True, there seemed to be a connection between Walker and Morgan and Garrison. But Vanderbilt himself would grind those two into their own dirt. Walker was not that much of a fool to side with those two against the power of Cornelius Vanderbilt.

Then there was the incident in San Francisco when

that newspaperman associated with Walker, a Byron Cole, had tried extortion on the Accessory Transit Company. Veiled threats that the Transit Company might need the friendship of William Walker, who was shortly leaving with an expeditionary force of armed men for Nicaragua. The Cole wretch had the insolence to demand that the company finance this madcap expedition. The manager, quite rightly of course, had shown Cole the door and reported the incident to the New York office.

That should have been that. Every business which maintains access to the public has its share of lunatics who drift in from the street. One in ten thousand will have a valid proposal. It was no fault of the manager's that this particular demand turned out to be well-grounded. Vanderbilt himself might have spotted this one among all the others, but that was why he was Cornelius Vanderbilt and the other man was an office manager.

Vanderbilt picked up the sheet of paper from his desk and studied it. He shook a small brass bell and the office door opened.

"Yes, sir?"

"You may show the gentleman in," he told his secretary, a bald, worried-looking man in late middle age.

Three serious men were shown in to the office and seated before the desk. They waited for Vanderbilt to speak. He was looking at the sheet of paper.

He did not greet his employees. "You have all seen this letter. It came with our steamer from Nicaragua this morning." Vanderbilt nodded in the direction of one of the men. "What do you think?"

"From an accounting point of view, Mr. Vanderbilt, I think we should stay away from disputing the actual sum they say is due from the Transit Company to Nicaragua."

Vanderbilt sputtered, "They say we owe them thirty-two thousand dollars!"

"They could have claimed a lot more," the man said mildly. "I would not dispute that figure. I'm certain they would settle the debt with a sum half that amount paid in gold. Sixteen thousand dollars."

Another of the men said, "From an accounting point of view, I have no doubt my colleague here is right. But from a legal point of view, which is my specialty, where will that payment leave us? To whom are we paying this money? Not the Legitimists, with whom we have a written contract and who have not demanded the money. Not the Liberals, who in all probability would continue to honor our contract as they have done before, and who also have not demanded money. But to a filibuster, a freebooter with a bunch of vagabonds—"

Vanderbilt interrupted. "He may have been that before. Now he is in possession of the Transit Road."

The lawyer smiled. "He has risen in the world. In view of the extortion effort by this man Cole in San Francisco, you may wish to pay the sixteen thousand to keep the route open. However, I would not recommend it for these reasons. If you pay Walker, you will strengthen his position by enabling him to buy arms and supplies. Of course, the money you pay him will not be recognized as a payment by the Nicaraguan government when they oust Walker. That's the crux of the matter. We cannot risk antagonizing the Legitimists by appearing to support this American, and by refusing Walker we risk his interference with the Transit. I say we sit still and do nothing for a while."

"I notice," Vanderbilt said, picking up the letter, "that Cole signs himself Transit Commissioner, presumably with Liberal consent. Yet I think you are correct in doubting he has their authorization to collect this money."

Vanderbilt's gaze shifted to the third man. Unlike the accountant and lawyer, this man had a non-sedentary outdoors look to him.

"I say we get off the fence," this man said with vehemence and finality. "We either back Walker to the hilt and surreptitiously send him arms and supplies—that is, make him an employee, Mr. Vanderbilt—or we raise and finance a force of our own to go down and boot him off the Transit Road."

The lawyer and accountant shuddered visibly at this kind of talk.

Cornelius Vanderbilt paused. Finally he said, "As you know, I surrendered the presidency of the Transit Company. It seems I must go about getting it back. In the meantime we have no choice but to wait." He turned to the accountant. "Send Cole and Walker a reply that the matter is under consideration. Sign it with your name. Do not mention mine."

Solange de Brissot glanced across at Thornton Mc-Clintock. She realized that if he ever learned the truth, she would take her life. From the first, his physical presence had excited her. That had developed into a schoolgirl's infatuation for him. Those months he had been in Leon before Walker's arrival in Nicaragua, she had been content to walk with him, occasionally allowing their hands to brush and even more occasionally allowing him to steal a kiss from her cheek. That was only a fraction of what her body wanted—but polite upbringing and convention had so deeply imprinted themselves on her since early girlhood that Solange had difficulty in separating what she wanted from what she knew was expected from her.

Now, day by day, a terrible choice was being presented to her, with no escape except through death. Solange's convent education had persuaded her that if she took her own life, she would be sent to Hell forever. So if Thornton found out, she would do something dangerous and be killed that way. Unless Thornton rescued her and she blurted everything out to him and he forgave her.

Could he ever forgive her? She glanced at him again. She could not tell. He was unpredictable to her. He came and went and did all the things men were free to do, while she and her sister remained penned up here like two albino mice in a cage.

San Juan del Sur had not much in the way of polite society. The few families in that category were so old-fashioned and backward socially by the standards of Paris, and even of New Orleans, that the two sisters felt almost as freakish among them as they did among the working class girls of the town who came and went as they pleased, just like the men. It was not fair.

Gaston de Brissot kept a close watch over his daughters. Whether they wanted to disobey him or not hardly mattered since they were under such close supervision at all times. As dutiful daughters, the very thought of disobeying their father or countering his wishes should be foreign to their natures, he surmised. The French aristocrat looked across the table at the perennial truant who had finally showed up—Harry Drayberry. His daughter Brigitte was batting her eyelashes and cooing to the fellow. He could never resist her. To hell with him if he did. Thornton McClintock was firmly on the hook.

Solange saw her father's shrewd appraisal of how things were going at the dinner table. Her sister was being sickly sweet to Harry—no wonder he did not show up for weeks at a time. But Brigitte had her father's instructions; she was obeying him. Solange wondered what her father's reactions would be if he could read her mind.

She remembered how, five or six years before, after her mother had died, her father, sister and she had been presented at Court. She had been proud of her father on that occasion because of his worldly graces and knowledge of how to behave—never, never to be disconcerted by any circumstances, whether lofty or from the gutter. An aristocrat transcends all. He showed this at Court, where everyone knew that the de Brissot family had a noble lineage of six hundred years, which was a great deal more than could be said for the Bonapartes.

Louis Napoleon, the nephew of the great Napoleon and now Emperor Napoleon III, was a pompous fool in velvet britches and silk stockings. In Solange's eyes, the old nobility as represented by her father could only smile bleakly at this fop with pretensions of being king. Solange had been brought up to believe that Louis XVI had been a decent, honorable monarch, undeservedly savaged by the unwashed mob.

She had to admit that Louis Napoleon's wife, the Empress Eugenie, was pretty. But Solange had heard, like everyone else, that Eugenie's mother, a Spanish countess, was little better than a courtesan—one joke had it that there was no doubt about who Eugenie's mother was, but that only God knew who her father was, and it wasn't Him! It was public knowledge that when Louis Napoleon announced his wish to marry Eugenie, one well-meaning cousin told him, "One does not *marry* women like Eugenie, one makes love to them."

Solange and Brigitte, in spite of their youth, had heard how assassins could be hired for just a few francs, how society belles were expected to change their dresses more than half a dozen times a day, how young officers in the *Garde Imperiale* circulated as male prostitutes, how women made love to each other instead of to men. To Solange, this was not Babylon—merely a tacky imitation of the Sun King, for whom all had been permissible. With her mother dead and such people ruling her beloved France, she and her sister had looked forward to departure when they heard they would accompany their father to the New World.

She had never questioned her father's doings over the years while she and her sister had been at the convent school in New Orleans. Now that they had outgrown

that, they could see him at closer range for themselves.
Byron Cole, she knew, had used them as a lure to
recruit Thornton and Harry. But she had been a willing
accomplice in this, since it was the only way she could
think of to keep Thornton leaving for California.

Then William Walker had done the unexpected. He
had given battle commands to these two inexperienced
fellow Southerners. De Brissot had been given a mean-
ingless title and position. Incoming intelligence never
got beyond Walker and Cole. The end result was that
Gaston de Brissot was at the very heart of things but
knew nothing—not the most enviable position for an
agent of Louis Napoleon.

Yes, if Thornton ever found out that her father was
a spy for the French, she would kill herself rather than
live on, having lost his love. And he would certainly
hate her if he found out that she, a spy's daughter, was
helping her father. That was the terrible truth Solange
was convinced which sooner or later would cause her
death.

Brigitte did not really love Harry. Their father had
demanded that she stay close to him as a source of
information. That she could not hold him was a blow
to her pride. But she had no conflict of loyalties to
endure.

Solange loved Thornton. Of course she loved her
father too. And she loved France, her motherland.
What would she do? Wait in trembling. . . . And when
all was lost, die. . . .

21

"CHOLERA IN Leon?" Walker said. "Damn! You know what to do, Byron. No one from Leon enters here into San Juan or into La Virgen. No food comes from the Leon area. Boil the drinking water."

Byron Cole nodded. Sometimes he found it hard to keep a straight face while he listened to the eccentric notions of this little man. But Walker had already had three of the townspeople of San Juan shot for disobeying him by drinking water direct from a well. Now no one argued anymore. They feared William Walker more than cholera.

Walker continued, holding up a letter from the table, "This doesn't say that the matter was ever brought before Cornelius Vanderbilt. I find it hard to believe that I could sit here on his Transit Road and tell him he owes thirty-two thousand dollars and receive a stupid letter from some lowly clerk—"

"Chief accountant," Cole pointed out.

"—whatever, telling me that they will consider my request at their leisure, as if I were asking them for a job."

'That's not exactly what it says in the letter," Cole objected. "But I see your point about the deliberate omission of Vanderbilt's name."

"Perhaps he feels I am beneath his attention," Walker said grimly.

Cole said nothing. One of Byron Cole's great powers was knowing when to hold back, seeming never to contribute directly to the decision he wanted.

After a while Cole said, "Well, we got the twenty thousand from Morgan and Garrison as promised."

Walker glowered at him suspiciously. "I heard about that already. I'm still waiting to hear what they want in return."

"I expect we'll be hearing from them shortly," Cole agreed casually. "Their sending the money as promised says more for their intentions than Vanderbilt's."

The gray eyes settled on Byron Cole, and he shifted uncomfortably under their stare.

A knock sounded on the door. A Nicaraguan who had recently been elevated to the rank of sergeant entered and handed a battered envelope with a broken seal to Walker. The man stood stiffly at attention until the general told him to sit and smoke.

Byron Cole looked mildly curious about this.

Walker read the letter and asked the sergeant, "How sure can you be that this is genuine?"

"I trust the men who captured the letter and I believe they took it from the man they say they did."

"But who did that man get it from?"

The sergeant answered, "It could have been given to him as a decoy. But it was just by chance our men happened to be there and caught the messenger. They would not have sent a message they wanted intercepted by that route."

"Unless they were very clever," Walker suggested.

"They would have been too clever then in ninety-nine times out of a hundred. The message would have been safe."

"Who else knows about this?"

"My men and I. The messenger is dead."

"No one else in San Juan must know. You will be

well rewarded if this message is true. On your way out, tell the orderly that Mr. Cole and I will take our lunch in my office."

The sergeant saluted and left.

"One of your secret agents?" Cole asked sardonically.

Walker ignored the remark. "The message is from the mayor of Granada to General Corral. From the head of the Legitimist capital to the commander of the Legitimist forces. Can you believe this? Through some incredible blunder, Granada has no troops there at the moment to protect it. They want Corral to rush soldiers there immediately."

" 'Incredible blunder' is the term I would use also," Cole said disparagingly. "I find it impossible to believe."

"If you didn't know otherwise, you'd find the civil war hard to believe also."

"True," Cole granted. "But I still think this is a trap of some kind."

"A faint-hearted man grows cautious with modest gains," Walker taunted him. "I'm going to take Granada."

Cole paled. "You can't mean that. We hold the Transit Road."

"The twenty thousand dollars puts me in a new position, Byron. I can now pay my own men, fund my own expedition."

"Think of all the letters Castellon has sent telling you to restrict your activities to the Transit zone."

"I often think of those letters, Byron. I have good reason to be grateful for them. But don't you think all those letters are enough to make attractive what they warn against?"

"What will Castellon do when he hears of this in Leon?" Cole asked in a voice of rising panic.

"Don't you remember? There is cholera in Leon." He was examining a timetable. "The lake steamer arrives in La Virgen this afternoon. We will ride there after lunch. You, as Transit Commissioner, will requisition the steamer for the Transit Company. McClintock and Drayberry have their companies in the town. I'll make the military arrangements."

"William, you can't just seize the capital of Nicaragua!"

"Byron, don't let it give you indigestion. It's almost lunch time."

Walker took Von Satzner and his Lancer Squadron with him without telling the Prussian their ultimate destination. In La Virgen he calmly ordered McClintock to fetch the Transit Company manager to the military enclosure. Cole's orders were clear from that point on—he was to force the manager, Cyrus Figgis, to sign the requisition order for the lake steamer. This was another of Walker's quirks, no doubt resulting from his legal training. There was nothing to stop him from seizing the lake steamer in the first place, and since he was using it to grab the nation's capital, it was hardly of interest to anyone whether he had a signed chit for use of the boat or not.

Forcing Figgis to sign the requisition order would give Byron pleasure, but it would not be much fun sitting with him in the military enclosure for the next twenty-four hours without telling him or anyone else what was going on. Figgis was not to be treated as a prisoner, Walker insisted, but as their guest. He was just not to be allowed to leave, that was all.

General Walker briefed Von Satzner, McClintock and Drayberry, but no one else. Drayberry and Walker would round up the men. Von Satzner and McClintock would prepare the boat.

Thornton rode to the building in the military enclosure where Cole and Figgis were. He apologized for not stopping to chat after collecting the signed paper. Cyrus Figgis was too dumbstruck with the enormity of the deed he had just perpetrated—at the stroke of a pen, he had just *lent* one of Mr. Vanderbilt's ships to these freebooters!—to reply to this person he had once considered a gentleman.

Thornton brought a group of men with him to the wharf, where Von Satzner was waiting for him. Captain Scott of the lake steamer, named *La Virgen* after the whore-infested town, did not approve, but the combination of the manager's signature and the presence of armed men overcame his doubts. Following Walker's instructions, Thornton ordered the captain to sail south on the lake until the town was out of sight.

When the steamer had anchored offshore, the two officers and their men draped all of the ship's deck with sailcloth, canvas and sacking. That evening they steamed back to La Virgen. The troops started boarding at eight P.M. and they steamed north at ten. The men cheered when Walker told them where they were going. After that they lay down to rest.

It was almost three in the morning as the steamer, with navigation lights and every possible other light extinguished, crept almost silently past the fort guarding the approach to Granada. From burning torches on the battlements, Walker could see that these ramparts were well manned. The flickering flames reflected in the gunmetal of the big barrels aimed out over the water. A couple of hits from these guns would send La Virgen rapidly to the bottom. But the sailcloth and canvas seemed to effectively hide whatever light or movement might have attracted attention from the battlements, and the ship's engine sound was muffled as it barely turned over. They passed on their way unseen. To Granada!

Walker stood alone and purposeful in the prow of the ship, as if he were ready to jump forward at anything that might rear out of the darkness to challenge their progress.

Walker shouted to the bridge to put in to shore. The

captain ordered the engines cut back and nosed in toward land. When he could get no farther into the shallow without running aground, he turned off the engines. They were only a mile or so from Granada, where lamps could be seen in the windows of buildings. At this hour, few were awake.

Walker conferred with Von Satzner, who had experience with this type of landing. The Prussian insisted that no loud sounds be made which could be heard across the water. He had steel cables stretched from the ship to land, a distance of about four hundred yards. In the pitch darkness, boats were lowered into the water at the steamer's side. Ten men got in each boat and used the cable to guide it to land, eight of the men disembarked and two brought the boat back for another eight men.

The process was laborious but preferable to the chaos of a night landing in water by a force of men the majority of whom were nonswimmers, which was the rule in those times. The horses were suspended in cinches from the cable and pulled struggling to the shore. In all, the operation took five hours to complete.

Dawn revealed to the frightened townspeople what was taking place, but by this time Walker had led an advance guard of troops into the town.

There was no resistance. Little happened, except that all political prisoners were released from the town's jail and all Legitimist members of parliament replaced them. The Legitimist president of the country, Fruto Chamorro, happened to be away from Granada at the time.

Again Walker showed his lack of interest in recrimination against his enemies. He released all the Legitimist politicans he had jailed, who now discovered something new. They had not, as previously thought, fallen into the hands of a mere hireling of their enemies, the Liberals. The Liberals would never have consented to their release. William Walker was in command here.

Word came from Leon. Cholera still ravaged the Liberal capital. Its latest victim had been Francisco Castellon himself, who had invited Walker to bring his "colonists" to Nicaragua. He had died without hearing about Walker's latest exploit. Walker ordered the town of Leon sealed off until the fever subsided. No one could enter or leave for any reason whatever. Walker attended a High Mass in Granada's cathedral of San Francisco for the repose of the soul of his beloved leader.

22

NOTHING HAPPENED. Nicaragua went on being Nicaragua. William Walker controlled the Transit Road from the southwestern corner of Lake Nicaragua to the Pacific, and the ex-Legitimist capital of Granada at the northwestern corner of the lake. Rivas, the first town to be attacked in Nicaragua by Walker, where Colonel Gonzalez had failed to show up with the additional men, had now become the Legitimist stronghold. Gonzalez was in Leon, along with other Liberals who were more than mildly suspicious by now of Walker's motives. They had no one of power great enough to challenge him since Castellon's death.

General Walker was still commander-in-chief of the Liberal forces. But Walker seemed interested in using only American troops and those Nicaraguans he recruited himself. Whereas if before there had been two sides locked in endless civil war, Nicaragua now had three armed camps.

Corral recognized the weakness of his position. The Legitimist-held cities were now scattered since Granada was in Walker's possession, and the Americans could launch a surprise attack on one or more of them at any time. Corral's strength lay in that he held Rivas, from where he could attack any part of the Transit

Road. This kept much of Walker's forces pinned down in the southern part of the country, protecting La Virgen and San Juan del Sur.

Walker's present position was strong, his adversaries quaked with fear at where he might turn next, and he himself had won a wide reputation of being personally invulnerable to bullets, knives and poisons. But Walker was a foreigner in this land and saw the possibility of his so-called allies in Leon joining with Corral long enough to expel him from Nicaragua by force of arms.

Also, Walker saw he had achieved more by his unexpected acts of mercy than even he could have foreseen. He had spared the besieged Legitimist garrison at La Virgen and allowed them to depart with their weapons as honorable men. He had freed the Legitimist members of parliament in Granada. He had not involved himself in Liberal intrigues in Leon; even those most outspoken against him there had not been silenced.

Nicaragua had not seen politics like this before. The general opinion was that Walker would live to regret the day he had not weeded out his opponents when given the chance to do so. In the meantime his lenient attitude lent credence to his efforts to make peace with Corral.

General Ponciano Corral was a prickly individual, a professional soldier rather than a politician, given to talking war, not peace. But the morale of his troops was low, the capital was lost, his treasury was empty. . . . If he could not make war, it might be time to talk peace.

Messengers galloped back and forth between Granada and Rivas bearing the handwritten proposals of the two men. It would be a gentlemen's agreement, but in writing, and between the two generals only—no politicians involved. Just the two of them. Where should they meet? Corral was welcome in Granada. Never! They would meet halfway. No, that was not possible—

Corral must come to Granada. He would not set foot in the capital while they were still at war. Outside Granada, then. He was not sure. Corral could write the peace treaty himself and bring it with him for Walker to sign. Outside Granada, then.

An awning stretched on poles kept the sun off a card table with a green cloth top, at which stood two upright chairs and a small circular stand for refreshments. Walker's officers and representatives of the Legitimist and Liberal parties formed a wide circle at a respectful distance about the table and two empty chairs. All three groups formed into their own small cliques and chatted as they stood in the hot sun.

General Corral arrived first. He dismounted at the edge of the circle of men, shook hands and spoke a few words with prominent Legitimists, and then strode purposefully to the table and sat with a rigid back in one of the chairs. The peppery general kept motionless but looked as if at any minute he might leap up and return without a word to Rivas.

General Walker did not keep him waiting long. As he walked to the table, Corral rose to greet him. Both men removed their right gloves and shook hands warmly.

"I apologize if I have kept you waiting, general."

"Not at all, general. It was a moment in which to organize my thoughts."

"A drink perhaps?"

"Not for me. By all means, have one yourself."

"I will wait," Walker said. "To business, then. You brought the treaty for me to sign?"

Corral noted that Walker had not said "draft of a treaty" but "treaty" for him to sign. Corral pulled out a folded paper from his pocket and smoothed it on the table before handing it to Walker.

"It's a straightforward soldiers' agreement," Corral said. "I wrote it myself last night."

Walker read the document.

As of this day, October 22, 1855, the state of war has ceased; for a period of fourteen months, or until general elections can be held, a provisional president of the republic will be appointed, as well as a provisional cabinet, the members of which will be furnished in equal numbers by both parties; there will be a general amnesty for political crimes, unification of both armies, abolition of all party colors and brassards, to be replaced by a blue patch bearing the inscription "*Nicaragua Independiente.*"

Walker nodded that he was willing to sign, much to Corral's amazement, since the treaty guaranteed Walker nothing, not even his personal safety.

"Bring me a pen and ink," Walker called enthusiastically to an aide.

While these were being supplied, Corral pressed home his advantage by asking, "What do you say we name the provisional president in this treaty?"

"By all means," Walker concurred.

"Then, General, tell me who you think should be provisional president."

"You," Walker said.

"Me?" Corral was taken aback.

"Certainly."

"As a signer of the treaty, I don't feel I could nominate myself," Corral said slowly.

Walker made no effort to dissuade him. "Who do you name then?"

"Patricio Arribas is a name that occurs to me," Corral said carefully.

"Arribas." Walker ran his finger down a list among the papers before him on the table. "Arribas . . . yes, here it is. He was a tax collector, not high up in the Legitimist party."

Walker did not read aloud the complete short biography opposite Arribas' name, which scathingly described him as a "weakling and minion of Corral."

Walker asked in a concerned, naive voice, "Do you think he will be neutral between the parties?"

"Absolutely," Corral assured him. "Arribas is a man of honor and sterling reputation."

"You see, poor Francisco Castellon, Lord rest his soul, was my only close friend in Leon—the only man I could trust. Now that he is gone. . . ." Walker raised his hands in hopeless resignation.

"You can depend on Patricio Arribas."

"Write his name in as provisional president then," Walker said, handing Corral the pen.

Walker waited for him to finish writing before asking, "But what about you, General? Surely you do not intend to deprive your country of your services?"

Corral shrugged wearily. "What use am I to anybody? I am a soldier, not a politician. The army is all I know. Perhaps the new army—"

"I agree," Walker interrupted. "If you wish, we could add the name of the new permanent, not provisional, commander-in-chief of the army to the treaty."

Corral smiled. "My dear friend, what an excellent idea! I can volunteer—"

Walker again interrupted. "Fine, that's settled then. A few words will cover it."

Corral dipped the pen in ink and held it expectantly. It was only courteous to allow Walker to choose these words.

Walker went on, "The *Falange Americana* will be solved as a separate unit and will be incorporated into the army as a division bearing the same name." He waited for Corral to get this on paper before continuing, "The general of the *Falange Americana*, William Walker, will assume the permanent command of the combined armies of the independent Republic of Nicaragua."

Corral faltered only a moment before adding this to

the treaty. He had been given his own man as president, and then he had gotten overconfident, only to be outwitted. Who cared who was President if you controlled the army? Corral could have refused to write Walker's name in, but the reason behind this would have been so transparent to all, after he had written everything this far, that Corral had no choice but, like a brave soldier, accept a major defeat and a little victory.

23

BYRON COLE had himself appointed Secretary of the Treasury. The change this made in the man in just a few short weeks was noticed by all. Initially Cole's critics expressed trepidation about the placing of what they called "an entrepreneurial type" in charge of the nation's finances. But even they had to admit that his previously somewhat evasive demeanor had changed into one of respectability, gravity and an air of responsibility eminently befitting a member of the cabinet of such a great nation as Nicaragua.

The secret behind Byron Cole's newborn forthrightness and accountability was simple. He had found the Treasury cupboard bare.

Like one newly converted to the ways of the righteous, Cole now exposed the multiple frauds and embezzlements that were eating up the tax revenues. He suggested new budget cutbacks and demanded detailed accounts from all who received government monies. No coin was thin enough to fall through the cracks in his system. Some who saw his serious countenance said jokingly that for countries in the financial state of Nicaragua, it might be a mistake to look at things too closely.

William Walker was not a great help. The money

owed the government by Vanderbilt's Accessory Transit Company had been snatched from the Treasury's grasp by the company's acceptance of Walker's proposition that they work the debt off in reduced fares to "colonists" arriving in Nicaragua by their steamers. This would give the company years to work the debt off and, more importantly, an excellent excuse to avoid all further discussions of cash owed. Walker, in his desperate need for more Americans, could not or would not see this, much to Cole's frustration.

Cole was not too blinded by his own affairs to notice all was not well with the new administration. Walker's constant demand for more Americans was a symptom of this. President Arribas was weak, so weak in fact he was not even much use to Corral as a pawn since he was equally terrified of offending Walker. Arribas presided over the cabinet meetings, which often amounted to nothing more than litanies of recriminations by Cole about funds extravagantly spent, lost or stolen.

The army, although nominally united as one with General Walker as commander in chief, was divided into three clearly mutually hostile camps—those under Walker, those under Corral, and those under Gonzalez, who was now a general at the insistence of Liberals in Leon. Cole saw definite signs that Corral and Gonzalez had grown closer. He mentioned this to Walker, asking him why he did not unite the army under his firm rule.

Walker laughed. "Because I know, and they know, that I could beat all their troops united with a quarter of my American forces. Let them plot in Leon. Let them plot in Rivas. I don't want them here in Granada close to me."

So, more Americans was the solution. It had required Cole's hard-nosed money policies to keep things going before, and he could see that it was going to be necessary again. He had already sent feelers back to the States. Morgan and Garrison had let it be known they might be ready for a big move very soon. Then there were the Southern politicians in Washington and their business associates in New Orleans, who had big ideas but who so far had proved more generous in words than in dollars. Dammit, they needed cash, and Cole saw it as his job to make Walker recognize this very hard and cold fact.

Then again, previously Walker had wanted to be left to play soldier without asking who paid the bills. Cole began to see this as his only sensible course of action. Such a course would, needless to say, require a somewhat less frank and open financial policy on his part in the future, but possibly a more successful one.

He wearily tramped up the steps of the government building. Early morning cabinet meetings were not to Cole's liking at all, but he had no choice. Walker had summoned him to this one, calling it an emergency session, so that it promised to be a little more interesting than their usual weekly meetings.

Cole was early. At least he was not late, which meant early in Granada. The conference room was empty except for William Walker, who sat gloomily at the long, highly polished table whose surface reflected the room's furnishings. Walker glanced at him moodily and nodded a dour greeting.

"Is it money?" Cole enquired with a trace of anxiety in his voice.

"Treason," Walker answered shortly.

Cole did not want to hear anything more. There was no doubt that Walker was becoming progressively unpredictable. Power is supposed to corrupt men; in Cole's opinion all it did to Walker was make him stranger, harder to fathom. But power was changing him. Treason! That was a good one, coming from William Walker.

Cole pulled out a sheaf of work papers from a pocket and busily reviewed them. He hoped he was making it very clear to Walker that he wanted no part in any drama involving so-called treason.

Arribas arrived, relieved to find he was not keeping them waiting, and assumed his place at the head of the table.

The seven other members gradually arrived, including Corral and Gonzalez.

"Gentlemen," Walker addressed them, "I've taken the liberty in calling this emergency meeting in the name of the President because of an extremely serious matter. I think it will be best explained by this." He held aloft a paper package. "Our men intercepted this message on its way across the border to General Guardiola, more popularly known as the Butcher of Honduras." He handed the package suddenly to General Gonzalez. "If you would be so kind to open it for us, general."

Gonzalez curiously turned the package over in his hands and pulled it open. The outer paper contained an inner, tightly folded paper. There was handwriting on the inside of the outer paper.

"Do you wish me to read it aloud?" Gonzalez enquired.

"If you would be so kind," Walker told him.

Gonzalez read aloud:

Sir:
The letter enclosed is from a man known to you and me, to you as a friend and to me as an adversary. However, the foreign invasion of our country has now united him and me in an alliance which places the national interest above our personal differences. We think that we can rely on your goodwill and sense of honor when we ask you to assist us in liberating our fatherland.

A Patriot

"I wonder who this 'patriot' could be," Walker said. "Have you any idea who he might be, General Gonzalez?"

"A very angry man," Gonzalez replied, looking unperturbed.

"Have you read this enclosed letter?" Walker persisted.

"You have not given me a chance to do so, sir," Gonzalez answered, meeting the gray eyes with his own calm brown eyes.

A crooked smile flitted across Walker's face. "Hand me the enclosed letter."

Gonzalez did so.

"Might I ask you to read this letter, General Corral?" Walker enquired.

There was silence.

All eyes turned to look at Corral.

His face was pale, but his eyes burned in anger. He rasped, "I consider what you ask beneath my dignity."

Walker shrugged lightly. "Well, although it's beneath your dignity, I'm sure it's not beneath that of President Arribas." He tossed the letter to the startled man at the head of the table, and said with an edge of command in his voice: "Read it, sir."

The President's nervous fingers took some time to unfold the letter. He peered at it shortsightedly and began to read in a barely audible murmur.

"Louder!" Walker barked. "We would all like to hear you, sir. If you would be so kind as to begin again."

Cole sighed and thought to himself that Arribas is not such a fool as men think—he senses Walker is now at his most dangerous, and he is correct. As for Gonzalez, it was obvious to everyone that the man had written the covering letter—or more probably dictated it to another to eliminate the risk of using his own handwriting. Cole had to admire his coolness under

Walker's pressure. Gonzalez had the nerve to make a perfect liar—something Cole regarded as a rare and valuable personal attribute—yet had not allowed Walker to force him into direct lies.

President Arribas obediently began the letter again in a high, nasal voice:

Don Santos:

As you already know, my trusted friend, Nicaragua is in the grip of a foreign demon who will never loosen his talons until he clutches all our beloved republics. Remember, as soon as your neighbor Nicaragua can no longer resist, this demon will seek more prey. Strike now, before it is too late. We can all rise up to support you, Legitimists and Liberals, so long as you do not wait too long. If you wait, we will all be dead. I know, as your lifelong friend, you will not let Nicaragua down.

The President stopped reading, his eyes glued in horror to the letter inches from his face.

"Go on, sir," Walker commanded coldly. "Whose name is signed at the bottom?"

"Mine!" came a voice from down the table.

They all looked at Corral, whose eyes shone with hatred at Walker for this tragicomedy he had insisted on staging.

"I wrote it and meant every word in it for the good of my country, Nicaragua!" Corral proclaimed proudly.

In the silence which followed this declaration, Walker calmly devoted his attention to recovering the two letters, folding one and inserting it within the other, then folding that and pocketing the packet.

Walker allowed his eyes to roam up and down the table. He said finally in a quiet voice, "A cabinet meeting is not the place to judge whether this man is innocent or guilty. We should, however, decide whether he stands military trial for high treason. Mr. Cole, what do you think?"

Cole's heart thumped. The bastard! Leave me out of this! "I agree that this is not the place to judge General Corral. He should have the benefit of a court martial. I say yes."

Walker polled the members of the cabinet one by one, pointedly skipping Gonzalez. A single man said no, and in Walker's pause after this could be heard withering the man's future health, happiness and fortune. He left the President till last.

Arribas' eyes wavered and his lips trembled. "Yes."

Corral stared straight in front of him as if waiting to hear the cock crow thrice.

24

A KNOCK sounded on the door.

"Come in," William Walker called.

Byron Cole entered. "The American envoy wishes to see you."

"Bring him in and join us yourself."

When the envoy was comfortably seated and the requisite amount of small talk had been exchanged, Walker lapsed into an expectant silence.

The envoy came to the point. "The U.S. government has decided for the time being not to recognize the administration of Patricio Arribas."

Walker nodded after a moment's thought. "Surely you should be telling this to the President rather than to me."

"I already have. He sent me to you."

"I see," Walker said. "Can you give me any reason for the refusal?"

"The turbulent political conditions that prevail here," the envoy replied.

"Did Washington mention any specific turbulent conditions?"

"No. But I feel certain that the forthcoming execution of General Corral must be one of them."

"Corral was found guilty of high treason before a

court martial," Walker said angrily. "The punishment for that crime is the same here as in the United States —death before a firing squad, for a soldier. Why should America intervene here?"

"There will be no intervention," the envoy was quick to correct him. "This is simply a request for clemency. A request for that most elevated of all human qualities in the breast of man—mercy."

"You speak beautifully, sir," Walker said sarcastically. "Yet I don't think there can be much doubt in either of our minds what the American attitude would be if the Nicaraguan envoy in Washington tried to interfere in the execution of an American traitor. To understate it, his plea would go unheeded."

Another silence settled between the two men.

Cole waited a few moments before speaking. He asked the envoy, "Off the record, sir, in your opinion would clemency toward General Corral be sufficient to ensure American recognition of the Arribas regime?"

"An interesting question. . . ." The envoy took his time. "I think it would be looked upon more as a gesture of compliance on your part than as an act sufficient in itself to warrant recognition."

Cole continued, "Suppose the execution took place as scheduled, what punitive measures could it result in?"

"It's hard to say." The envoy shifted his position in the chair. "It's a Presidential election year and General Walker's popularity has grown amazingly in the South. . . . No one wants to upset them with the election coming up. My guess would be that withholding recognition would be the most serious retaliation for the present. I must stress that this is a personal opinion, based not on any—"

"We understand," Walker interrupted. "We also appreciate your advice, sir, and recognize its confidential nature."

After the envoy had left, Cole returned to the general's office.

"Interesting, what he said about the government fearing your popularity in the South," he said. "It fits in with those other reports we have been receiving."

"The envoy has proved himself a reliable source before, hasn't he?"

Cole grinned. "Absolutely. We certainly pay him enough for it."

Walker nodded. "He gave us the go-ahead with Corral's execution."

Cole sighed. "Why don't you just grant him mercy? Remember how well it worked when you let scores of people off before?"

Walker ignored the question. "Don't ask me. Only the President can commute the sentence."

"Arribas will do whatever you tell him," Cole said in exasperation. "He won't get the credit. You will."

"I can't allow Corral to survive," Walker said gravely. "He is the nucleus around which my opponents gather."

Cole thought that from the tone of Walker's voice he could have been talking about a decision to poison rats. He remembered only too well how recently he had given this penniless man a job on his newspaper and pushed him into his present role. Already Walker was deciding that anyone who stood in his way had forfeited the right to live. No doubt Cole's own fate would be similar if he tried to thwart him now.

Cole spoke in a reasonable tone. "If Corral has to die, do it in an acceptable way. Come out publicly in favor of granting him mercy and add your plea to all the others that have gone to the President. Then secretly forbid Arribas to pardon him. That way you will look good."

"Sometimes, Byron, you become undone by your own cleverness. Corral must die because he broke a treaty that he made with me. Everyone must know William Walker was the bullet which slew Ponciano Corral."

Solange de Brissot grasped his arm and begged him, "Thornton, please, you must talk to him!"

He looked into her eyes and felt himself softened by a woman's compassion.

"As I promised you," he said, "I spoke to Byron Cole about it and he said there was absolutely no chance. Cole said the American envoy had gone down on his knees before Walker to try to persuade him to spare Corral, but that it had been a waste of his time."

. "You promised you would talk to the general yourself," she said. "You promised me that!"

"I will."

"General Corral's two daughters are the same ages as Brigitte and I are. They're insane with fear and grief. The only thing that saves them is they cannot bring themselves to believe it will really happen. Like us, they have lost their mother and have no brothers. If their father is taken from them in this brutal way, I don't think they will ever recover."

After Thornton had gone, Solange justified her actions to herself. Her father had told her to persuade Thornton to plead with Walker, as one Southerner to another, for Corral's life. De Brissot recognized as clearly as Walker himself had done that Corral represented the only effective opposition to him in Nicaragua. With Corral removed as a rallying point, the French had no one else to support against the American usurper. Solange had done her father's bidding.

But she really did know and feel compassion for Corral's daughters. Every word she had spoken to Thornton about them had been true. She would have asked Thornton to do something for their sake even if her father had said nothing. Yet he had asked her to. And she had deceived Thornton. As usual Solange made herself miserable by searching desperately within her mind and heart for a solution to this conflict.

As Thornton waited in the outer office, he saw President Arribas come out of Walker's inner sanctum with quick, awkward strides and with tears running down his cheeks. Thornton was aware that these were not tears of gratitude, but sobs of bitterness and the unsteady walk of a man given over to grief or shame.

Then his name was called and he went in to see the commander in chief. Walker sat behind his desk, looking much more hostile than usual. The gray eyes swept over Thornton.

"Is this about the execution set for this afternoon?" the general snapped.

"Yes, sir."

"You want me to commute the sentence?"

"Yes, sir."

"Any particular reason? Or just a merciful attitude in general?"

"For the sake of his two daughters."

"They are both pretty girls, McClintock. I have had them in here for an hour with me, weeping and praying along with their priest. What's your interest in them? I thought you and one of de Brissot's daughters were a pair."

"Solange is a friend of these girls. Like hers, their mother is dead. They have no one in the world but their father."

"He should have thought of that before he tried to betray me."

"I'm sure he did, sir."

Walker paused and looked at McClintock carefully. "Like the English poet who wrote to his lady as he left for war, 'I could not love thee, dear, so much, loved I not honor more.' I have no doubt Ponciano Corral saw some nobility in his deed. And that others do too. Do you?"

"No, sir. I am not interested in the ethics involved. If I had caught Corral on the battlefield doing what he did, I would have shot him then and there."

Walker nodded in agreement. "We are both soldiers, McClintock. The rules are harder to apply in civilian life."

The general got up from his desk and paced the floor. Outside in the hot sun, the cathedral bell struck two. One hour till the time of execution.

Walker sat down again. "I have refused this man's two daughters, I have refused the President of Nicaragua, I have refused assorted ambassadors, envoys, advisors, priests, army officers, politicians, but I will not refuse a gentleman from Tennessee. On one condition."

"I am grateful, sir. What is the condition?"

"That I get some form of capitulation from Corral—that he does not emerge untainted from this, smelling like a rose."

"What can I do?"

"Get him to confess to you the name of the man who wrote the letter enclosing his. I know it was Gonzalez, and both Corral and Gonzalez know that I know this."

"You want him to betray Gonzalez?" Thornton asked incredulously.

"I want him to capitulate."

"You are asking him to dishonor himself to save his own life."

"You may or may not convey my message as you please, McClintock," Walker shot back angrily. "A traitor can bear the weight of one more dishonor heaped upon his back."

As soon as Thornton had left his office, the general called in a sergeant. "General Gonzalez was to be here at two o'clock to see me. Where is he?"

"I don't know, sir. Never showed up. I heard nothing."

"Put out a warrant for his arrest."

Thornton walked angrily from the building out into the early afternoon sunshine. He felt disgust at what he had become involved in. He reasoned that the decision whether Corral died honorably or lived by betraying an accomplice was one only Corral could make. Therefore he had to present the choice to him. He clutched the signed pass that would permit him to visit the condemned man in his cell beneath the old monastery of San Francisco.

The crowds were already gathering in the Grand Plaza to witness the execution. They stood tightly squeezed into the shade on one side of the plaza. Beneath the blazing sun, near the center, stood a temporary wall of sandbags about eight feet high and twelve feet long. The soldiers on guard about the plaza had bayonets fixed to their rifles.

As Thornton passed them, he noticed the faces in the crowd were impassive. Only an occasional glance, lingering for a fraction of a second, revealed to him the fear and hatred these people now felt for the foreigners in their midst. That had never been the case before. The Americans had been greeted by the poor as liberators! Today that was changed, and all because of one man. Ponciano Corral. A fellow countryman martyred by the foreigners. There was no doubt that this was the feeling of the crowd. They could do nothing but come to show their silent respect and support of Corral.

McClintock realized that Walker was making a terrible mistake if he thought that this public execution of a traitor was going to frighten the people into loyalty to him. Walker was creating a martyr here, and in doing that was unifying public opinion against himself, just as his acts of public generosity had once attracted public favor. Another thing stayed in Thornton's mind. This had been the first time he had ever seen Walker emotionally charged rather than calm and calculating.

Displaying his pass to the guards, Thornton went

down the rough-hewn stone steps into the cool cellars which had probably served the long-departed monks of the monastery as a produce and wine cellar. The vaulted passageways were high and opened off into short blind ends, which were now barred from stone floor to stone ceiling and served as cells.

Thornton was led by a prison guard to Corral's cell. The general, in drab, loose-fitting prison clothes, sat on a wooden bench between his two daughters. They were pretty, although their eyes were swollen from weeping and they had already dressed in mourning. One daughter looked up as Thornton approached in his military uniform.

"No!" she screamed. "It is not time yet! It is not three! I will not allow you!"

The other daughter had jumped to her feet and stared at him in mute anguish.

Thornton made no attempt to enter the cell. "That is not what I have come for. I am a friend of Solange de Brissot, and she asked me to speak on your father's behalf with General Walker. I have a message for your father."

"What did he say? Has he delayed it?" The two women asked questions simultaneously.

Thornton held up his hand for quiet. "I have a message for your father. It will take only a moment for his decision."

"What has he to decide?" one daughter demanded.

Their father quieted them and sent them outside his cell door and beckoned Thornton in.

"General Walker is willing to commute the sentence on one condition, sir," Thornton said rapidly, realizing that time was all-important now for this man, whatever the outcome. "He demands that you reveal the name of the man who wrote the covering letter with yours."

"Never!" Corral bellowed. "Let me die with honor rather than live under a man who demands that from me. You may tell the little foreigner that Ponciano Corral, a loyal Nicaraguan, spits in his face!"

Thornton nodded respectfully and left the cell, as Corral's daughters rushed back inside.

As Thornton climbed the rough stone steps out of the cool cellar toward the hot fierce daylight at the top of the flight, he heard the screams and anguished cries of the two young women as they abandoned all hope in the depth of the cells.

25

IN THE weeks following Corral's death before the firing squad, a small flurry of military changes occurred, but soon things reverted to their normal state of lethargy. Thornton McClintock had been deliberately passed over when the new duties were assigned. This fitted in perfectly with his mood of disillusionment with William Walker, and he spent his days wandering Granada and the pretty lakeside country outside the town in the company of Solange de Brissot. Since his appointment to the rank of colonel after the fall of La Virgen, his only duties had been to keep his troops in battle-ready condition.

Harry Drayberry and some of the others fared differently. Appointed a colonel at the same time as Thornton, Harry now found himself inducted into William Walker's inner circle. He went all over the country on special, confidential missions for his commander in chief, and was apologetic he could not talk about where he had been to Thornton. The rift between the two men, at first narrow, was gradually widening.

Although dissatisfied, Thornton still had good reasons to stay in Nicaragua. He knew by now that California was no longer the land of easy opportunity he had once fancied it to be. He was still penniless, apart

from his army pay. There was no talk yet about award-
ing the land promised to the original "colonists," but
this would be worth staying on for to sell, if he wished
to then. Even if he wanted to go back empty-handed
to Tennessee, which he would be ashamed to do, he
could hardly return and leave Harry behind him in
Nicaragua. Harry was on top of the world in his new
role as confidential agent to the commander-in-chief,
and would certainly refuse to leave. And then of
course, there was Solange. . . .

Thornton did not quite know what to think about
her. He had never felt this way about a woman before.
Since he had nothing to offer her, as a matter of habit
he refused to think in matrimonial terms about her. He
had no idea where he would be or what he would be
doing one year from now, but suspected he would not
be in either the same place or same occupation. Meanwhile the sun beat down day after day, and life took
its languorous, graceful course of early morning army
duties, a long walk with Solange, lunch with fellow
officers, his siesta, early evening drinks and billiards
again with fellow officers, and then late dinner with
Solange at either her family's or a friend's home. His
days of revelry were over. He never even missed them
except when teased by other officers on his turning over
a new leaf.

Then the military activity and special missions began
to fizzle out.

"I can't understand what Walker is doing," Thornton
said after dinner one night to de Brissot. "He's allowing all the old Legitimist officers whose loyalties are to
the memory of Corral to keep their commands. You
could say he's letting the old Legitimist and Liberal
camps remain separate and intact."

De Brissot looked at him quizzically. "It's called
benign neglect. What do the officers want? Their pay
and a bit of occasional flattery, such as a parade or an
invitation to a state occasion. What do the enlisted men

want? Their pay and less work. Walker gives them both what they want. So long as he has the wherewithal to continue doing so, they will be reasonably contented. No one wants to revolt or fight a war if given the choice of having a good time doing nothing."

"What was all the fuss over then?" Thornton asked.

The French aristocrat swirled the imported brandy in his glass and looked at its colors in the light. "Neither you nor I were confided in about that. I can't say what went on at first hand, but there were some disappearances of Nicaraguan officers and politicians who were thought to be inflexible in their views. A coincidence, probably."

"Assassinations?"

De Brissot parried the question. "Don't you talk to the other officers? Don't you hear rumors?"

"Yes, but. . . . I didn't want to believe them."

"Perhaps you are right," de Brissot said with Gallic acid.

"I've been naive. Things have changed. It's no longer like it was when we started out."

De Brissot made no comment.

The de Brissots moved into a large villa reminiscent of the one they had lived in in Leon before Walker's arrival. Their house in San Juan del Sur and the one they had been occupying until now in Granada were humble in comparison to this new one. Thornton had chivvied them about never finding enough furniture to cover the huge bare areas in the rooms. He was told they would be leaving early the next morning to pick up belongings they had left in storage in Leon upon their move to San Juan del Sur.

"But you can't go!" Thornton told Solange, showing her an invitation card. "I forgot to show it to you when I got it, and then it passed out of my mind."

"Oh, it's for dinner and an overnight stay at the Huidobro hacienda," Solange said gleefully. "It's in honor of William Walker."

Brigitte pouted. She knew the reason she had not been asked was because Harry Drayberry was taking another girl. "We'll need you in Leon," she told Solange, "to help select what to bring to Granada."

"Bring everything!" her sister responded gaily.

"Father, make her come with us to help," Brigitte whined.

"Brigitte, don't be a child," he said tolerantly.

This was the first de Brissot had heard about Walker's trip to the Huidobro estate. Walker and Cole as usual made sure he was excluded when something of importance was going on. And this was no casual friendly visit. Huidobro was one of the most influential of the great northern cattle ranchers. Although his huge land holdings were far to the north, his family lived most of the year within easy reach of the cities on a ranch between Lake Nicaragua and Lake Managua. General Gonzalez and his supporters had escaped north across the border into Honduras on the day Corral faced the firing squad. Now, with the assistance of the Butcher of Honduras, they formed a constant threat of invasion from the north. But the invaders would need the help of the wealthy men whose lands they would have to pass through—the big northern cattle ranchers.

De Brissot decided that this had to be Walker's peace mission. The general had to be offering the ranchers something in exchange for their loyalty. McClintock, even if he knew about it, would not be interested since it did not involve horses, hunting or farming. But other men liked to chat with Solange on social occasions, and often a pretty woman made a man boast of his own self-importance. She picked up much information for him by telling him so-and-so was such a pompous fool, without realizing what she was doing.

In a surge of paternal feeling, de Brissot decided that Solange and Thornton were well suited to each other.

They were both outgoing, uncomplicated and good-natured.

"I think Solange should go," de Brissot said. "I assume proper accomodations have been set aside for the single ladies."

"I don't know," Thornton announced. "If there isn't a room for her, I suppose I'll let her share mine."

Solange blushed and hit him with her napkin.

Walker's group consisted of three carriages and an escort of twenty heavily armed mounted soldiers. On the way a stop was made for lunch at a large hacienda. The reception was chilly, but the importance of their unexpected guests, the rules of hospitality and the presence of armed men soon caused food and wine to be served on a long dining table.

Walker ignored the unfriendly host and his family, and chatted with Solange and other ladies of his group. The commander-in-chief's good humor and the ladies' high spirits soon caused everyone to forget their sullen hosts—father, mother, three daughters in their late teens and a son, younger than his sisters. The boy, fifteen or sixteen years old, sat next to his father and nearly opposite William Walker.

The youth suddenly jumped to his feet, pulled a pistol from beneath his coat and leveled it across the table at Walker's head. The boy took a deep breath, scrunched up his face and began to squeeze the trigger.

"Think of your mother and sisters!"

The voice was that of Harry Drayberry, and its level, sinister tone caused the youth to pause.

"The soldiers outside will savage your mother and sisters," Harry said in the same menacing voice. "They will satisfy their rage for what you have done on your own family—I don't have to describe how. Just pull that trigger and you'll see for yourself. They'll almost certainly force you and your father to watch."

Female gasps of horror accompanied the calm recital of facts.

The youth's hand which held the pistol was trembling. He was still listening.

Harry went on, "The officers present in this room, including myself, have behaved as gentlemen and we expect to continue to do so if permitted. Although the hospitality of your family is enforced, it would be better for all concerned to make the best of it and treat this as a proper social occasion. We will leave you, your family, your house and property unharmed."

The youth slowly put the pistol on the table before him and sat down.

An old male family servant unhurriedly removed the pistol from the tablecloth, placed it on a tray and left with it for the kitchen as if it were an empty soup dish.

The fish was served, and an excellent dry white wine. Walker chatted on pleasantly with the ladies as if nothing had happened. The youth and his father were silent.

The rest of the journey to the Huidobro ranch was uneventful. Harry was the hero of the day. Although Walker did not mention the incident at any time, he made it clear that Harry had risen high in his estimation.

Only Solange expressed doubts. She told them to Thornton in a quiet corner of the hacienda garden, and he found that her words put form to a certain vague uneasiness in his mind.

"How could Harry talk like that?" she asked. "He used never to be like that. He used to go along with whatever you wanted to do. If that boy had shot Walker, I think he really would have set the soldiers on those poor women. Harry has changed." She shuddered. "I think he has become an evil man." She took Thornton's arm and looked in his eyes. "I hope the same will never happen to you, Thornton."

He took her in his arms and kissed her softly on the lips. He felt her body yield to his, and she quivered as his lips brushed her neck and bare shoulders. Thornton breathed in her perfumed body scent and enjoyed the warm luxury of her soft skin.

Dinner at the Huidobro hacienda was lavish. Afterward they danced in the courtyard beneath the stars to a vaquero band. It was not far from dawn, while they were reviving their spirits with a breakfast grilled over charcoal and strong black coffee when a horseman galloped into the stable area. He spoke for a moment with the soldiers on guard and then came forward to General Walker.

The man saluted. "There's been a big earthquake in Managua, sir. Just hours ago. As I left the town to bring the news to you, they were pulling the dead and injured from the fallen buildings. There were already fifty bodies laid out on the floor of the church."

Solange's eyes grew wide with alarm. She uttered a strangled sob and fell in a dead faint against Thornton.

26

THE HUIDOBROS lent Thornton a lightweight open carriage and a pair of fast horses, and he and Solange left at first light. She was certain that her father and sister must have stayed overnight in Managua on their way to Leon. Managua was about thirty miles from Granada, and Leon about another fifty after that. While an individual horseman could do better, the heavy de Brissot carriage would have had rough going on the rutted roads, and the chances were they had put up at Managua for the night. What their chances had been after that, Thornton was afraid to think about.

Walker and a few others would arrive in Managua later that day. Thornton figured that just the two of them traveling together was quickest, since she would not agree to his going on alone by horseback and bringing the news back to her. They expected they would feel foolish and relieved after their mad rush to Managua, only to find her father and sister had not stayed there or had survived uninjured and were on their way to Leon.

Although both Solange and Thornton had experienced major earth tremors since they had arrived in Nicaragua, they had never witnessed one of destructive strength. But they had heard all about them. Every few years a major earthquake killed scores of people, and every generation or so a catastrophic quake almost leveled a city, killing thousands. From the messenger's account, this earthquake at Managua was relatively small-scale. Yet all it had to do was harm two particular people to make it a horrible tragedy for Solange.

Earthquakes were common in this land of smoking volcanoes, lava beds, dramatic mountains, steep hills, abrupt valleys. Thornton, from the beginning, had been struck by how the mountain folds seemed flexed and knotted like muscles beneath a thin skin of earth. It was easy for him to imagine the landscape, even though it was cloaked with lush vegetation, as the result of violent upheavals.

They spoke little as they traveled, even when they stopped to water and rest the horses. After five hours of dust and heat, both riders and horses neared Managua in a state of exhaustion. Solange wept when they looked down from a hill outside the town and saw the crumpled buildings in one section of the town. There seemed to be little damage elsewhere. The tiny figures of men moved in the rubble. They saw one group carrying three bodies to a horse-drawn cart. Most were digging and prying aside slabs of fallen masonry.

In the destruction zone the only buildings not razed by the shock were the oldest ones—the Spanish colonial edifices with walls four to eight feet thick, which with each massive tremor over the years only readjusted themselves like the fat on an obese dreamer.

Only the larger collapsed buildings remained not fully searched. These included the hotel, which was badly damaged. A man told Thornton that the dead and injured so far recovered from the hotel were on the church floor or in the hospital, but that no list was available of those who had escaped uninjured. If they did not find who they were looking for at either the church or the hospital, he said, they were probably all right—with the offchance they were still buried. Solange began weeping at this, and the man apologized for his insensitivity. He had seen so much in the last few hours, he said, that he had become unaware of the feelings of others. Thornton was reminded of what a gracious, courteous people Nicaraguans were.

On the way to the hospital, they had to pass the church.

"I suppose I should go in, just in case," Thornton told her. "Wait here. I'll be back in a moment."

The dead were in four rows on the church floor, lying on their backs, so that it was possible to walk along by the uncovered faces for the purpose of identification. Men and women, the small twisted bodies of children, two babies, one old man like a piece of gnarled wood. . . . There were about twenty-five bodies in each row.

Brigitte de Brissot lay with dust on her clothes and a smear of dirt on her cheek. It was as if she were asleep in the midst of death and mutilation. Gaston de Brissot was separated from her by two other bodies. The left side of his forehead was crushed, and congealed blood had formed a brown crust over his left ear with dried rivulets down his neck. Thornton removed his own hat and covered the man's wound. He then touched the cheek of Brigitte. She looked so unharmed, simply dusty and pale. Her skin was as cold as the stone floor on which she lay.

Thornton went out the church door. Solange, sitting in their open carriage, stared at his face and knew the awful truth.

He nodded to her and said only, "Both of them."

He held her tightly on the carriage seat until he felt her stirring again in his arms.

"I'll take care of everything," Thornton said. "I'll take you to an inn now."

"No." Her voice was firm. "I will help. What can we do?"

"They must be buried as soon as possible," Thornton

told her quietly. "I'm sorry, but it's the best thing."

"I want to see them."

He did not argue, and helped her from the carriage and through the church door. She held tightly to him as she viewed the bodies of her father and sister, and he felt her trembling transmitted by her hand clutching him. Then she went forward, bent down and kissed her father on the right cheek. Thornton was thankful the hat stayed in place. Solange kissed her sister's cheek also, and came back and stood next to Thornton, clutching his arm again.

The poor are always present. Their survival often depends on their skill at turning even crisis and destruction to some advantage. A coffinmaker, two gravediggers and a priest came forward to offer their services. To an outsider, they might have appeared as heartless vultures. To Thornton and Solange, they were what they most needed.

Thornton explained to the priest that although they were foreigners, de Brissot and his daughter were Catholics. The cleric said the Latin prayers for the dead and shook holy water on the bodies as the coffinmaker banged pine boards together into two simple coffins. The gravediggers lifted each body, and after another prayer and Solange's final farewell, the coffin lids were nailed shut.

The coffins were balanced on top of the open carriage, and they walked behind it as one of the men led the horses slowly to the cemetery outside the town. The gravediggers had a row of eight empty holes ready. De Brissot and his daughter were buried side by side. As the graves were being filled, the priest prayed and the coffinmaker painted their names on two wooden headstones.

Small children came by to sell them flowers with which to decorate the graves. Thornton bought all they had and strewed them over the two mounds of black earth. Then he paid off the priest, gravediggers and coffinmaker in gold. He was generous, and they promised to pray for the souls of the deceased. They had been gentle and respectful in the face of death and sorrow.

At last Thornton and Solange were alone with the two sad monuments to the last of her family. Round about, crosses and statues stretched away in this thickly populated city of the dead. Six open holes waited, each with its pile of earth to cover the remnants of a once vital human being.

This evidence of universal death at the end of life's cycle calmed Solange, and set her emotions on their first step of accepting her terrible loss.

Thornton let her linger there.

"I will stand by you," he told her quietly.

It seemed to him that for some reason this upset her further, although he knew she loved him. In a little while, she told him about the real role of her father, as a spy for Louis Napoleon—how the French and English took William Walker much more seriously than he was taken in Washington, and how both countries independently were supplying arms to Nicaragua's enemies and increasing their naval presence in the Caribbean.

She explained how ironically her father's presence as a spy had actually helped Walker, insofar as the two European powers had been convinced in the beginning that Walker was an agent of the U.S. government bent on expansion of its territories. Her father had convinced Paris that Walker was a soldier of fortune, and the European powers had decided against a confrontation which would almost certainly have forced Washington to intervene militarily.

Solange did not try to hide her own role and how she had betrayed Thornton's trust in her. They laughed together when she told him her father's criticisms of him as someone whose information on horses and hunting could not be questioned, but who had little other information. The Frenchman had been frustrated by the fact that Harry, the ambitious power-seeking officer, had escaped one daughter's charms, while the officer ensnared by the other daughter did not give a damn for Walker's plans or politics and was of little use as a source of information.

27

"WHAT ABOUT Emily?"

"Harry, I told Emily not to wait for me when we left Antrimville," Thornton said.

"But Emily is heiress to a big plantation. Solange is almost penniless and has no property. How could you marry her instead of Emily? You must be mad. The sun must have affected your brain."

Thornton could see that Harry was seriously considering whether he had taken leave of his senses.

"Remember when I used to say I couldn't imagine living all the time with Emily?" he said. "She was nice, but she didn't make my blood race. Well, Solange does. I really want her."

Harry shook his head sadly. "All duty and responsibility, that's you, Thornton. Just because her father and sister died, which was not your fault, and now she's all alone in the world, you feel here is your chance to be a hero and step in to protect the damsel in distress. Now, heroics are a fine thing and I myself claim to be as hellfire reckless as the best man you could put up against me—but even I know that a hero has to be able to look back on his daring deed the next day, not wake up beside his folly every morning with nothing but gallantry to show for it."

Thornton laughed. "You've become quite a talker, Harry. Folks won't know you when you get back to Antrimville."

"They're going to be hard put to recognize you as well. Especially if you return with this foreign Catholic as your wife. I can't see the pair of you becoming the social hit of the county."

Thornton knew that this was an accurate observation. He said nothing.

"Where will you live?" Harry asked. "What will you live on? You can't go back to Tennessee with a woman nobody knows, even if she is a French aristocrat's daughter. Not without a penny in your pocket or an acre to call your own. How long can you stay here? If William Walker died tomorrow, the next day we would be running for our lives out of Nicaragua. I know you don't approve of my approach. But at least I stand something to gain—and if I lose, I've kept Elizabeth, like money in the bank for a rainy day. In the meantime, who knows what chance and good fortune will bring to me?"

Thornton nodded. "I see your point, Harry. When opportunity knocks, you will be ready. For me, Solange is this good fortune. She is my opportunity. While I have her, everything else will fall into place."

Harry snorted derisively. "Brain fever. Tropical delirium. Have another drink. This rum is terrible, but it can't make you any worse off than you already are."

William Walker strode up the center isle of the cathedral of San Francisco with Solange on his arm. Thornton waited for his bride at the altar. Walker, in an uncharacteristic burst of human feeling, had insisted on taking de Brissot's place in giving away the bride. Of course, since Walker was now involved in the ceremony, the cathedral had to be used instead of the small church they had planned on, the Archbishop had to officiate instead of the nice curate they had spoken with earlier, and Solange had a white veil and bridal train supported by children instead of the black dress of mourning she had worn only the day before.

Thornton had persuaded her to break the traditional period of one year's mourning by pointing out that it was ridiculous for the two of them to live alone while waiting for twelve calendar months to pass before marrying. They had decided to wed in a quiet ceremony attended by a few close friends. However, Thornton as an army officer had to have his commander-in-chief's permission to marry, which was when Walker unexpectedly appointed himself as the bride's father and their marriage began to take on aspects of a state occasion.

After the ceremony the couple walked down the central aisle of the huge old cathedral, in slants of light filtering through the stained glass windows, with the ghostly strains of organ music echoing from the high stone choirs and arches. Outside the church door the bride and groom passed beneath an arch formed by the swords of army officers in full ceremonial uniform.

The wedding reception was indeed a state occasion. It had by now become obvious to Thornton that Walker was using their marriage for his own purposes, primarily as an excuse to bring opposing factions together on neutral ground. Thornton ruefully remembered accepting Byron Cole's suggestion, at Harry's urging, that the army pay for the reception and that Cole send out the invitations. Thornton had not known these would go to President Arribas, cabinet members and top army officers, many of whom Thornton knew only slightly and some not at all.

Solange was delighted at the splendor and the number of important people gathered for her marriage. Thornton did not have the heart to tell her that none of them cared.

The bride and groom, after a time, left the revelers

and made their way back to Solange's, now their, house. At least Walker's participation had that advantage, the festivities were not held there and so they had a quiet place to which they could retreat and be alone together.

Both were newly shy of each other. Solange was a virgin. She had never even seen a man with all his clothes off. Of course she had had long, intimate discussions with married women friends, and knew exactly what to expect on her wedding night—well, not exactly, since the accounts she had heard differed so much. To many women it had been *awful*, with fear, embarrassment and finally pain. To others it had been warm, calming, beyond what they had dreamed. . . . Solange had been unable to guess how much personality came into all this, what had been caused by brutal handling on the part of an inexperienced man, what had been caused by the woman's nerves, how much of the so-called wonderful experiences had been lies. . . . She knew what would happen, but had no idea how she would feel. And she was frightened.

Thornton, despite his whoring or perhaps because of it, had little idea how to go about seducing a woman who was not brazenly willing to offer him her charms in self-confident abandon. He was tender with Solange. She undressed as modestly and quickly as she could, and then appeared in a lace-frilled nightgown. She hid beneath the covers of the big bed.

She turned her back as Thornton slid in beside her naked. Solange waited for him to touch her. His hand touched her waist and gently caressed her body. He snuggled up close to her body and affectionately stroked her. She relaxed to find he had not turned into a rutting goat once in bed, and almost without realizing it she turned on her back to present her body to his caresses, put her arms about his neck and kissed him passionately. They lingered over each other, kissing and fondling without being restricted by propriety for the first time. Thornton suddenly realized that Solange's urges and need for affection were quite as strong as his own.

Soon her nightgown seemed to be more awkward hindrance than protective covering and she let him help her out of it and sank gratefully into his full embrace. His finger crept over her soft skin and stroked her flesh so that she sighed with pleasure. Her breasts were very sensitive to his touch; her nipples stood erect at the brush of his fingertips. Then his hand wandered down over her belly and upper thighs, tantalizing her until she presented herself to his touch. She moaned at the intensity of feeling he aroused in her.

She moved rhythmically against his touch and in a little while pulled him on top of her, parting her legs submissively to allow him to enter her body. He moved into her slowly, waiting for her to press him farther inward when she was ready. He felt the wall of her maidenhead, broke it quickly, and smoothly sank into the blissful warmth of her body.

28

FOR THORNTON and Solange the weeks passed in a dream state. They hardly remembered whom they had seen, what they had done, where they had gone, outside the intimate aura of their own two selves. For several days they had worried Thornton might have to leave to repel a Costa Rican invasion across the southern border, but Walker seemed content to let the invaders remain there, even though they posed a threat to the Transit Road. Neither of them bothered to wonder why. They now had themselves to think about, and that was turning out to be a full-time occupation.

However, in spite of the self-absorption of the two newly wedded lovers, Nicaragua went its way, though slowly as usual. General opinion had it that when Walker moved his troops south to fight the Costa Ricans, Honduras would attack from the north. If Walker did not move south to repel the Costa Ricans, they would gradually move northward. At some point Walker would be forced to move his American troops out to meet them.

Then the Transit Road fell to the Costa Ricans. They moved north and captured Rivas. The invading force numbered three thousand men, far outnumbering Walker's American forces. Whatever support he could have mustered among Nicaraguan soldiers disappeared when President Arribas denounced Walker and welcomed the Costa Ricans as liberators. Walker had allowed Arribas a great deal of freedom. And now strong opponents of Walker had set up the weak Arribas in Leon as a figurehead of resistance. Walker had made no effort to quell the intrigues or crush the plots against him, which were centered in Leon and supported to a great extent by General Gonzalez from exile in Honduras.

The Costa Ricans were unable to move farther north than Rivas, faced by a determined force of the *Falange Americana*. But the Americans did not have enough men to advance against them, and were hard put to hold them where they were. Walker refused to take men from the north and send them south.

Cholera broke out again, this time in a small town near the Pacific coast. The United States had been devastated by cholera more than twenty years previously, in 1832. This Asiatic cholera epidemic originated in the marshes at the mouth of the Ganges in India. After confining its ravages for some years to India, it gradually spread, till it reached London in 1831, where it occasioned widespread panic. Crossing the Atlantic the following year, it appeared first in Canada, and from there spread south to Chicago and down the Mississippi Valley, appearing also in Boston and New York and spreading south and west. The disease "set medical skill at defiance and hurried thousands into eternity," according to one nineteenth-century account. The American epidemic did not subside until 1838. Although a few cases had occurred every summer since then in the States, they lacked the original virulence of the disease.

Not so in the tropics. Here, outbreaks were sudden, were often confined to a single locality, and claimed many lives. Since cholera struck respectable towns as well as dissolute ones, it was not recognized as a direct punishment from God for loose living. The mystery of why it struck in one place and not in another occupied some of the best minds of the day. Obviously the disease could be caught by contact with someone who already had it. But why did people catch it from just being in the same place as those afflicted without direct contact with any of them?

There were those with theories about the dangers of breathing "pestilential airs." There were even more exotic explanations, such as vapors escaping from cracks in the ground caused by earthquakes. Many recognized cholera as simply the prelude to the end of the world as prophesied in the Bible, although they saw the actual end itself as something a bit more climactic than the population expiring merely of vomit and watery diarrhea. And there were a few eccentric souls who insisted that cholera resulted from a contaminated food or water supply, most often the latter.

William Walker was one of these eccentrics. As a medical doctor he based his opinion on the facts then known, and as the commander-in-chief of an army he could have his recommendations followed without serious opposition. The result, he had been pleased to observe, was that the *Falange Americana* was free of cholera.

Harry Drayberry had been summoned by General Walker.

"Drayberry, when you first joined my command not so very long ago," Walker said reflectively as they sat in his office, "you were a raw country youth."

Harry did not respond to this.

Walker had not meant to cause offense and quickly amended what he had said. "But a gentleman, yes, without doubt, fine as they come, yet inexperienced in the ways of the world."

"Yes, sir."

"You are shrewd enough to see the dangers of the military problem that we face. We must fight the Costa

Ricans. All three thousand of them. But this time not with guns. I think I know a way we can cause an even greater devastation of their ranks. But it will take an uncommonly dedicated and courageous man to perform the deed. Let me be honest with you, Drayberry: you are the only man I have I could fully trust with this confidential mission."

Harry volunteered.

He rode out of Granada with eight of his most trusted American soldiers, sixteen Nicaraguan criminals condemned to death for nonpolitical crimes and six large wagons, each drawn by four horses. Two feet of chain connected each prisoner's left wrist to his right. Walker had given Harry lurid descriptions of the cholera disease and had left it up to Harry himself as to how he would carry out the assignment. No one other than Walker and Harry knew a thing. Harry was elated at the trust his commander-in-chief placed in him. It did not occur to him that his being granted the entire responsibility of the mission in secrecy was only to ensure that nothing could be traced back to Walker, particularly in case things went wrong.

Harry had warned them, yet guessed one of the criminals would make a break for freedom anyway. He was prepared. A lowering giant with glittering deepset eyes ran for the undergrowth about five miles outside the town. Two of the American soldiers raised their rifles.

"No!" Harry yelled and cantered his horse after the man running for the bush and holding his chained hands out before him.

Harry looped a noose about the running man's neck, secured the other end of the rope around the saddle horn and trotted back to the group with his captive running and stumbling at the end of the taut rope.

His men and the other fifteen convicts watched. Harry could see from the leers on some of the prisoners' faces that this would be the test as to whether he meant business as the officer in charge or whether he was too much of a gentleman to control them.

Harry rode his horse beneath an old spreading oak and, before the man could loosen the noose about his neck, tossed the other end of the rope over a stout tree limb, caught and reattached it to the saddle horn and spurred his horse forward. The convict was dragged from his feet and hoisted up by his neck. He began to slowly strangle at the end of the rope, his feet kicking in the air.

In a regular hanging, the drop of the trapdoor causes the weight of the falling body to break the neck, resulting in a reasonably painless death when performed properly. Allowing someone to strangle slowly by their own weight is neither a pretty sight nor a painless death.

The big convict was strong. He reached above him and pulled himself hand over hand up the rope. Harry watched until he was nearly to the bough, when he nudged his horse several paces closer to the tree, thereby lowering the rope. The convict was ready for this. He let go of the rope and landed with his feet on the ground at the end of the slack rope. He tried to loosen the rope about his neck, only to be hauled off his feet again and hoisted by the neck as Harry spurred his horse away.

They went through this complete procedure a second time. The third time the convict did not have the strength to pull his body hand over hand up the rope. He slowly strangled, twirling at the end of the rope, his nails raking his constricted throat, his mouth gasping for air like a fish at the surface of a muddy pool. . . .

Harry cut the rope above the noose and left the body on the ground for animals and vultures. There were no more attempted escapes.

Outside the miserable little town of San Pablo, Harry gave the convicts their orders. "Don't touch any of them—not even kick them, no matter whether they're sick or well. Don't eat or drink anything or put your hands near your mouth, not even if you wash them first. Then you'll be all right. No danger. Now remember, the ones we want are those who have just started vomiting and shitting, at most for six or seven hours. The ones lying around collapsed are too far gone—they'll either die or recover, but if we make them travel we'll kill them almost immediately. Just get the others up here and I'll make them an offer."

Harry and the eight American soldiers waited outside the town. They knew the convicts would not escape in this cholera-ravaged area. They had been promised, when the mission was complete, they would be paid with a pardon for their work and in gold for their silence. They could go home again, to murder, rape or rob again, perhaps. But that was not Harry's concern.

Over the next few hours the fifteen prisoners, still in wrist chains, brought back eighty-three people. Harry was unsure that all were infected—some looked quite healthy to him—so he ordered half a dozen water bottles filled and passed from one to another of the group. The healthy ones drank from the same container as the infected. They all looked terrified, and Harry did not enquire what methods his prisoners had used to persuade them to gather here.

Harry stood on a wagon in front of them. He held up a cloth bag of gold pieces, dipped his hand in and pulled out a fistful of coins to let them fall between his fingers back into the bag. Then he hefted the bag to show its weight and turned it so the assembled crowd could look inside at its gleaming contents. Harry now had their full and closest attention.

"I need you all as spies for your country against the invading Costa Ricans in the south. Some of you will make your way into Rivas, some to San Juan del Sur and some to other towns. Just tell us everything you see there. When you set out, each of you will be paid two gold pieces for your expenses." Harry held up two gold pieces in his fingers to shine in the sun. He knew this was more than most of them made in a year of drudgery. "You will receive three more gold coins when you return if you stay more than two days."

He added three gold pieces to the two already glittering in his fingers. Any questions or doubts on the part of his listeners were quelled by the awesome prospect of soon holding such wealth in their own hands for a few days' work.

They piled willingly into the wagons while Harry took the prisoners out of their earshot. He felt it was time to reinforce their good behavior.

"What you see me holding here," he told them, waving a sheaf of documents at them, "are pardons in each of your names signed by the military governor of the city of Granada."

The military governor was a Nicaraguan toady left over from the Legitimist administration who had not even questioned. Harry's demand that he sign the papers. Each man got to see the paper with his own name on it.

"You've seen the gold," Harry announced. "Now you've seen your pardons. You know I'm telling you the truth. You each get a pardon and seven pieces of gold when you finish this job. You keep your mouth shut now, and keep it shut after you go home too, if you know what's good for you."

The convicts said nothing. Freedom and gold were almost within their grasp, and the chains on their wrists rattled as they shifted restlessly, anxious to be on the move.

Harry dropped the sick residents of San Pablo off at various points near the Costa Rican occupied territory and sent convicts part way with them to make sure they went where they were supposed to. The wagons were a putrid mess from the vomit and diarrhea of the cholera victims. Four had died on the way, and Harry had refused to allow their bodies to be dumped.

Nine had been shot while trying to escape, and their bodies had been loaded back on the wagons by their fellow townsmen, again on Harry's orders. He could not risk spreading the disease, intending to deliver this package of pestilence complete and entire to the Costa Ricans alone.

He did not wait for the return of the cholera victims from the occupied territory, he burned the infected wagons. He knew that most of them would be killed by fearful townspeople who would recognize their symptoms. Others would be tortured and shot as spies by the Costa Ricans. Harry had starved them for a day and let them go without water for six hours before releasing them. They each had a small fortune of two gold pieces with which to buy food and water. Many would be so desperate they would dip their head into the nearest well.

Within the space of a month, two-thirds of the invading Costa Rican troops, two thousand out of three thousand men, had died of cholera. Costa Rica withdrew the tattered remnants of its army and begged William Walker for peace. He graciously consented to a cessation of military hostilities. The Transit was back under his control.

President Arribas, who had denounced Walker when the Costa Ricans invaded in strength, now waited in Leon for the ax to fall. He remembered how he had treacherously consented to the death of his sponsor and friend, Ponciano Corral, before a firing squad in the Grand Plaza of Granada. Arribas could hardly expect his friends to come forward to help him now. There was no escape from Leon, and a terrible silence from William Walker.

29

"Urgent message for you, sir," the clerk called out in the hall.

Cornelius Vanderbilt stopped in his greatcoat, top hat and spats, and waved his stick at the man. "Give it to me. Where is it from?"

"Just came in on the Transit steamer from Greytown, Nicaragua, sir."

Vanderbilt read the message where he stood. His eyes protruded, his cheeks grew crimson, his lips quivered. He lashed out with his stick at the wretch cringing before him who had brought the bad news.

"I'm sorry, sir," the man apologized and scuttled away to some cranny to nurse his bruised shoulder.

This was impossible! He was Cornelius Vanderbilt! A soldier of fortune at the head of a band of desperadoes could not take away what rightfully belonged to Cornelius Vanderbilt!

He threw things about his office and bellowed. The first prices were coming in from the Stock Exchange. They had got word. The price quoted for the Accessory Transit Company had dropped by one third in a single hour! This was disaster! Those mealy-mouthed toadies in Washington would hear from him about this. Not that he could expect them to do anything about it. He could depend on a few of them. The rest was afraid of the Southerners. Or had been bribed by Morgan and Garrison.

He looked at the message again. This was March 14, 1856, right at the start of the busiest season of emigration to California. The bloody man had seized *his* Transit. ". . . Rescind the charter of 1851 . . . on behalf of the government of the Republic of Nicaragua . . . expropriate the Transit . . ." The message did not have to say the charter would be resold to Morgan and Garrison.

Vanderbilt had had himself elected president of the Transit Company again at the January meeting of the board of directors. He had immediately engineered the ouster of Morgan and Garrison from the board. Now the company was one hundred percent under his control again. Until this! Right at the start of the peak season!

His executive secretary, a circumspect man, nervously suggested that he send messengers to cancel Mr. Vanderbilt's luncheon appointment for that day with a German merchant and the *vernissage* of new landscapes of the Hudson River he was to attend that afternoon.

"My God, man, this is a business setback, not a personal tragedy! Of course I shall have lunch, and a very good one too, and then attend to my artistic needs."

"The gentlemen you summoned are outside now, sir."

"Send them in."

Vanderbilt's chief accountant, senior counsel and chief field engineer entered. They stood until waved into chairs.

"Well, gentlemen," Vanderbilt addressed them in orotund tones, "you have all heard of this preposterous act of brigandage that has been perpetrated upon my person—a crime which cries in the face of the Almighty for His vengeance, and an insult to our glorious Union, the United States of America. Every red-blooded American who fears God and loves his country will demand the privilege of striking back at these cowardly thieves who so perfidiously follow their sinister trade under foreign skies . . ."

Vanderbilt stopped here, possibly because he had lost the thread of his argument, but more probably because he realized that his fine flood of verbal passion was being wasted on these calculating, stone-faced employees of his.

"What really galls me," he said in an entirely different tone, "is that the message is signed by one Byron Cole, who has, you will have noticed in his missives to us, moved up from Transit Commissioner to Secretary of the Treasury, no less. You will also not forget that our first contact with this gentleman was when he tried to extort money from us for this mad scheme. It is now clear that Morgan and Garrison have reached a point with him which we could not—a financial arrangement."

"Sir," the chief accountant defended himself, "Mr. Cole's demands have been outrageous. His most recent estimate of the Transit Company's debt to Nicaragua is $425,000!"

Vanderbilt snorted. "I wouldn't pay that for the whole stretch of land between Texas and the continent of South America."

They all laughed at the great man's little joke.

"I am not trying to assign blame to anyone for the actions of this unpredictable soldier of fortune, William Walker. In fact, it's probably my own lack of foresight which allowed him to seize the Transit in the first place, if any blame must be assigned. No, gentlemen, let us not grow wary of each other. Let us band together, as friends, as comrades, so that together we can stamp this varmint out."

"Hear, hear," the lawyer seconded warmly.

Vanderbilt pointed a stubby finger at the accountant. "What are your ideas?"

The accountant swallowed. "Keep the company stock afloat on the Exchange as best we can, sir. By doing this, we can offer some challenge to the legality of any company which Morgan and Garrison try to raise funds for. If we can cast enough aspersions against them and raise enough doubts about the safety of investments in their operation, I think we can seriously hamper their fund-raising efforts for a new transit enterprise."

"Very good," Vanderbilt said. "I have a few ideas of my own along those lines to try out on the market, too."

Vanderbilt nodded to the lawyer.

"We've been lucky with the ocean-going steamers, sir," his senior counsel said. "All are presently outside Nicaraguan waters and we will be able to turn them back before Walker can seize them. This means that although Walker has the river and like steamers, he has no transport back and forth between the States and Nicaragua in either the Atlantic or the Pacific. I think we have to move quickly, sir, to corner whatever suitable ships are in the marketplace by buying them outright, putting a down payment on them or chartering them for an extended period. As well as paralyzing the Transit system, this lack of ships will leave Walker totally without supplies."

Vanderbilt was smiling. His loyal employees had made him smile pleasurably with the fruit of their industrious and fertile minds—which was what he paid the bastards for.

The third was not a man who had spent his best years at a desk. His rugged athletic-bearing distinguished him from the others. Vanderbilt grunted at him to proceed.

"As you may remember," the engineer said in a relaxed way, "the last time we discussed this Walker critter, I suggested we go down there with a force of men and dig him out. I know now I was right then, and I think all of you do too. This time"—he paused for emphasis—"I think you should do business with him."

The accountant and the lawyer sat upright with their hands placed on their knees and tried not to look at the dreadful way Mr. Vanderbilt's eyes were popping from his head and at the red flush that crept like a stain along his jowls.

The engineer went on, apparently oblivious to the disastrous effect his words were having upon the magnate, "Walker, whether we like what he is doing or not, has proved himself militarily. He and his corps of Americans would be unbeatable in the area with proper support from home. I'm certain Walker knows this, and that all his maneuvers could be seen as overtures to you. If you threw your lot in with him, sir, even at this late stage, there is no end to what you could gain in the area."

Vanderbilt found his voice. "If it takes my last dollar, I'm going to ruin that cheap tin soldier in Nicaraguey. You watch me!"

"Well, if that's the course you're going to take, sir," the engineer replied nonchalantly, as if it mattered little to him which course Vanderbilt followed, "and since you've turned down my previous request for the intervention of our own mercenaries, I think your best bet would be to arm Walker's enemies in Central America—the political factions against him in Nicaragua and the Indian tribes on the Mosquito Coast, some of whom have already received guns from the British. Most important though would be to pour rifles and ammunition into the two neighboring countries of Honduras and Costa Rica. If you supply the playthings, the game will get under way by itself."

Vanderbilt growled, "Goddam tin soldier! I'll show him!"

30

WILLIAM WALKER had not avenged himself on Patricio Arribas for denouncing him during the heighth of the Costa Rican invasion. However, Walker had suspended Arribas' powers as President—thereby managing to suspend something which had never existed—and declared a presidential election for Sunday, June 27, 1856. Arribas was permitted to run for office in this election. Three others joined him in this race, one of whom was William Walker. Byron Cole, although already overworked, agreed as a loyal new citizen of Nicaragua to supervise the elections and guarantee fair play for all contenders.

Privately Cole was dead-set against Walker running for president. "So long as you have a Nicaraguan-born puppet in office, no one can say you came in and seized the country. Nicaragua is run by Nicaraguans, and so forth. The United States has to—"

Walker harshly interrupted. "Tell your friends in New Orleans and Washington that they have an ally here."

"You mean it, William? You'll go all the way with them?"

Walker nodded.

Cole brightened. "Those old boys are going to be

209

pleased. Still and all, William, you've been a mite standoffish with them up till now. They'll be suspicious of your sudden friendliness."

"No, they won't," Walker replied bitterly. "They know that Vanderbilt has cut us off by sea. In spite of everything I have achieved here, one word in New York City is enough to finish me. Or so Vanderbilt thinks."

"Morgan and Garrison are trying to buy ships, but Vanderbilt snaps up everything that comes on the market."

Walker laughed scornfully. "We would be foolish to bet our lives on those two." He drove his right fist into the palm of his left hand with awesome force. "No supplies. No further men. No income from the Transit. How long can we last?"

"You think then my Southern friends will not be surprised to hear from us," Cole said by way of a statement rather than a question. "I guess you are right. What will I tell them?"

"Send us arms, powder, lead, dried food and someone with enough authority to negotiate with us and pay in gold."

"They'll want us to side with them against the North, if it came to that," Cole cautioned.

"My pleasure," was the curt reply.

"It stands to reason that if you are President of Nicaragua, down South they could perceive that you might be in a position to be very accommodating."

"Precisely," Walker said. "That is, of course, if I am elected."

Cole smiled. "I think you have a very good chance."

In the last week of June 1856, it gave Byron Cole great pleasure to announce the results of a landslide election: Walker, 15,835; Ferrer, 4,447; Salazar, 2,087; Arribas, 867.

* * *

The joy of President Walker's men was soon cut short in the capital city of Granada. Despite all precautions, the townspeople began to vomit and have watery diarrhea. Asiatic cholera, the deadly kind, was hard to diagnose with certainty in individuals. In isolated cases the condition was easy to confuse with certain types of dysentery and malaria, or with food or even mushroom poisoning, all very common at that time in Nicaragua. Only when great numbers fell ill did it become evident that a cholera epidemic had struck. Then, of course, it was too late to do much about it.

As soon as cases of sickness began to rise and be noticed, Walker ordered the immediate transportation of those afflicted to islands in Lake Nicaragua. On the average, the disease lasted five days. To be certain, Walker decreed that after a period of ten days' exile, but not before, the victims would be picked up by boat and returned to the city. They were left on the islands to survive as best they could.

Walker selected the man he knew he could trust to handle this—General Harry Drayberry.

Harry was the first officer under Walker's command to receive the single star of a general. Thornton remained a colonel, and the two friends joked about their relative ranks every time Harry paid a visit to Thornton's home. Thornton had become a bit of a joke among the officers. They snickered at the faraway look in his eyes and over the way he ran home to "wifey". Harry had defended his friend on several occasions, most effectively by pointing out that if any of them had a woman half as pretty as Solange, they too would run home to see her.

Yet, to tell the truth, it bored the hell out of Harry to sit and sip tea and chatter with Solange and Thornton. They were so proud of their shiny furniture, he didn't know where to get rid of the cup and saucer.

And if he wanted to smoke, the men had to retire to the anteroom. Solange didn't like the smell! Damn, it made him want to spit on the carpet.

Catching the sick ones was a problem. Their families tried to hide them. Especially the children. Harry solved this problem by moving the whole family to an island for ten days' quarantine if even one member became ill. It was moving entire families which Walker later credited with keeping the outbreak of cholera from reaching epidemic proportions in Granada, although it had been done for other reasons.

Admittedly there were some problems. Several of the larger islands to which the sick were transported were already inhabited and the residents, as soon as the government boats had left, attacked and killed the newly arrived city people and burned the bodies to protect themselves from infection. Word of this soon spread to Granada, probably deliberately on the part of the islanders, and often the ill had to be physically restrained in order to be transported to what they regarded as certain death. Since their handlers, non-political criminals earning a pardon, had been warned to come in contact with the sick persons as little as possible, it had to be expected that sticks, goads and other somewhat cruel methods would be used against those who resisted. It was unavoidable, Harry explained to anyone who would listen, and all for the good of the city.

Most died of the disease itself. Many died of exposure and malnutrition, and a lesser number from murder, snakebite, and drowning while trying to swim to shore. The rest seemed to have disappeared without a trace. A small percentage made their way back to the city and raised loud complaints that the army had looted their homes while they were away. But this was a minority.

* * *

"You may be a general, Harry," Thornton said bitterly, "but if this is how you have to earn your star, you'd be better off a private."

"What are you talking about?" Harry's voice was cold and menacing.

"You know damn well what I'm talking about. All those people you shuttled out to the island and left to die."

Harry looked him in the eyes. "I didn't hear you and Solange inviting them to stay with you."

"They didn't have to be dumped like that. A lot would have survived."

"And infected others," Harry said. "Maybe we saved Solange's life by what we did."

"Leave her out of this!" Thornton raised his voice.

Harry tipped himself another drink from the bottle of rum. "You think your happy little home puts you beyond reality. Give you another couple of years and you'll be standing with your back to the fireplace sermonizing about morality and love of Jesus to your slaves."

Thornton grabbed the bottle and sloshed a drink into his glass. He thought to himself he should have gone home long ago, except for what he had to say to Harry Drayberry. The others in the officers' lounge pretended to pay no attention to the dispute, but since there was little in the way of entertainment, every disagreement was followed and recounted with great interest. Both Thornton and Harry had consumed enough alcohol to have shed their self-consciousness and had already forgotten their audience.

"You started going downhill with those so-called special missions," Thornton said. "Murders would be a better word to describe them."

"Several wars are going on here at the same time, in case you haven't noticed, Thornton. Everyone who got killed wore a military uniform. That's the risk they took. That's the risk you and I take. Not a single civilian was assassinated."

"Just a selection of honest men," Thornton said.

"By their lights, perhaps. Not by ours."

"You know, when I heard about the Costa Ricans and the cholera, I hit the man who said you had done it. I'd have shot him if I hadn't already suspected he was telling the truth."

Harry smirked. "It must be rough down here on someone with your sensitivity. You've gotten soft, Mc-Clintock. Face it, you were terrified you would be sent down to fight the Costa Ricans. You didn't want to miss your warm bed and homecooked meals. So people like me had to take care of them for you while you stayed home and tickled your Frenchwoman's—"

"Damn you!" Thornton shouted. "I told you to leave her out of this. You say I'm soft. You think I'm a coward. I'll show you. I challenge you to a duel."

Harry was taken aback. "You know duelling is forbidden between officers in the *Falange Americana*."

"But not drunken quarrels!" Thornton jumped to his feet. "I'll fight you right now. In the street outside, you bastard. One shot apiece at twenty paces."

Harry shook his head.

"Coward!" Thornton shouted. "How dare you insult my wife!"

He struck Harry across the face.

Harry leaped to his feet in a rage.

Thornton pointed at him and addressed the other officers, who could no longer pretend they noticed nothing. "You see here General Drayberry, who attacks the sick and dying and insults women, but who refuses to fight an able-bodied man in a matter of honor." Thornton raised his glass in a toast. "I am asking you to drink to the prosperity and short life of this popinjay."

Thornton laughed mirthlessly and tossed off the glass of rum.

None of the officers dared laugh or join in the toast. They were jealous of Harry, but did not dislike him. And they feared him. But this row between two old friends was too good to let die quietly, and they knew their quiet snickers would further incense Harry.

"Let's go," Harry snapped, walking to the door.

Outside in the dusty street, the setting sun made long shadows and townspeople hurried away from the two uniformed Americans staggering about with drawn pistols.

The two men stood unsteadily back to back in the middle of the street.

"I take first shot since you challenged me," Harry said over his shoulder in an angry voice. "When I say 'now,' we count out ten paces together. Now!"

The men counted out as they stepped ten paces in opposite directions. They turned to present a side view to each other. Thornton held his pistol barrel to the sky before his face and pulled his belly in. He swayed slightly, but was not aware of this.

Neither was Harry, who seemed to be having difficulty getting a line of sight with his pistol. The gun discharged and the shot echoed and re-echoed among the stone houses. Harry peered through the blue smoke. Thornton was still standing, so he raised his smoking pistol barrel upward before his face and prepared to take his opponent's shot. He belched.

This man had insulted Solange. Thornton raised the pistol and squinted along the top of the barrel, placing the head of Harry Drayberry in the sights. This man had insulted his wife. He lowered the pistol a fraction of an inch so the recoil of the barrel would not cause the bullet to overfly the head. He couldn't remember exactly how Harry had insulted Solange. His right finger squeezed off a perfect shot. Harry and he had been friends since childhood. The gun barrel jerked slightly to the right as the hammer struck.

The lead ball whistled in front of Harry's nose. The

middle of the street behind him had been cleared, and people pointed at the wall of a building where the bullet tore away a patch of stucco—then the pedestrians and wagons which had crowded back against the sides of the street flowed on again, the combat between the foreigners already forgotten.

Thornton shook hands with Harry. "Want to finish the bottle?"

"Sure. That's why I deliberately missed you," Harry answered.

"I waited till the last minute before moving the barrel aside," Thornton confessed. "I wanted you to see the bullet."

"I saw it!"

They both roared with laughter and returned to their table at the officers' club. Harry bought drinks for everyone in the house.

Thornton looked happily at his old friend and said in a slurred voice, "You know, I'm very pleased I didn't aim to hit you. I'd be miserable now if my bullet had hit you."

"I was just thinking along those lines," Harry told him. He looked at Thornton seriously. "Because what I told you a while ago was a lie. I aimed for your heart."

31

THE SKY had not fallen when William Walker was
elected President of Nicaragua, and the cholera outbreak in the capital city of Granada had not been as
bad as elsewhere. For the time being, the epidemic
disease seemed to be quiescent. Not all the news was
good. Spies, travelers and merchants brought stories of
American arms shipments to Honduras and Costa Rica
and elsewhere, all paid for, it was said, by Cornelius
Vanderbilt.

Morgan and Garrison had been able to get ships, and
supplies had now been resumed on an irregular basis.
Welcome new shipments were arriving from the port of
New Orleans. This was considered a very favorable
omen by Byron Cole. The disquieting rumors continued of Vanderbilt's efforts to arm Walker's enemies
and even to mount a naval blockade. There were even
stories that columns of armed Guatemalans had been
admitted to Honduras to join with them in an attack
on Nicaragua.

The city of Leon remained a hotbed of opposition
to Walker. As before, he made no effort to stamp out
internal dissent. Walker's policy in this direction had
paid off to all appearances, because there were no
armed groups in the country in open rebellion against

him—there were the usual bandits and hostile Indian groups in the east, but they would be there in any case, and their loyalties could not be depended upon by Walker's enemies.

Then the invasion came. From the north. The Hondurans marched south with a force of men intent on taking the capital of Granada. Lake Managua formed a barrier which the Hondurans had to march around. They received supplies from Walker's foes in Leon and arrived in Managua, at the lake's southwestern corner. From there it was two days' march to Granada, about thirty-five miles.

Walker decided to meet them on the way in order to spare Granada the damage of the attack. The small town of Masaya was twelve miles north of the city. The troops had been ready for battle for some days now, since they had first been warned of the approach of the Hondurans. Walker moved almost his entire force out of the city so that he could vanquish the invaders in one decisive battle, rather than have their retreating forces lay waste to the northern parts of the country.

As he rode at the head of his company, Thornton wondered if he had indeed gone soft. It had been many months since he or his men had last seen action. He himself had put on weight, he could not deny that. Also, he now seemed to lack the blood-thirsty urge to fight. He would never admit that—here he was, a professional military man, a soldier of fortune, who would prefer to stay home with his wife rather than go to battle. He decided he must be getting old before his time.

Thornton looked in front of him to where William Walker and Harry Drayberry rode proudly to the right of the colors. They had not lost the passion to fight. A man could tell that, even from the way they sat on their horses—upright, in control, eager. Damn, he wished he were home with Solange.

They reached the town of Masaya in late afternoon. The men were assigned sleeping places for the night by their sergeants, who would shut down the inns and bordellos early that night. The officers gathered with Walker to review their strategy and the layout of the town.

"There's no reason they have to attack us in Masaya," Walker told them, "except they dare not move south and leave us behind them to cut off their escape route home, and more importantly, their supply route from the north. We have a large force of men here and they will need everything they've got to fight us. So if we just sit here in Masaya, they have only the choice of attacking us in full strength or of turning around and going home."

They had dismounted on the northern edge of the town. The road to the north, to Managua, ran through a broad valley. It was the obvious route for the Hondurans to take into the town.

"Let's assume," Walker went on, "that they are not going to pass us by and allow us to attack them from the rear before they get to Granada, and let us also assume they are not going to turn around and go home after they've come this far"—polite laughter from the assembled officers—"which leaves us with an attack on Masaya. This is the best way for them to come. They will approach warily, knowing that we are here to defend the town. I want one company of men out here to decoy the enemy into the town."

Walker waited for a volunteer. He waited in vain, since no officer was going to deliberately seek the opportunity to be overrun by the enemy and flee before him. Such playacting was too close to the real thing, and there was no glamor in pretending to be a coward.

Walker grinned knowingly. His gray eyes flicked from man to man, and settled on Thornton McClintock. Thornton knew he was being given a gentleman's opportunity to volunteer for this duty before being ordered to if necessary.

"Very well, sir," he said unenthusiastically.

"Good man. Retreat before the Hondurans as if you are the town's only defense. Naturally they would expect us to defend the outskirts of Masaya to stop them causing damage inside. I'll leave it up to your judgment, McClintock, but get those Hondurans into the streets of the town."

Word soon got around Thornton's company that they were to be made sacrificial lambs the next day, and as he walked the streets of Masaya late that night, Thornton recognized many of the very drunk soldiers as members of his company. He did not blame them.

The next morning he rode up and down before a miserable, hungover company of men, except for a cheerful few who either had not been drunk the night before or were continuing into today.

"I've never allowed my men to be cannon-fodder and I'm not doing so now," Thornton announced in a loud voice.

The men paid attention. They had expected some nonsense about duty and God's will. This was much more to their liking.

"We fire on their advance men and maintain our positions," Thornton continued. "When their main force arrives, we retreat before them in orderly manner —the trick is, it must not seem orderly to the Hondurans. All we have to do is lure them into the town. I don't want a single man hit, so forget all this talk you have heard about them overrunning us in hand-to-hand fighting. Right now, we rehearse our moves."

He spent the next two hours supervising the sergeants and corporals as they agreed among themselves in what order to withdraw, how far, who would cover for whom, how best to simulate panic. Sentries posted around the practice area kept outside observers away. They did a complete run-through of their make-believe rout and flight, which made everyone laugh. The men were then fed. After that they erected shelters against the sun and rested until the enemy showed.

Refugees had been streaming down the road all morning—rugged country people, with much Indian blood, who had placed all they possessed on mule-drawn carts and headed south before the Honduran army with their children and farm animals. The stream of refugees slowed to a trickle, and finally there were none at all. Only the dusty road stretching off up the valley. And silence. Silence everywhere in the afternoon heat.

Thornton lay in the shade of a rock watching a lizard move slowly across a smooth stone. The reptile was hunting insects, he supposed, but was not having much luck. There was no shortage of flies, mosquitoes and bugs of all sort, but in this part of Nicaragua the insects seemed to know all about lizards and kept away from this one's darting tongue. They had no fear of humans, however, and hungrily traversed on Thornton's skin, biting and stinging.

The Honduran army appeared miles away down the valley road, at the horizon, beneath a towering column of yellow dust. For a while it looked as if there were many thousands of men rolling forward like a giant, unstoppable ant formation. Then no more appeared over the horizon, and the size of their army suddenly seemed to shrink. Thornton estimated they numbered about two thousand men, and sent word of this back to Walker inside the town. Previous estimates by spies had placed the number of Hondurans at close to three thousand. Four hundred members of the *Falange Americana* were in Masaya. They weren't really worried about the odds anymore.

Thornton walked about among his men during the tense hour the invading army marched upon them.

"Let them know we're here," he told them. "Hold them off until I give the signal, and then we go into the drill we've rehearsed. That's all that's to it."

He laughingly answered one wisecracker who asked him where he would be, "If they bury your ass, they're

going to have to bury mine first, because I'll be right
here along with you."

The men cheered him and began yelling obscene
names and threats at the advancing enemy, who were
out of earshot and probably would not have understood
such English words anyway.

The Honduran infantry units came first, followed by
cavalry. The forward infantry units broke marching
formation just out of range and fanned out to prepare
an advance. A bugle blew and the men began to come
forward, about seven hundred of them against the
hundred in Thornton's company. The Hondurans
inched forward, using every cactus, shrub and rock as
cover. They obviously had orders to advance as far as
possible before firing.

That morning the sergeants and corporals of Thornton's company had tested the ranges of their guns and
marked the points at which their fire would be effective.
The defense of each area had been parceled out. When
the first Honduran crossed between two boulders which
marked the effective range of their weapons, a single
shot took him out. A second Honduran, another single
shot, and he bit the dust. There was no cheering or
abuse now. Just silence and concentration. This was
work for professionals.

The enemy foot soldiers moved forward relentlessly,
ignoring individual casualties, sweeping on in waves.
The barrels of the defenders' rifles grew hot from constant firing. Thornton had not given the signal to retreat. He could not, since the Honduran infantry were
being held in check by his men. Although the Hondurans outnumbered them by seven to one, the cover
was poor. The attackers could advance to a certain
point, but beyond that it was suicide.

Thornton kept a close eye on the maneuvers of the
opposing officers. He guessed their move before it came.

He shouted the order, "Quick! Close formations! A
cavalry charge!"

His men darted from behind cover to form a much more densely packed central core which would discourage a cavalry charge because of the huge losses of attackers it would involve. Spread out thinly, as they had been before, the horsemen could have broken through their lines and turned to attack from behind while their infantry charged from in front.

The cavalry were called off, but now the Honduran infantry had a much more centralized target and open flanks upon which they could advance.

Thornton sounded the retreat. As the captain is last man to leave his sinking vessel, Thornton made sure his men saw he was the last man in the retreat, the one still in the most forward position. This kept the retreat orderly. It also conveyed to the enemy the impression that more men were involved than actually were, allowing them to think, as the plan called for, they were driving Walker's entire force before them.

In calm reflection the Honduran officers would of course have suspected a trap. But in the heat of battle, nothing encourages a man to move forward more than to see his enemy back down before him, and few things could have appealed more to the Honduran officers' vanity than to claim victory over the man who was now the world's most notorious soldier of fortune—William Walker!

Sensing conquest in their grasp, smelling the blood of their enemy, feeling already the weight of medals and gold awards, the Honduran officers did an unexpected thing which nearly brought disaster to McClintock and his carefully staged retreat. They brought their flags and pennants up, ordered another cavalry charge and galloped forward waving their sabers in the air.

"Run!" Thornton yelled. "Make for the side streets!"

By this time they had retreated to the very edge of the town. There was no point in slaughtering and being slaughtered by these clowns. Give them the highway! Ride on!

The enemy officers and cavalry thundered into the deserted streets of the town. They ignored the fleeing defenders on the side streets and galloped forward in a colorful cluster, more than seventy horsemen in uniform with swords, flags and bugles and the infantry running behind them, thick in the narrow streets.

The horsemen wheeled into the central plaza—and met William Walker's main force. Walker's infantry stood in tiers like an enormous firing squad. In the first ten seconds a third of the horsemen had fallen. The others turned and tried to ride back the way they had come, but could not because of the multitudes of their own infantry filling the narrow street behind them. In less than two minutes not a single horseman survived. Only three horses were hit, and then only by accident. They were valuable.

Then the shuttered second-story windows above the Honduran infantrymen opened, gun barrels emerged and fired buckshot and bullets into them. Ancient blunderbusses were taken from walls, loaded with powder and nails, small brass objects, anything small, hard and heavy, causing death and injury on the scale of modern antipersonnel fragmentation grenades.

The Hondurans panicked. Many were trampled to death in their rush to escape the city's narrow streets. More were picked off like goldfish in a bowl by snipers in the buildings on either side of them. Most had dropped or lost their weapons by the time they reached the valley road stretching away to the north.

A sound of hoofs. Von Satzner led his Lancer Squadron in pursuit. His cavalry men hunted down their running prey, leaned down from the saddle to swipe at the fleeing men with razor-sharp sabers. They cut, hacked and chopped indiscriminately, and left the valley floor around them strewn with dismembered groaning men, some of whom crawled pitifully about in their searing agony. Thornton watched until sickened by the sight.

His horse had been brought to him and he rode

into the town to the plaza. Walker met him on the way.

"You brought them in beautifully, McClintock," Walker congratulated him. The gray eyes gave him a quizzical look. "Glad to see you can still fight."

Thornton laughed. So Walker had heard talk that Thornton's domestic life might be interfering with his soldiering. As Thornton suspected, there was not much that happened in Granada that did not reach Walker's ears.

A galloping horse approached in a cloud of dust. A scout reined in his sweat-covered horse. He saluted and shouted to Walker, "They've gone south, sir."

Walker tensed. He dismissed the man and turned to Thornton. "They've outflanked us. General Astrada and six hundred Guatemalans. They were with the Hondurans, but split off before you sighted them. Remember the original estimates of nearly three thousand men?"

Thornton was pale. He spoke in a sorrowing voice. "We'll never catch them now before they reach Granada."

He meant before they reached Solange.

32

GRANADA LAY about two miles distant, and from the hill they could overlook the entire small city. The fighting had stopped. A pall of dust and smoke hung over the roofs, the result of combat. A few houses were still burning, but the fires were not spreading. A flag flew partway up the spire of the cathedral, which dominated the town, pointing to Heaven as evidence to God of the aspirations of the people. Estrada and his six hundred Guatemalans had taken the capital literally behind their backs.

Where was Solange? Had she died? Was she lying injured, a bullet lodged in her tender body, softly calling out his name? Were the Guatemalan soldiers sexually savaging her at this very moment, passing her body from one to the other? Thornton could stand it no more.

"Let's counterattack without delay, sir," he said to Walker.

Walker's gray eyes looked at him sadly. "That's what they expect us to do, McClintock. That's why their soldiers are not in the streets looting and raping. They've been put in a position to defend the city. Which is where we'll keep them, under pressure, till they crack."

"Lay siege to the city?"

Walker nodded.

Keep them too busy to rape. . . . Thornton had to agree that was the best plan. He had left Solange under the protection of the sergeant in charge of the twenty *Falange Americana* soldiers left in Granada when they had marched on Masaya. They could not have offered much resistence to the six hundred Guatemalans, but judging by the smoke and damage that could be seen from where they were, they had offered some. If only Solange were unharmed. . . .

Thornton got his company moving quickly over the remaining distance to Granada. Each company was assigned one-fourth of the ring about the city as the siege was laid. Thornton's company was nearest the cathedral, and as his men occupied their positions, volleys of shots rang out from the cathedral tower into the streets of the town. They were not shooting at Thornton's men, but at the Guatemalans inside. Thornton got a spyglass and focused on the flag on the spire of the huge fortress-cathedral. He sent for the commander-in-chief to come urgently. He wanted Walker to see this for himself. The flag was blue and white with a red star. Walker's emblem.

Was Solange in the church, too? Had the sergeant evacuated her? Had they been taken by surprise, with no time to rescue her? Probably not. They would have been watching out for messengers from Masaya to learn how the battle had gone there. And there had been fighting. No doubt this was what had given them time to withdraw into the fortress-cathedral, within which they could hold out against the Guatemalans indefinitely. In the cellar beneath the church, a well specially dug for the purpose many years before provided drinking water that could not be poisoned or diverted from the outside. They had sacks of dried beans and rice in other parts of the cellars, which were in use as storerooms by Walker's forces. Had Solange managed to find refuge there?

William Walker had no intention of waiting to starve the Guatemalans into submission. Too many of his own troops had women in Granada, and the men could hardly be expected to wait outside while their women starved within. Walker brought up four artillery pieces he had received a few weeks previously from New Orleans. Walker ordered his gunners to fire on the houses between the cathedral and the lake. They began at one end of a row of houses, and having demolished three dwellings, waited until the townspeople could evacuate the area. Then they methodically set about leveling the buildings.

The deadly duel continued among the infantrymen of both sides. Walker's men were now using rifles captured from the Hondurans at Masaya. These new weapons fired the minie ball, a rifle bullet with a conical head that had much superior flight characteristics to the projectiles of the guns they had been using. The Guatemalans were using minie rifles, too.

Walker remarked laconically, "Every shot you hear, both ours and theirs, was paid for from the purse of Cornelius Vanderbilt."

The huge amounts of brand-new weapons and ammunition captured at Masaya would greatly build up Walker's arsenal. And he had proved against the Hondurans that even with new weapons against his old, with many more men than he, the Central American armies could not beat the *Falange Americana.*

But General Estrada and the Guatemalans had outwitted William Walker. He could not forgive them for that. His men noticed the implacably cold way he was going about this siege to destroy his enemies—and a good part of the city of Granada along with them.

"Shall we offer them terms to surrender, sir?" Harry Drayberry asked Walker. "They've taken heavy losses.

I think they would lay down their arms if we granted them a safe conduct out of Nicaragua."

Walker stared at him in contempt. "General Estrada will never live to boast he took Granada while I was looking the other way."

The President walked away in a cold fury. Nothing further was mentioned to him on the subject.

Walker next presented Harry with his plan of attack, which explained why the artillery had leveled the buildings between the cathedral and the lake shore. The Guatemalans had been forced to abandon the flattened area as no-man's-land. Harry made Thornton his second-in-command and they set about the project. Farther up Lake Nicaragua, out of sight of Granada, their men chopped down trees and bound the trunks together to make two large rafts.

At night, in complete darkness, they poled the rafts along the shore with twelve soldiers aboard each. They landed at the rubble-strewn area that the artillery had leveled, and the twenty-four armed soldiers crept from the raft into the ruins of the razed buildings. They stumbled, fell and cursed softly in the darkness as they felt their way in the direction of the cathedral. A sergeant went ahead and banged on the great metal-studded oak doors. A sentry inside recognized him, and one of the great doors opened a few inches to admit him. A minute later the door opened again and the sergeant called to his men. They slipped inside without being noticed by the Guatemalans.

Thornton anchored his raft out of sight of Granada and returned to camp to await the dawn. That was when he would get the signal. If Solange was safe and in the cathedral, three shots exactly one minute apart would be fired in the last darkness before dawn, before the sounds would be drowned out by other weapons in combat. If her whereabouts were unknown, two shots spaced two minutes apart. If she were dead, four shots half a minute apart. Thornton thought he saw daylight breaking over the hills to the east. He would soon know.

With just a few gray streaks in the lower sky and silence all around, except for the cry of an occasional coyote or other night animal, a shot rang out. From the direction of the cathedral. With a shaking hand, Thornton pulled out his watch but could not see its face. He tried to count instead. His heart was thumping so hard, he was not sure whether he was counting too fast or too slow.

At the count of thirty, if he heard a second shot, she would be dead. He counted to thirty. Nothing. Had he been counting too fast?

At the count of fifty, the second shot rang out. Was that the second shot at thirty seconds, meaning Solange was dead, or was it the second shot at sixty seconds, meaning she was alive and well in the cathedral?

He tried to count to the third shot, but he found he could not remember the numbers after eleven. When he finally did remember, he had lost track of how long he had paused in his counting. He walked up and down like a beast in a cage. The third shot sounded. That must have been one minute! She was all right.

Or had the three shots been separated by only half a minute which just seemed like a minute to him? The fourth shot would tell. He waited.

A sergeant checking his men on watch found him still standing there a half hour later.

They ferried in another twenty-four armed men to the cathedral that night. On the third night they made a double trip, with forty-eight men. That gave them ninety-six men plus fifteen to twenty inside the cathedral.

Harry passed on Walker's orders to the last group of men that entered the cathedral. At one the next afternoon, the hottest hour of the day, when all the townspeople would be indoors taking their siesta, and the Guatemalans would be recovering from a heavy midday meal and feel least like fighting, they were to rush from the cathedral, take over the streets as they went, and head for the northwest side of the city. There they would attack the defenders from behind while Walker attacked from in front. Harry stressed to them that the success of the maneuver depended on their timing, silence and speed.

At one the next afternoon, the sun was so hot that even the lizards did not come out on the stones. Walker's men had surreptitiously fixed bayonets to their rifles, but moved about as little as possible so as not to attract special notice on the part of the enemy.

With a suddenness that surprised even Walker's men outside the city, their comrades appeared behind the defensive positions and started shooting the Guatemalans in the back. Then the men inside charged at the survivors with their bayonets. A great roar sounded as Walker's entire force surged forward.

Thornton had seen the savagery of hand-to-hand combat before, but this surpassed anything he had thought possible in viciousness and butchery. His own men, whom he worked with every day and knew well, were transformed into raging beasts who slit bellies open with their bayonets, gouged out eyes with their thumbs, made necklaces of sliced off ears, threw severed genitals at each other in savage fun, did everything but drink the blood of the slaughtered Guatemalans.

Walker was upset because no one was sure which of the carcasses was that of General Estrada. He had hoped to put his head on a spike for display in Leon.

33

THORNTON AND Solange's house had not been occupied or looted by the Guatemalan soldiers, as had many others. At first the couple were just wordlessly grateful to find each other alive and unharmed. Solange was a soldier's daughter, and so was accustomed to hear of war, gallant fights and heroism, but this had been the first time she had actually seen a military engagement.

She was horrified. "I just can't believe that men would let this happen over and and over again—just continue killing each other. What does William Walker want? Why is the President here?"

Thornton had no answers that made much sense. "That's why men must protect women from the world. Your sensibilities are too refined to withstand reality. Try to think about pleasant things, about flowers or cats, or perhaps new wallpaper."

"Why?" Solange demanded to know. "So that I won't notice what a mess you and other men are making of the world?"

Thornton grinned. "Something like that."

She threw her arms about him. "Darling, I'm sorry for blaming you. I know you are not happy about what is happening here any more than I am."

"How do you know that?"

"I can tell."

Neither had any immediate solution to their problem, and most of their conversations about what they were doing in Nicaragua were as inconclusive as this one. Then Thornton's duties grew heavier. He was made military commander of the capital city, responsible for its defense and for keeping all troops in that area in combat readiness.

Harry Drayberry was sent to the southern zone as general in command of the Transit and the city of Rivas. Walker now began to fortify his positions at selected points throughout the country. Militarily, Walker was strong and, as President of Nicaragua, he could do as he wished politically. But by this point, there was no question that his troops represented a foreign army of occupation and enjoyed almost no local support.

Walker's opponents, centered in Leon, were helpless and disorganized. Walker could have had them lined up against walls in the streets of Leon and shot in the heart, but this would have achieved nothing for him. The Legitimists and Liberals had laid aside all their old quarrels to unite in silent opposition to him— silent at least in Nicaragua, where they dared say little and do nothing, but loud in warning other Central American states that Walker had designs on their independence and loud in pleading with them to invade Nicaragua.

To the north, Honduras was told Walker would seize it to use as a base to conquer Guatemala. To the south, Costa Rica still lived with the shame of having had to beg Walker for peace after their previous invasion had ended in a disastrous cholera epidemic. Guns from Queen Victoria, guns from Emperor Napoleon III, guns from Commodore Cornelius Vanderbilt. . . . Supplies flowed to Walker's enemies.

Thornton put his troops to clearing some of the wartorn parts of Granada. He and Solange had spent many hours wandering the streets, and it seemed to Thornton now that every empty shell of a burned-out building was like a skull and put unanswerable questions to him.

One afternoon in the cathedral, standing in the central aisle before the high altar, where they had stood not long before as groom and bride, they looked about at the damage caused by the recent fighting. The damage was not as heavy as they had expected.

Many gouges in the stonework were not fresh enough to have been caused that recently. For the first time they noticed just how battered the venerable walls were. Thornton remarked on this to a priest who had come out to chat with them.

The priest smiled resignedly. "I don't know what caused most of the damage. Trouble over the years, I suppose, now all forgotten. Just like the recent trouble will be. Forgotten. Nothing learned."

Sad news came from Tennessee. Thornton's elder brother, Jeremiah, had been killed in a fall from his horse. His neck had been broken and he had died instantly. Thornton and his elder brother had been close. His death was like some kind of omen to Thornton. He had better watch out. He began to think about his brother constantly, especially while in the ruined areas of the city. He knew it was not the carnage itself at Granada which had upset him even before his brother's death, it was seeing it through Solange's eyes which made him aware of how hardened and unconcerned he was in danger of becoming. He felt it was not yet too late for him to become master of his own destiny, no matter how quiet or modest that turned ou to be, rather than allow William Walker's ambitions to control his future.

A week later a second letter came, this time a summons home. Since Thornton was now the heir to the family plantation, that was where his duty lay. The trouble over the Congressman's sons was now forgotten. They looked forward, the letter said, to meeting Solange.

She wanted to leave immediately. All Thornton had to do was resign his commission, pick up and go. There were some ships getting in and out of Nicaragua, as the receipt of his two letters showed.

"I can't go back without Harry," Thornton told her.

"Then you're going to be here for the next ten years!" Solange retorted. "General Drayberry"—she waved an imaginary saber—"is having the time of his life and refuses to go home to his mother or wash his face and hands before meals. How can you possibly feel responsible for someone like Harry?"

"Because I brought him here! And he wasn't like that when I brought him. I've changed too, I suppose."

"For the better."

"Perhaps. There's also the postscript my father added to my mother's second letter. How did it go? 'We are all proud of you here, my boy, and of gallant President Walker. Do your duty first by him, your mother and I will wait.' "

"Your father doesn't know what he's talking about."

Thornton laughed. "I'd like to hear you tell him that! My daddy is a fierce old Southerner. I know you. When he's around, you'll be Little Miss Demure."

"Maybe for the first few weeks. Then I'll work up enough nerve—"

"No you won't!"

Solange became serious. "How long will you stay here with Walker?"

Thornton's face became gloomy. "There's going to be major trouble soon. We all know that. We're just sitting here waiting for it. Once we beat our opponents decisively, I think I can persuade Harry to pay a short visit to Antrimville—he can be a visiting hero, he will never be able to resist that. We'll stay on there, you and I, and if Harry returns to Nicaragua after that, he does it on his own. I won't feel I'm responsible. Also, I won't feel I'm deserting Walker while the clouds loom on the horizon."

Solange knew that even if she argued with him now and persuaded him to leave in the face of what he felt he should do, she would be the ultimate loser since he would forever after resent her for it. In her opinion Thornton was mistaken, but she knew better than to question his code of honor.

Thornton sniffed the air. "What are you cooking?"

"Wait and see."

After an initial period of criticizing Central American food, Solange had taken to preparing it herself in her own way. They had an abundance of servants, but if they were not expecting people to dinner, Solange preferred to prepare it herself and to send the servants home.

As appetizers, they had quesadillas, which were cheese-stuffed tortillas. For the main course, she served grilled fish Yucatan-style, a big lake fish grilled over the open fire and smothered in a chili-and-garlic paste with lime wedges. Along with the fish came humitas, a puree of corn with tomatoes and raisins.

"Back in France, I never even imagined food like this existed."

Thornton smiled. "Wait till you get to Tennessee."

"I went to school in New Orleans. The food there was like it was in France, wonderful. Tennessee food can't be that different."

"You're in for a bit of a surprise."

They lingered over their wine as the candles burnt low on the table. The first candle sputtered out. Then the second. They talked and laughed, enjoying the pleasure of each other's company, as one by one the candles went out and darkness closed in around them. They held hands and watched the last flame flicker, almost become extinguished, send up a tongue of blue flame with a white tip, shrink back, almost die, make a tiny leap again. . . . Then they sat in the dark, watching a few glowing embers in the fireplace.

Thornton picked Solange up and carried her to their bedroom. He foraged his way through the darkness and finally felt the side of their bed against his knees. He laid her on top of the bed.

He opened a window shutter and the moon shone in on her bare shoulders above her low-cut dress. Her breasts were firm, high mounds. It was as if he had never seen her body before. He found himself feverish to run his hands over her smooth beauty, to feel her tremble as his lips brushed a sensitive place, to take his time with her and arouse her passion with a slow hand, to gain her ultimate response with a new, unleashed passion of her own.

But Solange did not want this.

"Take me!" she hissed.

He grabbed her. She struggled free on the bed and fiercely pushed him away.

"You see, you can't!" she taunted him. "You're not strong enough! You can't force me!"

Thornton leaped on her, pinning her down. She bucked beneath him as he half-unfastened, half-tore her dress from her body. He yelped when she bit his arm. He pulled off his own shirt and pants as he held her down on the bed with one hand, and then used the weight of his body to pin her beneath him.

She refused to part her legs. He forced his right knee between her knees, levering her soft limbs apart, and squeezed in his left knee also. His muscular legs gently forced her shapely thighs apart, revealing for him her secret garden.

He let his member slide in deep and slow right up to the hilt in her warm, soft depths.

She gasped, and her hips began to work in a circular motion. She squealed and trembled convulsively as he entered and withdrew and entered her in long, measured strokes. She wept. She scratched him. She bit. Cursed.

Arched her back. Thrashed. And shook from head to toe in repeated orgasms.

When she sobbed with exhaustion and begged for him to finish, Thornton delivered himself into the hot, dripping, honeyed vent of love.

34

CORNELIUS VANDERBILT glowered across his huge desk at his chief accountant and senior counsel. The lawyer's eyes blinked as alternatives and counterploys flashed rapidly across his mind as he desperately sought a rag of some color to divert this bull. The accountant quaked silently within himself and could not at that moment have added three and five. The engineer, the outdoors man who had been with them here before, seemed unaware as usual of the highly charged atmosphere generated by the irate millionaire. A fourth man sat beside him. He too seemed unperturbed.

Vanderbilt swiveled his gimlet eyes onto the engineer and scowled at him.

"That swine Walker has wiped out the Hondurans *and* the Guatamalans," Vanderbilt ground out. He spat accurately into a large ceramic spitoon some distance from his desk. "What have you got to say for yourself?"

"My tune remains unchanged, sir," the engineer replied.

"What tune? What the hell are you talking about?"

"Whatever else Walker may be, he is a competent military man. He has proved it a number of times, and he will prove it again if we allow it. I recommend an alliance with him. Short of that, you will have to mount an organized force against him. Either the U.S. Army or troops of your own. And Walker knows this."

Vanderbilt ignored what he had said. He pointed at the fourth man but spoke to the engineer. "Who's he?"

"The gentleman I mentioned in my memo to you, sir. You gave permission for him to be present."

"I did?" Vanderbilt looked the man over, as if regretting such easily granted permission. "Does he work for me?"

"No, sir," the engineer answered.

"What's his name?"

"The Honorable W.R.C. Webster."

The Honorable W.R.C. Webster remained impassive throughout this exchange—not looking away, not looking aloof, simply not responding.

"Honorable . . . ," Vanderbilt muttered the man's title. That must have been why he let the fellow in. Might have met some of his relatives on his European jaunt aboard the *North Star*. He addressed himself to Webster for the first time. "You the younger son of a lord or something?"

"An earl."

To hell with him, Vanderbilt thought. British snot. He's here for dollars, like anyone else. *My* dollars. He spat in the spitoon again, a perfect shot.

"Very well, Webster, you know I've got a problem. Spencer here"—he pointed to the engineer—"thinks you can help me. Make it brief."

Webster spoke in a languid Oxford tone. "I slip down the coast with a force of men, land on the Atlantic side of Costa Rica and take over the San Juan River."

"Just like that! I see," Vanderbilt said in a mocking tone. "Tell me, Webster, did you ever do anything like this before?"

"Many times, my dear fellow. Ask around. At times I wish I were a little less well known."

Vanderbilt snorted. "You're no better than this Walker fellow yourself. You're another—"

"Soldier of fortune," Webster cut in.

Vanderbilt paused. "You as good at it as Walker?"

"Probably not," Webster replied. "However, I don't think I need to be if we take advantage of Walker's present situation."

Vanderbilt made one of those sudden decisions that so amazed and terrified his accountants and lawyers. He jumped to his feet, strode around his desk and vigorously shook the hand of Webster, who had half-risen at his approach.

"I like a man who can realistically size up an opponent," Vanderbilt said. "Before you shoot Walker—you hear?—I want you to cut that little gigolo's balls off."

"Both of them," Webster replied debonairly.

Charles Frederick Henningsen was the son-in-law of a Southern senator and lived with his pretty wife, a genuine belle, in the best section of Atlanta, Georgia. Henningsen was well satisfied with his lot, which was not bad at all, he thought, for an English soldier of fortune in his early forties. He had seen better men end up a great deal worse off than himself. He was handsome and cosmopolitan. He was also bored as hell. After all, he had fought in Spain, Russia, Poland, Italy and Hungary. The only place so far he had found himself in dread of dying had been Atlanta, Georgia.

Naturally he had leaped at the opportunity when his father-in-law had mentioned the possibilities in Nicaragua. Much as he would miss being away from his own dear wife and the wonderful friends they had in Atlanta, he would make the sacrifice of leaving them all to deal with Walker himself.

"I know of Webster," Henningsen told the Senator. "Never met the fellow, but I've heard he's dangerous. When Walker hears Vanderbilt has hired him, it should make him more receptive to our offer."

"Remember," the senator told him, "we want that gesture from Walker. Tell him we know all about him."

Charles Henningsen leaned over the rail of the steamer as it crossed Lake Nicaragua. His crates of "machinery" lay safely stowed below. The swamps he had seen so far had not done much to cheer him, but this looked much better. He had always liked smoking volcanoes and such. Probably would have stayed in jolly old England if it had been a bit livelier, he thought. Funny how you leave one place because you're bored and end up in another which is even more boring than the place you left. The greater the changes, the more it all begins to look alike. A Frenchman said that. Typical. Damn, if he ever came to believe that, he'd shoot himself.

Walker was pleased with his visitor. The man was urbane, yet did not beat around the bush.

The President said, "You've brought five hundred minie rifles and two of the latest field howitzers. And thirty thousand dollars."

Henningsen nodded.

Walker continued, "In exchange for this, you want my loyalty to a confederacy of Southern states that will secede from the Union?"

"Correct."

"Words are easy in exchange for guns and dollars."

"We will ask you to make a gesture of goodwill, Mr. President."

"How would I stand in this confederacy?" Walker asked. "I am President of a sovereign republic already."

"The Senator and his associates foresee the Central American Confederacy, composed of Nicaragua, Honduras, Guatemala, El Salvador, Costa Rica and Panama. This confederacy would be loosely allied with the confederacy in the South. I assume you would be President down here."

Walker seemed skeptical.

Byron Cole added his piece. "Indeed, I have discussed the possibility of such a confederation of Central American states by messenger with associates in New Orleans. If the break comes with the Yankees and we have an independent South, we could prove a valuable ally to them.

"You have no treaties or agreements for me to sign?" Walker asked Henningsen.

Henningsen shrugged. "Why bother? Anything we agree to do together will be to our mutual benefit. There is one gesture of goodwill—"

"Five hundred rifles, two artillery pieces, thirty thousand dollars . . . ," Walker mused.

Henningsen tried another tack. "Some people in Washington raised questions about you, on a personal level, sir."

Walker bristled but said nothing.

Henningsen resumed. "It seems that as a journalist in New Orleans and again in San Francisco you published articles supporting the Abolitionist cause."

"I can't say anything for New Orleans," Cole butted in, "but as you know I was publisher of the journal in San Francisco, I can assure you that although those articles appeared over William Walker's name, he did not write them. It's a common journalistic practice that when the journalist whose byline the column bears is not available, a junior writes the column for that day. Some of these young men have an ax to grind. I'm sure the same happened in New Orleans."

Henningsen waited a moment for Walker to speak without looking at him directly. When Walker remained silent, Henningsen said smoothly, "I know the individuals concerned in Washington will be extremely relieved to hear this. The Senator, I might add, never doubted you for a moment, Mr. President."

Walker remained silent.

"Nicaragua abolished slavery thirty years ago," Henningsen said. "As President of Nicaragua, Mr. Walker, you could restore slavery in this country with paper, pen and ink. It need not go beyond that. Make this political gesture and announce your support for the South against the North, and a collection across the Southern states will be made for you. It will net at least half a million dollars."

Cole audibly whistled.

Walker's gray eyes were intense and still. He calmly studied the man opposite him. He finally asked, "Will you return with my answer, Mr. Henningsen?"

"If something could be found for me here, I would gladly stay. You know I am a soldier, like yourself. But this would be a personal thing—it would come as a bit of a surprise to the Senator."

"And also to his daughter, your wife, I would imagine," Walker added drily. "I'm ten years younger than you, yet I don't mind tell you I already dread the day of being put out to pasture."

Henningsen grimaced. "Not having anything to do all day is not half as bad as having to sip tea with clergymen and watch where you put your feet when you walk in case you damage flowers."

Walker laughed. "I could never send you back to that, Mr. Henningsen. In fact, let our Southern friends see your joining the *Falange Americana* as an additional gesture of my goodwill to those already agreed upon." Walker stood and the two men warmly shook hands. "Welcome to Nicaragua, General Henningsen."

35

Sylvanus H. Spencer, the engineer who had sat with the accountant and the lawyer in Vanderbilt's office, shared one attitude with his boss—he felt he was being robbed of his personal stake in the Transit. Spencer had been on the project from the very beginning and knew every foot of the Transit. He had been on the original survey team on the San Juan River, between the Atlantic and Lake Nicaragua, and again on the Transit Road, between the lake and the Pacific. Spencer had seen the great business potential of the Transit and had invested his savings in Accessory Transit Company shares. He had persuaded his father to do likewise, and when the old man died, through his inheritance Spencer found himself to be a moderately large shareholder in the company. Indeed, Cornelius Vanderbilt had found it necessary to ask for his support in his fight to regain control of the company.

When Walker revoked the Transit Company's charter, the price of its shares plummeted on the New York Stock Exchange. Spencer saw his savings and inheritance turn to dust, plus the work and time he himself had put into the Transit. All because of one man. William Walker.

Sylvanus Spencer had not gone off the deep end at

this. He had sat quietly while Vanderbilt had allowed clerks and lawyers to pussyfoot around, whimper and sit on the fence, because he was secure in the knowledge that Vanderbilt's rage would not die down. With Walker's increasing success, Spencer had been the only one with courage enough to suggest to the Commodore that he strike a deal with this outrageous soldier of fortune. Such a notion offended Spencer as much as it did Vanderbilt, but it went without saying that Vanderbilt would come out on top of any deal that was made. Vanderbilt would not listen. That was all right with Spencer. If Cornelius was willing to pay to have Walker's testicles cut off, Spencer would gladly be there to sharpen and pass the knife.

Spencer had met Webster at a gambling house in New York City. They had nodded to each other at brothels, restaurants, sporting events. When special ships to ascend the San Juan River were being designed for the Transit Company, Spencer was called in to deliver survey data to the shipbuilders. Webster was one of the naval architects working on the project.

They were both men about town, but with a taste also for the wilderness, or at least the wild side of life. They despised fashion, overly good manners, and Victorian hypocrisy, although both of them, being of good family and being without question gentlemen, always dressed fashionably, had excellent manners and were openly and even charmingly hyprocritical.

Spencer was aware of Webster's frequent lengthy disappearances and also of the generous amounts of cash he had to spend. Through mutual friends, Spencer heard of Webster's exploits as a soldier of fortune, and how he used his English citizenship to ignore the restrictions placed on Americans by the Neutrality Act. Spencer never mentioned what he had heard to the young Englishman, any more than he ever voiced his doubts as to whether he was really the son of an earl.

When it seemed to Spencer that Vanderbilt was

finally ready to take some action, he had brought
Webster to him more as a goad than as a serious prospect. He had hoped that the Commodore might begin
to think along those lines, of finding someone to over-
throw Walker and retrieve the Transit.

Millionaires have a way of acting unpredictably;
Vanderbilt had proved that. The magnate had simply
taken a liking to Webster—with the result that a few
weeks later Sylvanus Spencer sat on the bank of the
San Carlos River in Costa Rica, listening to the Honorable W.R.C. Webster explain to a local *generalissimo*
how they were going to invade Nicaragua.

Spencer grinned with pleasure, opened his pocket
knife, and began to sharpen its blade on a stone beside
him.

The Costa Rican military officer was being pleasant.
"I agree, Señor Vanderbilt has shown us his generosity
and commitment by his previous gifts of weapons to
us. Certainly three thousand new minie rifles will
change our military strength considerably.

Webster nodded. "You told the President that Vanderbilt has authorized me to spend up to a hundred
thousand U.S. dollars if I can get things going here in
less than two weeks?"

"Yes, yes. If you can pay the army, you start in two
days."

"I want to take a thousand men down this river on
rafts," Webster told him.

The Costa Rican officer said nothing. A loco Yanqui
had taken over Nicaragua to the north of him, and
now he had another of his own to deal with here. A
thousand men on rafts down a river!

"And I want many times that number ready in a
few weeks to invade the north."

"*Si, señor.*"

But if the Costa Ricans for the most part were
openly pessimistic about Webster as a leader, Vanderbilt's dollars and new guns combined with their own

desire for revenge for their previous humiliating effort
to invade Nicaragua to make them willing, industrious
and reliable.

The rafts were built in a few days. The soldiers took
their supplies and weapons, and poled out into the
currents of the San Carlos River, which flowed north
into the San Juan River, which in turn was the first
leg of the Transit.

The San Juan River formed the border between
Costa Rica and Nicaragua, and Walker's soldiers defended its northern bank in scattered small forts. As
soon as Webster's scouts located a fort, he pulled the
rafts to shore before they were sighted, and sent a
raiding party downstream along the river bank. His
men had two orders—don't destroy the forts because
they would need them, and take no prisoners so there
would be no warning to the next fort downstream.

There was little resistance. Webster left a detail of
Costa Ricans in each fort to guard the river as he
made his bloody progress toward the sea.

The rafts crowded with men floated down into the
Atlantic port of Greytown one evening just before
dark. Those who saw them from the embankments
could not make out their uniforms or see their weapons
in the fading light. No one spread the alarm.

The armed men climbed up on the wharves and
walked through the streets of the town casually to the
army barracks. The Nicaraguan soldiers there said they
were pleased to see the Costa Ricans and laid down
their arms. Webster had four Americans they caught
in uniform put before the firing squad. The other fifteen
Americans in Greytown who belonged to Walker's
forces claimed to be civilian employees of the Transit
Company. The townspeople happened to like them, so
no one gave them away.

36

IT WAS New Year's Day of 1857, but no one at William Walker's headquarters in Granada was celebrating.

"I never even knew this Webster existed while he was floating down the San Juan River," Harry Drayberry told Walker. "He had taken Greytown before I knew we had an invasion on our hands."

"What happened to our spies in Costa Rica?"

"Bought with Vanderbilt dollars."

"Losing the San Juan River seals us off from all supplies," Byron Cole remarked mournfully.

"Whatever is on its way from New Orleans is headed for Greytown," Henningsen told them. "They'll capture the ships. Even if we managed to get word to the vessels, and they pulled in elsewhere along the coast, we could never get supplies through the damn swamps —not to mention the Indians and their English guns."

"What about down the Pacific from California?" Harry asked.

Cole laughed mirthlessly. "Supplies are more valuable than gold in California. Certainly scarcer."

"We need a military victory, Drayberrry," Walker said quietly.

"Sir, the enemy refuses to engage with us," Harry said. "That's why I'm here. So far as I know, this

Webster and an engineer who surveyed the original Transit and knows every hill and valley—his name is Spencer—they came right back after taking Greytown and brought an invading force across the border as far as the Transit Road. When we attack them, they withdraw. If we follow them, the others on our flanks close in and try to encircle us. So we withdraw, and the ones we drove back advance again as far as the Transit Road. They're playing a game."

Walker nodded. "The Hondurans have flooded arms into the area around Leon. A lot of exiles have returned. Even Gonzalez is rumored to be back. Webster is trying to give them time to get organized."

Cole remarked, "He'll be there for the next year then."

The men laughed, lightening the tension.

"You have to get them to fight you," Walker said emphatically to Harry. "You'd cut them to pieces. That would change the attitude of the rest. They'd all go home with their tails between their legs, no matter what new toys Vanderbilt has given them."

Henningsen nodded. "We must not let them gain confidence."

"What do you want me to do?" Harry demanded in frustration. "They're scattered everywhere, far outnumbering us, and they run away when we come near. If I attack Costa Rica, they'll cut me off from the rear. It's like trying to catch mosquitoes with your bare hands. What do you want me to do?"

A silence followed.

Walker spoke finally. "Give them Rivas."

"What?" Harry was shocked.

"It would gather them into one place," Walker went on. "Withdraw your forces from Rivas. Retreat to the north. When they take the town, counterattack. You'll have a battle on your hands."

Harry nodded his head doubtfully. "I'll try it. Can I have some more men?"

Walker said, "I'll send you your old sidekick Mc-Clintock and his company."

Harry brightened. "He'll make a big difference. As soon as the Costa Ricans occupy Rivas, McClintock can set out from Granada. I'll talk to him today before I leave."

"That leaves Petrie, Von Satzner and you," Walker said to Henningsen, "to take care of Leon and the northern approaches."

"I estimate our total forces at a thousand men," Henningsen told Walker.

Harry listened. At first he had not liked the Englishman out of jealousy at his being made a general too. But he soon realized what a valuable addition the man was. He had even more battle experience than Von Satzner. Also, he was older than William Walker and not afraid to present his views to him. And Walker heeded him.

Henningsen went on, "I estimate the total opposing forces, all factions combined, at six thousand. They outnumber us six to one."

Walker's gray eyes were no longer friendly. They settled like those of an eagle on Henningsen. "So?" The voice was cold. "I took Nicaragua with sixty men."

Thornton McClintock was delighted to see his old friend Harry Drayberry as a surprise guest for their New Year's Day dinner, even if he had to leave early to get back to his troops. Solange had cooked some kind of large game bird, which they pretended was a turkey.

After the meal, Harry took Thornton to one side. "When I visit you two I might as well be a thousand miles from all this war. It's like being back home in Tennessee."

"Maybe we'll visit there soon," Thornton tested him.

Harry laughed. He dismissed Thornton's suggestion without even considering it and relayed Walker's orders for Thornton and his company to join him at Rivas.

"Sorry, Thornton, but I need you down there. You know, I saw Walker really worried today for the first time ever. When you come, maybe you should bring Solange with you rather than leaving her behind in Granada."

Thornton was startled. "I had no idea things were that bad. Walker would never allow me to bring her."

"Not if you tell him."

Harry withdrew his troops some distance from the Transit Road. A wave of Costa Ricans crept northward after him. When he stopped, so did they. He retreated to Rivas, and then ordered the evacuation of that town. His men backed down farther to the north. The Costa Ricans swept into Rivas, victorious. But instead of days of celebration and looting, as would be expected, Harry's spies informed him that the Costa Ricans were suspicious and staying on guard.

At least Harry had a number of them in one place. He reckoned there were about fifteen hundred of them in Rivas. He had less than five hundred men, and when Thornton arrived he would have a hundred more. Harry decided not to wait for him. The fifteen hundred in Rivas were not going to find it as easy to get away confined in the narrow streets of the town as they had in the open country.

Harry counterattacked. He had expected a complete rout. Instead he found that fighting the Costa Ricans was very different from this battle with the Hondurans. They were highly disciplined and stuck to their battle tactics by pinning his men down with a rearguard action while their major force withdrew from the town. They were giving Rivas back to him!

Harry realized suddenly that if they wanted to hold Rivas, he could not have recaptured it from them. Yet they apparently felt their strategy of avoiding a full-scale battle was more important than scoring a territorial gain.

Harry did not mince words in his report to Walker. The Costa Ricans were toying with him, and now rested in the hills south of Rivas, watching. Once they started a serious northerly advance with their thousands of men, he would fight them to his last man, but Walker should know the result was a foregone conclusion.

Harry had never communicated with Walker in such straightforward terms before. To hell with the man's pride, and with mine, he thought, now is the time to be realistic. Yet Harry could not help feeling he was letting his side down.

Thornton and his company arrived in Rivas. He had brought Solange with him. The enemy, south of the city, grew more insolently uncaring every day. They openly traded with farmers for fresh food almost within a rifle shot of the city's defenses. They ate and drank at tables outside inns on the outskirts of Rivas, in full view of the defenders. Such confidence and their numerical superiority began to take a toll on the morale of Harry's men. For the first time, the *Falange Americana* was beginning to lose its feeling of invincibility. Harry had not heard a word from Walker in Granada. He had to do something.

Harry formed a small group of expert horsemen and galloped out with them in a charge upon enemy strollers south of the city. They shot them with pistols, hacked them with sabers, trampled them beneath their horses' hooves, dragged them at the end of a rope around an ankle until coated in blood and dust, and then they returned to Rivas to the cheers of their fellow soldiers and watched with satisfaction as the Costa Ricans retrieved their dead.

This little display helped encourage the men and release some of Harry's own frustration. But the enemy was back again the next day. Harry decided on another punitive expedition.

"It's a trap," Thornton warned him.

"If I don't step into it," Harry responded, "they will have outbluffed us. I'm going to call them on their bet."

"You were always a bad poker player, Harry."

"This isn't poker, McClintock," Harry laughed and called his horsemen together. "If anything happens to me, you're in charge, Thornton. Although this command is not much of a gift to make to a friend."

With a series of whoops the horsemen rode through the city streets, cheered on by answering yells.

They bore down on some Costa Ricans eating outside an inn, when all at once bullets began to whistle through the air about them. In an instant Harry saw his mistake, how he had let impatience and frustration affect his judgment. The riflemen had crept into place during the night and remained hidden until the bait was taken.

"Back to Rivas!" Harry yelled and wheeled his horse about to lead his men out of the trap.

Some of his riders had already fallen. Before Harry could take stock of the situation, his horse was shot out from under him. He jumped clear of the animal before its side could pin his leg to the ground and joined three other of his men who had been similarly dismounted. Another half dozen lay sprawled in death. The rest of the group was galloping back to Rivas in a cloud of dust, following his orders.

The Costa Rican riflemen rose from behind rocks and out of gullies to encircle the four Americans. The circle grew tighter.

The four had only pistols and sabers.

"Let's go down fighting, men," Harry called out.

"We're with you all the way, General," one of the men shouted back as they faced the Costa Ricans.

Harry whooped and yelled, waving his saber, "Let's cut this pigmeat into bite-sized pieces!"

Sylvanus Spencer could hardly believe his ears and eyes. A Tennessee accent! One of his men had called him "General," and he had a gold star on his uniform! In his excitement Spencer forgot that William Walker was barely five feet tall and had fair hair, while Harry Drayberry was over six feet and had dark hair.

"Take the General alive," Spencer ordered the Costa Rican soldiers. "Shoot the other three."

The soldiers raised their rifles and shot the men down. Harry Drayberry stood untouched among his three dead companions. He could scarcely believe it. He clutched his saber and advanced alone on the enemy.

The Costa Rican soldiers mobbed him before he could seriously wound any of them. They held him to the ground while Spencer approached.

"This gives me great pleasure, General," Spencer told the restrained man.

"What does?" Harry snarled.

"This." Spencer held up the open blade of his pocket knife.

He knelt and sliced open Harry's pants, seized his testicles in his left hand, twisted them, reached underneath with the blade as Harry tried to kick and wrench himself away, and cut upward with savage strokes of the knife until the testicles came away in his blood-covered fingers.

Harry screamed once and lost consciousness from pain.

"Shoot him," Spencer said. "We don't want him living on, looking for revenge." He held the testicles up for the Costa Ricans to see. "I'll pickle these in whisky and bring them back to New York for Mr. Vanderbilt."

37

CORNELIUS VANDERBILT sent a message to Washington to tell the President-elect he would see him on Wednesday—lunch would be a pleasure if the President-elect's schedule permitted. The President-elect's schedule was adjusted so that it did. The Democrats, who were in favor of letting slavery extend wherever it found its way by the voice of the people, had nominated James Buchanan of Pennsylvania. He had won in a close three-man race and would be inaugurated on March 4, 1857, in five weeks' time. Vanderbilt's private railroad car was prepared for the trip.

The two men consumed barley soup, fried flounder, roast mallard duck, braised lamb chops, potatoes, cabbage, baked apple and cream, two bottles of white wine, two bottles of red, a bottle of port and a pot of coffee. The magnate and the lawyer-diplomat soon to be President got along well. Vanderbilt was pleased to note the man had not forgotten who had contributed to his campaign. Buchanan, at sixty-seven, three years older than Vanderbilt, and the only bachelor ever elected U.S. president, was not the kind of man to tolerate the antics of a scamp in the tropics.

* * *

Thornton McClintock collected the body of his friend under a white flag and buried him with full military honors in the cathedral in Rivas. Neither Walker nor anyone else from Granada appeared for the funeral. No wreaths came, no messages of regret. The men Thornton sent to Granada returned and swore to him they had delivered his dispatches to headquarters and had been sent away without a reply. Meanwhile the enemy continued to build up south of Rivas and seemed to be in a buoyant mood. Spies brought Thornton the reason why. The Costa Ricans believed they had killed William Walker and that nothing could stop them now. Rumors spread in Rivas itself. Thornton sent another message to Granada, duplicated in the hands of several messengers.

President William Walker:
The Costa Ricans are massing in unprecedented numbers below Rivas. Unless I hear otherwise from you, I will continue in command and hold Rivas against the enemy to the last drop of our blood. The hostile forces believe that the mutilated body in general's uniform was that of the President of the Republic, although it was that of my dear friend General Harry Drayberry. A variant of this story is presently gaining credence among your own men here in Rivas—that you were killed in action to the north. They feel the silence from headquarters substantiates this story and grow more dispirited by the day. Certainly a greeting from the President of the Republic would instantly banish this hollow tale and bring smiles to the faces of gallant men.

Yours, Col. Thornton McClintock

There was no reply. News filtered through of increasing threats from the north. Supposedly, Honduran, Guatemalan and Salvadoran troops, all armed by Vanderbilt, had crossed the border into Nicaragua and joined with Nicaraguan rebels centered about Leon.

From what Thornton could figure out, it seemed as if their enemies to the north and south of them were poised to attack, but suffered a failure of nerve. That was why they had wanted to believe William Walker was dead. Then they would have had the courage to attack.

"Try not to worry," Thornton comforted Solange. "I'm probably being more miserable than necessary because of Harry's death. I just can't get it out of my head that I brought him here."

"That's nonsense," Solange said. "Harry himself told me about the row which caused the duel with the midshipmen. If either of you were at fault, he was more than you."

At least he had her here with him. That had been a wise move—on Harry's advice, a parting gift.

More news came daily of unresolved skirmishes in the north. Finally a message came from headquarters that Walker and his forces were on their way to "relieve" him at Rivas. It sounded better that way, Thornton supposed, than admitting Granada was being abandoned. Thornton also got orders to spend whatever available funds he had on food purchases locally, where possible depriving the Costa Ricans of supplies. When his money ran out, which it would in a single day of large-scale buying, he was to go farther afield and "requisition" anything of the slightest possible value to Walker's forces in Rivas.

Thornton spent the next three days, with groups of his soldiers, literally stealing from farmers. This activity did nothing to improve his mood. He tried to imagine his father's and his own reactions if soldiers had tried to seize the produce of their plantation in Tennessee, but it was unimaginable that such a thing could take place there. Thornton, because he felt guilt at what he was doing, did less than a thorough job, always allowing the farmer to conceal a portion of his harvest and stock for his family's use.

This mattered little in the end since Walker's first act on arrival was to order a scorched earth policy around Rivas. Large numbers of troops seized what they could and burned or otherwise destroyed anything that might be of use in sustaining the enemy. This ring of scorched earth stretched out for six miles on all sides of Rivas except the southern part occupied heavily by the Costa Ricans, which had already been well picked over.

Walker then ordered the men to further strengthen the city's fortifications. Anyone who was not a resident of the town or a member of Walker's forces was expelled as an unnecessary mouth to feed. Walker ignored Cole's suggestion that they turn out many of the townspeople also, particularly young children, whom he saw as a useless burden.

Walker prepared for a long siege. What he hoped would come at the end of it, no one dared ask. No one had alternative suggestions to make. There was nowhere to run. As the enemy forces drew in on all sides on the burnt-over land to encircle the city with their camps, the last flow of information came from the outside.

Apparently this was to be it. All the Central American states had contributed to the siege in a united effort to rid themselves of the Yanqui in Nicaragua. If the Latin Americans lost here, they knew it could be a turning point in history.

One of the last spies coming in from the outside told a story that enraged Thornton. He said that when the American called Spencer who had castrated Harry Drayberry had heard they had cut the wrong general, he pulled the testicles from the whisky in which they had been preserved and fed them to a starving dog. The dog's empty stomach rejected the alcohol-soaked flesh and the dog regurgitated its grisly meal.

At that moment Thornton McClintock emerged from being an unwilling soldier in a war that no longer involved him and changed into a Tennessee fighting man, mad as hell and mean as a Cumberland polecat.

38

THE BEGINNING of February 1857 saw the siege of Rivas fully under way. Food and water were strictly rationed, although there was an unusual abundance of both because of the preparations. But the wet season was five months away, and the hot, dry spring was just beginning.

Walker instituted daily staff meetings, and the troops were drilled and inspected every day. Discipline was strict. This was the first contact most of the men ever had with army life in this sense. Before this, they had always been more or less free to live, eat and dress as they pleased. Many of the men were mavericks, and barracks life did not suit them. Yet there was little trouble, since every man could clearly see the necessities of the situation.

Thornton appreciated all the more the luxury of being able to return to the privacy of the small apartment he and Solange occupied overlooking the Grand Plaza. They often sat on their small second-floor balcony watching the sun set and the activity in the square below. The Americans had long since become thoroughly acclimatized and adapted to local ways. They took their evening walk and greeted friends as a brass band played on the bandstand in the plaza. Dinner was

not eaten until ten or eleven at night, and usually involved a large number of people.

The livelier spirits gathered in certain restaurants.
There were skittles, bowls, concerts, dances. . . . Rivas
had not seen livelier days and nights in living memory.
Walker was rarely seen in public. Cole or Henningsen
could sometimes persuade him to visit a restaurant,
and on two occasions he dined at Thornton's apartment, but mostly the President spent his evenings and
nights in solitude.

The carnival atmosphere lasted about a month in
the besieged city. Although food and water had been
strictly rationed, there had been no shortage of either
and no complaints. At the beginning of March, wine
ran out. Already at the restaurants the meat content
of the dishes was obviously shrinking and the rice and
bean levels rising. But there was still enough food and
water for everyone.

It cheered the besieged, soldiers and townspeople
alike, that the besiegers were having a much rougher
time of it. The encampments ringed about the city
were tattered and littered with offal in which dogs had
once roamed. Now dogs were scarce, having been eaten
by the soldiers, and there were no scavengers to clear
the stinking garbage among which the men lived.

On several occasions each day the attackers mounted
an offensive, more to keep their spirits up than to make
any progress. On orders from Walker, all such displays
of hostility were ignored by the defenders unless a
man presented himself within range as a clear target.
Every bullet fired from Rivas was to count.

Fights broke out among the attackers. Scuffles involving as many as fifty men and numerous pistol
shots were seen by the defenders. Walker paid close
attention to these stories and wanted to know each
time whether the factions fighting had been different
nationalities, Hondurans against Guatemalans, say, or
within one nationality.

Thornton told Solange, "I think Walker hopes that if we leave them out there long enough in the sun, half-starved and making no progress against us, they will turn on each other."

"Do you think they will?"

Thornton smiled. "That's what sieges are all about. To see who can hold out the longest."

"Do you think they can hold out another month?"

"I suppose so," Thornton answered. "Why?"

"I was at the storehouses today to get food. The meat is all gone. All they have is rice and beans. In a week the rice will be gone. Several of them said that in a month there will be nothing left to eat."

Thornton said, "Come on, you know how these old women moan and see the worst side of everything—"

"These were sergeants in the *Falange Americana*. And they weren't telling me for my information. They were discussing it among themselves, and I overheard."

"Oh."

The rice ran out a week later. By now the festive atmosphere that had once cheered the besieged city was only a memory. Solange claimed there was one thing that could be said for Nicaragua—it had about forty different kinds of beans. She prepared different varieties in every way she could think of, so that with a bit of imagination their diet of beans and water was nourishing and even entertaining as Solange met the challenge of creating diversity out of dried beans and water she had to boil before it could be drunk.

People who had never liked beans grew fond of them, for hunger loomed not far down the road. Byron Cole had lost thirty pounds since the start of the siege and claimed to his friends that he felt better now than he had in the last twenty years.

The portion of beans on each person's plate grew smaller. People were asked to stay out of the sun so they would not grow thirsty and need water. No one cared anymore about having different varieties of beans

or feared they might get bored with their unchanging
fare—this was food! People were hungry all the time
now, but no one in Rivas starved.

Conditions among the besiegers encircling the city
seemed no better, and they lacked the unifying command and discipline of the troops inside. The varying
nationalities and cliques within nationalities had broken
off into their own mutually hostile camps. Minor
skirmishes between them were commonplace. However,
there was no sign of the siege being lifted, or even of
the dissension weakening it.

One morning in late March at the officers' meeting
in Walker's headquarters in Rivas, the President announced, "The day after tomorrow we go on iron
rations. One plateful of beans per day per person. Unless we strike it lucky tomorrow."

The officers exchanged puzzled looks.

"Tomorrow we break out."

Walker said it as casually as someone suggesting an
afternoon outing. A murmur of voices rose in amazement, although it was not really a surprise. Everyone
had been waiting for Walker to come up with the unexpected—some daring maneuver to confound the
enemy.

Walker indicated the map of the city on the wall.
"We break out here and here and here tomorrow
morning at eleven."

After a moment of silence, Henningsen was first on
his feet. "With all due respect, sir, that sector is where
the enemy is most heavily positioned—the Costa Ricans
are there and they seem to be in the best shape of all."

"Which is precisely why we must attack them rather
than a weak sector. While we are occupied in breaking
through a weak place, the strong Costa Ricans would
invade the city behind our backs as well as attack on
our flanks."

"Why at eleven in the morning, sir?" another officer
asked. "It seems an odd hour."

"I agree," Walker answered. "That's what makes it an ideal hour."

That was the end of the discussion. Thereafter Walker instructed his officers in detail as to who was responsible for what. The next morning they would assemble the main body of troops in the Grand Plaza, out of sight of the enemy. They would then double the defenses all round their perimeter. After that, at eleven, they would break out against the enemy at three points. Any man who broke his silence about this plan before dawn the next day would be shot.

Thornton waited till dawn before telling Solange.

"Walker is mad!" she cried. "I've always known it. Now you have proof of it yourself."

"We have to do something, Solange. Maybe this will break the siege."

"Let the others do it then," she said. "I don't want you throwing away your life."

"You married a soldier."

She pouted. "I should have known better."

They embraced each other beneath the sheets in the first light of morning. She pulled him on top of her and lifted her nightdress above her hips. He entered her and drove his shaft home blindly and deeply within her until he felt his surge and then relief.

She kissed him, wriggled out from beneath him and whispered in his ear, "I've got to cook your beans before you leave."

The venom lingering in Thornton's system since Harry's death came to the surface as they prepared to break out against the Costa Ricans. He no longer cared whether he survived or not so long as he took vengeance, raised bedlam, wreaked bloody havoc. . . . His men saw the change in him, and even the perpetual whiners in his outfit, accustomed to taking advantage of his usual good nature, were silent this morning as

Thornton, grim and gray-faced, dourly checked men and equipment.

The sun, almost directly overhead, shone down on the rock-strewn earth and blackened, twisted trunks of small trees. A sparse groundcover of green plants had sprung up since the fires set by Walker to deprive his attackers of food and cover.

Three streams of men burst from the besieged city and ran across the open ground toward the enemy. Shots rang out. Men fell. The three streams spread into a great onrushing wave of men, bayonets fixed to their rifles, who shot and then fought hand to hand against their opponents. Most of the Costa Ricans had to pause to fix bayonets to their rifles, and many died from a thrust of cold steel before they could complete the task.

The encampments were thrown into confusion. Canvas blazed, horses bolted, men dropped their weapons and fled. . . . Von Satzner led his Lancer Squadron on a special mission—they were cavalrymen whose horses had long since been eaten. In short time the Prussian officer rode at the head of a band of mounted men. They drove through the enemy encampments ahead of Walker's infantry and cut down every living thing in their path with either their sabers on their horses' steel shoes.

The screams of men being struck by blades, the cries and moans of the fallen wounded, black smoke and orange flames from the burning tents, the sightless eyes of the discarded dead. . . . Thornton McClintock pressed on regardless. He rode his captured horse bareback ahead of his men, waving them onward and pointing the best way for them to advance. After a while he was joined by another rider. William Walker.

Walker as usual ignored flying bullets, flames and fighting men. He lived in a world of his own. While Thornton yelled and gestured to his men to increase their endeavors and not allow their courage to drop, Walker simply rode up and down in the most dangerous zones as if exercising his horse on a Sunday afternoon. If this diminutive, fierce man had the courage to do it, the great hulking ex-miners and ex-outlaws who composed his army were not going to be outdone. They slew all before them.

Thornton no longer cared whether Walker approved of what he was doing. His company forged ahead of the others in sheer, brutal crushing of all opposition and made for the village of San Jorge, which seemed to be the Costa Rican officers' headquarters and supply center. They could see the Costa Rican high command pulling out of the village in turmoil and panic at the unexpected sudden thrust forward of Thornton's company.

Thornton pointed and yelled, "That American! I want him alive!"

He cut off the retreat of the American and several Costa Ricans with his horse and saber, ducking two pistol bullets fired almost pointblank. A dozen of his men came rushing up on foot and killed the Costa Rican officers with bayonet thrusts.

Thornton dismounted and dragged the American into the courtyard of a building. He pushed the man against a wall and searched him. The man carried no weapons except for a long-bladed pocket knife. Papers in his pockets identified him as Sylvanus H. Spencer.

"I've been looking for you," Thornton told him, with catch of rage in his voice. He held up the pocket knife. "You used this on my friend, remember?"

Spencer grew very pale. "I thought he was William Walker. I swear it."

Thornton opened the blade and approached the man. "Do unto others as they do unto you, or however it goes."

"You can't—no! You wouldn't—"

Thornton stopped and handed him the knife, handle first. "You're right. I wouldn't."

Spencer took the knife warily, and Thornton stepped

back quickly and drew his own bowie knife. He gestured for his men to cut off the exits from the courtyard and moved in to stalk his opponent.

Spencer had time to look fearfully about him once as the buildings on all sides caught fire as Walker's men went about leveling the village of San Jorge. Then Thornton was upon him with a powerful thrust of the bowie which just missed his right arm.

Spencer drove his blade at Thornton's left shoulder and the tempered steel eased through the cloth of his coat just above his shoulder blade.

The two men squared off and resumed stalking each other. They stooped forward, legs well apart for balance, arms swinging loosely in front of their bodies, knives grasped in the right hand with the blade held flat by the thumb.

They parried. Back and forth. Thornton charged. This time he did not make the expected thrust, but slashed at Spencer's face with his bowie. The blade opened a diagonal line across the man's forehead, nose and right cheek, from which the blood welled, brimmed and spilled downward.

The swing of his arm threw Thornton off-balance, and he took a painful stab in the right upper chest, near his armpit. The wound to Spencer's face checked the force behind his thrust, and the blade did not reach the muscles of Thornton's right shoulder or arm. The urge to kill pumped into Thornton's system and soon blotted out the pain.

Thornton glared at his adversary, at the blood streaming down Spencer's face, steadied his knife and came at him again. He threw a series of right stabs to the head and body, not full thrusts that require a follow-through, but a succession of lightning slashes, too fast to be warded off in which the blade of the bowie penetrated only an inch or so into the flesh, but enough to traumatize his opponent and render him almost immobile.

Thornton drew back the bowie as if about to aim a massive thrust to Spencer's heart, but at the last moment stepped to Spencer's right side, clutched the man's knife arm in his left hand, leaned across in front of him and drew the sharp edge of the bowie across Spencer's shirt front.

The long coils of Spencer's intestines spilled out on the ground at his feet. The man staggered forward, looking down in horror, and tripped on his own steaming viscera.

Thornton's battle-hardened troops, inured as they were to slaughter, turned away from the sight. Except for one. William Walker did not move a muscle, and his face remained carved in stone as his gray eyes flicked from Thornton back to the disemboweled man.

39

THEY WERE back inside the barricades of Rivas. Now
the besiegers maintained a much more watchful stance.
The sun beat down as always, Walker's troops had
been forced to withdraw into Rivas from the wrecked
village of San Jorge as the Costa Rican forces re-
grouped and joined with the Guatemalans in a determined assault on the city. As Walker's troops rushed
back to meet this threat, the assault was aborted and
their enemies were content to close the circle of siege
again.

Thornton had his men drive back flocks of sheep
and goats as they left San Jorge, and almost every
man carried a sack of beans or rice on his back. The
breakout, apart from raising morale, had provided Rivas
with a few weeks' provisions.

At a simple and dignified ceremony, William Walker
named Thornton McClintock a general and presented
him with the star. Thornton said to all there that it was
Harry Drayberry's star he was accepting, in memory of
his departed friend.

The fiery sun of April grew a little higher in the sky
each day and burned down that much hotter as the
siege went into its third month. The vultures soared in

the sky above them, their numbers increasing each week, as if slowly gathering for a terrible feast.

Solange said to Thornton one evening, "If we ever survive this, I think we'll be able to put up with anything together."

Thornton squeezed her to him. "You're a very special woman. I was thinking earlier today that, because of you, I probably suffer less than any man here in the siege of Rivas. Then again, I thought, I probably suffer more than any of them, because I have more to lose."

She smiled and kissed his cheek.

"I promise you this, Solange. After this, it's back to the peace and quiet of Tennessee."

Her eyes lit up. "You mean that, Thornton? Truly?"

"There's nothing in Nicaragua for me anymore. I've lost my friend and I've done my duty."

Rivas was back on a diet of beans again. Of more concern was the water supply. The water table had dropped beneath the city, and some of the wells on higher ground had already run dry. Soldiers were assigned to strictly enforce rationing.

In the middle of April the besiegers launched a surprise attack. It started shortly after dawn with waves of men charging the defenses of the city. They could not be driven back with rifle fire, they were so numerous. But the men knew what to do. They had been instructed and drilled by their generals, McClintock and Henningsen, in the use of shrapnel barrages. They had modified artillery pieces and even found some old cannons, which were all loaded with small, sharp pieces of scrap metal on top of a tamped charge of black powder. These pieces were kept ready to fire at all times by special crews.

The first wave of attackers swarmed over the barricades, only to die by pistol shots and to be impaled on the bayonets of the defenders. The second and third waves of attacking infantrymen were covering the open ground between their lines and the city defenses when the shrapnel barrage caught them.

The black-powder explosions sent sprays of white-hot metal pieces from the barrels, spreading forward in a cone of inescapable destruction. The irregularly shaped, high-velocity and high-temperature metal fragments shredded flesh, rent tissue from bone, tunneled into the skulls and torsos of those unfortunates caught in their path.

The ground became heaped with corpses, some men still alive and twitching in their final agonies among their dead comrades. Succeeding waves of infantrymen jumped over these grisly hurdles on their way to the barricades as the artillery was hurriedly reloaded with fresh powder and buckets of projectiles.

The attackers broke through and swept over the defenders at many points around the city. By this time the sound of shooting had alerted everyone in Rivas, and armed troops ran from their quarters and came face to face with the enemy on the city's cobbled streets. The invaders at first had the advantage of surprise and cut down the home forces before they could collect their wits and respond. But they were now on strange turf, and each one in the end released his life blood into the open sewers that ran on each side of every street.

Walker's men let off their second shrapnel barrage and added to the pile of mangled bodies on the bare ground near the barricades. Defenders emerged to charge forward using the heaps of bodies as cover for closer shots against enemy positions, only to retreat in time for their side to deliver the next broadside of hot metal fragments into vulnerable human flesh.

Attacks and counterattacks raged hour after hour. In the afternoon the assaults showed signs of lagging, but then officers in the rear ranks began shooting those unwilling to join in the charges.

Thornton had little to do in the area of actual defense. He had trained his men intensively, and those of other companies too. They managed better under their sergeants and corporals without his interference. Thornton had learned a lesson in leadership from William Walker. Throughout the hours of fighting, he exposed himself to equal risks as any of his men and devoted his efforts to bringing the wounded back to where they could receive attention. Considering the way he had been feeling about his role in Nicaragua recently, helping the wounded caused him less guilt than being an instigator of assaults as he had been at San Jorge. He did not forget that the chillingly effective and bloody defense tactics of the shrapnel barrage resulted from his training.

A lull in the attacks occurred in the late afternoon. An assigned number of men cooled down their weapons and cleaned them, while the rest maintained a sharp eye out for a surprise move. Half a dozen enemy troops waving a white flag emerged onto open ground and carried a few wounded away. Thornton sounded a ceasefire, and the sergeants picked up the order and relayed it to the ring around the city.

Not a single shot was fired by either side as all the men on both sides abandoned cover, retrieved their wounded and dead, sometimes coming within touching distance of one another. Men stood and stretched their cramped limbs, and the field kitchens passed plates of beans around. Tonight every man would remain at his post, though all knew that the battle was over.

Nothing happened during the night. Both sides lit huge bonfires in the open ground between them, but not even a single pistol shot was exchanged. The defenders of Rivas ate another meal of beans before dawn and dug in for a long day of renewed fighting. Nothing happened in the first hour of daylight. Or in the second. Or all that morning. There was no doubt about it. The battle was over. But not the siege. They still held their hot and dusty positions in a ring about Rivas.

President Walker called an officers' staff meeting for the early afternoon. As usual, he succeeded in surprising Thornton by his attitude. By accurate counts, as the enemy removed their dead under the white flag, almost three thousand bodies had been consumed by the scrap metal of the Rivas artillery and the minie bullets of the riflemen. This represented half the enemy fighting force—lost in a single day of combat! A cause of jubilation as far as Thornton and everyone else was concerned. Not so with Walker.

"Why did they attack?" the President asked in mournful rhetoric. "Because they know something we do not? Remember, we know nothing of recent developments outside."

"Maybe it's good news for us," Thornton declared, "and that's why they tried to overrun us."

"Possibly," Walker grated pessimistically, "but I am not a believer in good news coming galloping over the hill to our rescue."

Walker added to the crestfallen Thornton, "McClintock, I'd like to take this opportunity to say before everyone that you earned your general's star yesterday with the way those troops performed."

A round of applause was given to Thornton.

"And to Henningsen also," Walker continued. "He commanded the less glamorous lines of supply, communication and other services, which we of course know are equally important."

Another round of applause.

Walker's mood changed back to pessimism. "I'm worried. We did well, we all know that. But *why* did they attack? Even if it was stupidity, it was in response to something. Especially because of the insistent way they kept coming at us for ten hours. Why?"

The meeting ended, as Walker intended it should, on this extended note of interrogation. Those who had come to the meeting filled with self-congratulation left it with a needling question. Walker did not put it in so many words, but every man there knew what the reality was. They could only hold out in the siege for a few more weeks at most. Why should the enemy sacrifice half of his men to end the siege quickly? Walker had posed a good question.

The answer did not come until May 1. And then dramatically. For the rest of April, a period of intense heat and humidity and almost unbearable insect infestations, which left both sides with little pretense of any military efficiency, almost nothing happened.

The day after the attack the men looked out on the familiar bare ground around Rivas. The day after that they guarded the same ground. And the day after that. In the blistering heat. The familiar dust clung to their lips, and the roof of their mouths was parched as usual. After several hours the reflection of the bright sun from the ground gave them their normal headache. The mosquitoes sucked their blood. Gnats bit. Snakes and scorpions ignored the siege lines as always. The vultures soared overhead, haggard black outlines against the chillingly innocent blue sky. And the days passed as the sun baked the ground and all on it.

Thornton often stood on the defense perimeter. It seemed to him as if the recent slaughter might all have been a dream. On this bare land before his eyes, on which hardly anything grew or moved, on which even the lowest forms of life could barely scrabble for existence, he had seen dead men heaped on each other, men cut down screaming and their red blood soaking into the dry yellow sand . . . yet here there was nothing. It could never have been. Beneath the white flags . . . the men lifting the rigid bodies locked in various attitudes of death, a knee that could not be unbent, an outthrust arm that would never calmly return to its owner's side, open eyes whose surface now bore hundreds of insect eggs and did not blink as bluebottles crawled across the irises . . . this could not have been. There was nothing here but stones and sand. Not even a thorny cactus.

Like many of the men, Thornton had grown increasingly silent. He looked out daily from the barricades at nothing in particular, as an old salt searches the ocean with an unfocused gaze, knowing his eye will fix upon any detail that does not belong to the everyday picture.

On May 1 he saw the Stars and Stripes. There could be no mistake. Thornton did not have to question his own eyes. Other men saw it too. Nor was this an enemy trick. The self-important posture of the American military officer on foreign soil as he marched beneath Old Glory could not be duplicated by any foreigner! This was the real thing.

After dispatching an emergency messenger to Walker, Thornton welcomed Commander C. H. Davis of the U.S. Navy warship *St. Mary's* and his contingent of men into Rivas. Tables and chairs were set out in a shaded courtyard. Since there was nothing to offer them, except water and beans, and both of those too scarce to lavish in hospitality, Thornton maintained a stiff formality until the President arrived, even refusing an offer of tobacco, which he had run out of a month before and often thought of wistfully, along with the magnolia blossoms of Tennessee.

The American naval commander was polite but firm with William Walker. As he was with all military men, Walker was considerate with the commander. If a note of condescension could be detected in Walker's manner, Commander Davis justified it by continually stressing he had no power to bargain or make terms, only to put his name to a preconceived agreement. As the commander pointed out, considering Walker's present position, the terms offered were favorable from his viewpoint.

Walker read the statement. He made additions and deletions which did not substantially change the agreement, and Commander Davis agreed to all of them. While a fresh copy of the agreement was being written for them, Walker questioned the naval officer.

"There will be no prosecution?"

"Of course not," Davis said.

"What do you mean by 'of course'? I have been prosecuted before."

The commander laughed and turned in his chair to beckon one of his men. The man immediately placed a bottle of Tennessee bourbon on the table with several glasses.

Davis uncorked the bottle. "Because we would not stand for it, President Walker. That is why Washington will not dare prosecute you."

Walker looked at Davis in amazement.

"You've been out of the States too long, President," Davis said, raising his glass in a toast to Walker. "I and all my men want to salute William Walker, and they join me here as I drink to your health, sir."

The Navy men cheered and Davis downed his glass in a single draft.

"Good Tennessee whiskey," he muttered.

William Walker stood with his untouched glass in his hand. "I want to thank Commander Davis and all you men for the things he has spoken just now. I know you have your duty to do. The fact that you can carry out the job you were sent to do and express your own" —he smiled—"perhaps mixed feelings about doing it is a great thing to hear and see. Thank you for your kind thoughts."

Walker downed his bourbon.

May 1, 1857

Between President William Walker and Commander C.H. Davis of the United States Navy, be it agreed that,

1. The President, his staff and the Guard Company, with arms and personal baggage, will leave Rivas under the protection of Commander Davis and will not be molested by the enemy. In San Juan del Sur the President and his staff will be taken aboard the vessel St. Mary's, *to be safely conducted to the United States of America via Panama. The Guard Company will await safe conduct to California in San Juan del Sur.*

2. All officers, noncommissioned officers, and enlisted men not natives of Nicaragua, wounded or not, together with their weapons, will place themselves under the protection of Commander Davis or of any United States naval officer designated by him, for the purpose of obtaining safe conduct to California.

> *The President thanks the* Falange.
> *He will not forget the* Falange.

As Walker was leaving Rivas, he turned to his assembled troops. "Remember, men, Washington politicians took us out of here. As soldiers, we never lost a battle."

40

THEY SAILED south on the Pacific and left the U.S. warship *St. Mary's* to cross the isthmus at Panama, twenty-four miles of rough journeying through steaming, fever-ridden jungles. Ironically this crossing was doing a booming trade because the crossing through Nicaragua had been closed for many months. They sailed north on the Atlantic side, bound for New Orleans.

Shipboard tailors worked overtime to replace the men's uniforms with civilian clothes. By the time the ship reached port, a respectably dressed party walked down the gangplank to the shore.

To the adulation of a cheering mob! Crowds lined the street leading from the dock at New Orleans, bands played, pistols were shot in the air. It was true! The rumors and what Commander Davis had said were not exaggerations. William Walker was a hero! The South had come to welcome its son home.

Thornton and Solange drifted along in the wake of Walker for the next few days, too dazed and gratified to do anything else. Thornton stumbled through speeches he was called upon to give at lunches, dinners, church meetings, literary societies, clubs whose names he could not remember—much to the amusement of their members.

Everywhere the cry was the same. The South! The South! We'll smash the Yankees!

In Nicaragua they had all been called Yanquis. Down there the States had seemed a peaceful tranquil place. Back here in New Orleans, all Thornton heard were calls for war, for victory. No one ever mentioned death or defeat.

He was tired. He wanted to go home.

It was early June by the time he and Solange got back to Antrimville. He had been gone a bit over two years. Not a great span in the life of a man, yet it seemed to him he had last seen Tennessee as a wild youth and now he was coming home as a reflective man.

"I never went to the university," he told Solange. "Hell, I barely scraped through country school, and the standards around us were none too high. But coming back, I feel as if I've taken a cram course with Professor Walker."

"I'm not sure I'd recommend that professor or his course to anyone else," Solange said.

"I won't."

Thornton's father and mother, sisters and younger brother were all at the Huntsville railroad station to meet them. So was half the town and a good section of that part of Alabama who wanted to set their eyes on the boy from Antrimville who had been a general with the great William Walker. Thornton listened to the mayor speak for half an hour, said thank you to the crowd, and left town to renewed cheers.

Their family coach was still twenty miles from Antrimville when Thornton had to climb out on the driver's seat to satisfy people who wanted to see him pass by. Antrimville itself seemed to hold more people than New Orleans that day. It seemed a holiday had been declared locally, and a good number of the menfolk had been celebrating while waiting for him to show up.

Women wept while he presented Harry Drayberry's parents with their son's ceremonial sword, general's star, medals and a personal letter from William Walker. He and Solange slipped away from the festivities after a while down to the churchyard, where they stood at his brother's grave.

"What can you say about fortune?" Thornton mumbled. "He stayed home and was a good boy. I liked him. He looked out for me. Yet, the terrible thing is, if he had not died, we would not be here."

"Thornton, you can't blame yourself for your brother's death."

"I know. It's just that I feel an injustice was done to him which I somehow escaped. Him, and then Harry. How did I survive?"

"It was God's will," Solange said.

Thornton knew better than to argue religion with a woman, especially a French Catholic one.

She watched him curiously as he knelt by the grave and loosened some soil with his fingers. With his other hand he drew out a small gold star from his pocket, dropped it in the little excavation and covered it with earth so quickly she almost missed seeing it. It was Thornton's own general's star. Solange pretended not to notice.

Thornton's eyes ran over the cotton crops on the fields on each side of the county road. He turned his horse and buggy into the cypress-lined avenue leading up to the plantation house whose columns shone white among the dark pines. He helped Solange down from the buggy in the gravel area before the house, and they were greeted by old Matthew Hardwick, their host for the all-day picnic and ball that night.

Solange joined Emily and Elizabeth and the other married women in the shade, while Thornton joined the men for a tall glass of bourbon with a sprig of mint and a spoon of sugar in it. The young unmarried folk flirted and giggled, and their laughter and screams filled the air. Thornton found it joyful, yet slightly disquieting. It all seemed so near and yet far away. . . . Emily and Elizabeth had married within a year of Thornton and Harry leaving. Word had never been sent to Harry. Or had he known? Thornton put these thoughts out of his mind and turned his attention to what the men were saying.

"I say we show these Yankees what real men are made of!" one man declared.

Another added, "We have our own real-life general to train our lads!"

"You'll lead us, won't you, Thornton? We'll wade in Yankee blood!"

"I don't think it will ever come to war," Thornton said. "Not in America. Americans fighting Americans? I could never believe that."

They had been home since early June, and now they were in the last humid, baking weeks of August. After Nicaragua, it seemed cool to them. Thornton, Solange and his family were eating their midday meal out of doors in the shade of a huge old tree. Solange had fitted in well. Since she was French, they accepted the fact she was Catholic, which they would not have done had she been born in America. It was a twist of logic Thornton was glad to accept and not question. Her manners and gentility, combined with a lack of hauteur and pretension, impressed even those who were jealous of her or disliked her. She had been accepted into the McClintock family as one of their own within a week of her arrival, and was now so well incorporated into the daily round of activities, an outsider might suppose she had never been outside Antrimville in her life, apart from her accent!

The postal service, with the little glued stamps on the envelopes, was still a novelty in Antrimville, and when a letter arrived for Thornton, everyone at the table fell silent in curiosity as he opened and read it.

Finally he laughed and tossed it to Solange. "It's from an old friend."

She picked up the letter and began to read it. And fainted off her chair into a crumpled heap on the ground.

Consternation reigned. Thornton and his mother helped her back into her chair, and a sister passed smelling salts beneath her nose. As soon as Solange recovered and remembered the letter, she began to weep bitterly.

Thornton was scolded by his mother, who demanded to know what he had done to upset his wife. There was no doubt whose side she was on! He gave the letter to his father to read.

"Walker wants you to join him in another expedition to Nicaragua leaving in a few days' time from New Orleans!" his father exclaimed.

"Tell Solange you're not going!" his mother demanded.

"I'm not going."

"I don't believe you," Solange sobbed.

Thornton spoke in exasperation. "Do you think I'd show you the letter if I meant to go?"

Solange thought about that. She smiled. "Now I believe you."

They avidly watched for news of the expedition. In September they heard that Walker had captured Greytown and the San Juan River—the whole eastern half of the Transit. Suddenly there was bad news. Commodore Paulding, the U.S. Navy officer holding the Caribbean command, had landed marines, disarmed Walker's troops and forced them aboard ships bound for the United States.

Three years later, in 1860, William Walker spirited a force of men aboard a ship and sailed out of New

Orleans. He planned to land in Honduras and march south into Nicaragua. The British Royal Navy intervened, captured Walker and handed him over to the Hondurans.

On September 12, 1860, outside the small town of Trujillo in Honduras, William Walker died before a firing squad.

THE GUNFIGHTERS

by Lee Davis Willoughby

Young Wes Cardigan meets Wild Bill Hickok, town marshal of Abilene, while helping him stand off a murderous band of outlaws. Under the legendary gunfighters tutelage, he learns the art of the fast-draw, and falls in love with Wild Bill's cousin, the beautiful Helen Butler.

But as Cardigan's star rises, Wild Bill's declines, as his incomparable skills fade and he gains one enemy too many. Jack McCall, a relentlessly evil man, plots a final showdown for Cardigan and Hickok, with all the cards stacked against them.